COSMOCOPIA

Frank Lazorg's gone mad!

The elderly, ego-driven dean of fine art fantasy illustrators has reached the end. His creative powers have failed him, his mistress spurned him, his younger rivals threaten to eclipse him.

But a strange new drug promises to reinvigorate him, as both man and artist. Reliance on the organic high soon results in addiction—an addiction in madness. He's suddenly plunged into a world inhabited by monstrous parodies of humanity, living in a culture that bears a skewed resemblance to the world Lazorg knows.

Yet, this new dimension exhibits its own, perhaps higher-level reality and tangibility, its own dangers and delights, enemies and lovers, including the remarkable being known as Crutchsump. What Lazord experiences with the alien being and her kind, however, is merely the first rung on the Cosmocopian ladder!

Borgo Press Books by PAUL DI FILIPPO

After the Collapse and Other Stories
Cosmocopia: A Science Fiction Novel

COSMOCOPIA

A SCIENCE FICTION NOVEL

PAUL DI FILIPPO

THE BORGO PRESS

MMXI

COSMOCOPIA

FIRST BORGO PRESS EDITION

Published by Wildside Press LLC

www.wildsidebooks.com

DEDICATION

To **Deborah**,

Whose nature informs every plane of the
Cosmocopia,

And thanks also

To **Michael Bishop**,

Who coined the title of this novel for his own
uses, and then generously passed it on to me.

CONTENTS

PART ONE

CHAPTER ONE
THROUGH THE CRIMSON PORTAL

"Will you ever paint again?"

Dense November Pennsylvania sunlight, molten white and descending through lofty windows, impasto'd the large modern room that held an old man and a young woman.

The woman had issued the query, in a tone both sincere and aggressive.

Frank Lazorg lifted his rheumy eyes to the tall walls of his home, hung with framed canvases and matted works on paper. Hardly any of the nubbly ivory plaster showed, twelve feet from hardwood floor to beamed ceiling, so thickly sown were his paintings and drawings.

Every phase of Lazorg's career was represented. He had always been a canny businessman, sharper than Eisner even, retaining as much of his original art as possible, given the predatory practices of pulp and paperback publishers. His foresight and artistic implacability had eventually made him a very rich man.

But fifty years ago, striving amidst poverty—

There had been only inner fire, the brush, and the women.

The full head of hair, the head full of visions, the muscular crook'd arms strong enough to serve as perches for bathing beauties hoisted skyward.

And today—?

Lazorg dismissed the comparison irritably, with a trace of fear, fear that grew larger and crept closer daily.

Instead of contemplating spectres, his gaze circumnavigated the two-dimensional archipelago of his career.

His early work for comics, from the 1950s: penciled and inked pages of original art rescued from company dumpsters, now safely under glass. Funny animals, noir molls, hillbillies, car-racing jocks.

His hyper-real yet fantastical book covers for paperback original novels of the 1960s and 1970s: a gallery of demons and brawny warriors, luscious-bottomed maidens and brawling barbarians, aliens and otherworldly explorers.

His fine art from the 1980s and 1990s: portraits, and abstract representations of mental landscapes, surreal collages, visions of dimensions beyond.

Lazorg dropped his watery grey eyes back to his interviewer.

The young woman's complexion was blanched, like the cloistered meat of shellfish. Dressed all in sharply cut black clothing, with raven-dyed hair and multiple piercings, she pinned her artist subject with her own intense dark gaze. Between them, atop a low table, her small recorder digitized their dialogue.

She had given him her name an hour ago, but he had forgotten it already.

"Seeing what hangs here," said Lazorg slowly, "you can still ask such a question? Isn't it plain that I breathe my art—bleed my art?"

"But the stroke you suffered. You haven't finished a painting since you left rehab. And that was over a year ago."

Ah, brutal youth. Had he ever been so mercilessly direct with his elders? He flinched as he recalled some long-gone encounters, lost now past wisdom's revisions.

Lazorg sighed wearily. "Suppose I never paint again? Haven't I done enough? Can't I coast or even rocket down that mortal slope, riding the runaway train of my old successes?"

"I can't say. That's up to you. From the outside, from my perspective, your accomplishments are tremendous. The whole world knows your work. You've spawned tons of imitators. Your name is an adjective for a certain style."

These words of praise soothed Lazorg with a hollow touch. But the woman's next words robbed him of even that ghostly solace.

"But did you ever get to the heart of your artistic quest? Are you done experimenting or pursuing old lines of inquiry? Is there no new place left for you to explore? Do you have any strength or desire left to go there? I can't answer these things, only you can."

Lazorg contemplated these painful questions for a few moments, attempting to formulate answers fit for an audience seeking happy endings. (Under whose auspices had this woman said she was conducting this interview?) But in the end, he couldn't prevaricate.

"Right at this moment, I'm afraid, I can't quite summon up my old energies. No subject appeals, no technique calls out to me, no unfinished business feels urgent. Just prior to my, ah, cerebral assault, I had a canvas underway. But now—well, we'll see what the future brings, I suppose…."

Lazorg's husky, quavering voice trailed off.

The woman sitting across from him seemed untroubled by the old man's pitiful despair and defeat. She did not express any overt sympathy, but neither did she goad him with his abject surrender to mortality. Instead, she merely displayed a small, enigmatic, witchy smile, and continued the interview along less fatalistic lines.

Lazorg found it within himself somewhere to continue to respond with intelligent albeit half-hearted answers to her questions, although he felt creeping over him a weariness typical of this hour of the day under his new stroke-imposed regimen.

But then a question triggered from the old man a burst of indignation.

"What do you think of the latest work by Rokesby Marrs?"

Lazorg had been a short, compact but burly man in his prime, crowned with a thick shock of auburn hair. His frame, now attenuated by age and illness, still faintly echoed that impressive physicality. And upon hearing the name of his younger rival,

Rokesby Marrs, Lazorg seemed to bulk out to his old dominance. Even the few remaining threads of color in his sparse bleached coiffure seemed to glow with renewed brilliance.

"Is that cheap hack still foisting his poisoned eye-candy on the hapless public?"

"But Mr. Lazorg, how can you speak so harshly of a man who calls himself your worshipful first disciple?"

"He's no disciple I would ever care to acknowledge. Judas was a better disciple! There has never been any substantial contact between us. Certainly, Marrs never studied directly with me. He simply learned to copy my most superficial mannerisms and themes imperfectly, like a trained ape, or one of those elephants that paints with a broomstick grasped clumsily in its trunk. He's debased everything he's ever touched. But he's never touched me."

"But his popularity—"

"The masses have no taste, Miss—Miss—"

"Hemphill. Nia Hemphill."

"Well, Miss Hemphill, if you're going to adduce Marrs's inflated sales and outrageous fees as a testament of his talent, then you're going to have to class him with artistic travesties like Thomas Kinkade. Or perhaps that British woman who put forward her unmade bed as art."

Nia Hemphill offered another wry smile. "I can see the topic's toxic, so we'll skip on to my final question—"

At that moment, however, Frank Lazorg's housekeeper intruded. A stout, plain, middle-aged woman named Anna Compton, she stood in the doorway, be-aproned and drying her hands on a dishcloth.

"Mr. Lazorg, your dinner will be ready in an hour. But you've got therapy scheduled before then. In fact, Mr. Kenton is already waiting."

Lazorg turned his attention back to Nia Hemphill, and found her already standing, pocketing her small recorder.

"I won't intrude on your time any longer," said the young woman. "Thank you so much for this opportunity. I've admired your work for so long, and it was a pleasure to finally meet the creator behind it."

Using his cane, Lazorg struggled to his feet. When had his favorite chair developed into such a deep ditch?

Now that Nia Hemphill stood on the point of departure, all the annoyances she and her questions had brought seemed negligible, and Lazorg suddenly felt that he wanted to prolong her stay. He got so little company these days. All his contemporaries were dead or distant, and his family equally so.

"You won't stay to share dinner?"

"I'm afraid I can't."

"But what about your last question?"

Nia Hemphill ventured another smile insusceptible to interpretation. "Oh, it can wait. I've got quite enough material otherwise."

Teetering, Lazorg managed a handshake with the woman, and then watched her leave.

Anna Compton lent her employer an arm to escort him to the room where a massage table and other equipment had been installed shortly after his return from the Rowanthorn rehab facility.

Dean Kenton, a young man with sand-colored hair and a crooked nose, possessed a supple physique honed by yoga. He greeted Lazorg heartily, and then put his client through an excruciating set of exercises alleviated only by a canny and caring massage at the end of the ordeal.

Kenton accompanied Lazorg to the big, green-tiled, brightly lit bathroom on the ground level, where the therapist stood watch while Lazorg showered the sweat of pain and exertion off his elderly frame, then reclined in a whirlpool bath to ease his aches. Once out and dressed, Lazorg dismissed the man with sincere thanks, and made his way unaccompanied to dinner table.

Mrs. Compton had everything arranged and waiting. Lazorg sat down to a perfect if bland repast, composed by his non-resident chef and nutritionist, Brian Foss, who, having cooked, had gone home for the night. Lean turkey breast sauced deliciously, several sides of steamed vegetables, a single glass of a light red wine. Fruit and cheese, decaffeinated coffee for dessert.

But despite the sensible acceptability of the meal, Lazorg could not resist thinking about repasts of his youth. Giant lobsters and steaks, washed down by quarts of beer. Whole loaves of bread smeared with brie and pâté. Champagne and zinfandel, hard liquor by the many jiggers. And always, it seemed in retrospect, in the company of women, beautiful women.

Lazorg sighed. The table cleared, his shrunken stomach filled and his debilitated frame supplied with more energy for another fruitless span of hours, he made slowly to rise. Perhaps he would pass the evening watching a DVD. He didn't sleep well, and so postponed bedtime until as late as possible.

Mrs. Compton had her coat on, ready to go. "You're wearing your medic-alert gadget, aren't you?"

Lazorg snaked a necklace'd lanyard partway out from under his sweater. Mrs. Compton came over and tugged it out all the way, revealing the ugly and bulky remote signaler attached to the cord.

"Leave it outside! How will you get at it if you need it?"

Lazorg smiled ruefully. "Yes, mother."

Mrs. Compton snorted. "You should be so lucky." She headed for the door, but stopped and turned while still in the dining room.

"The mail came during your interview. All the usual junk. I sent the bank statement over to your accountant, and the fan letters on to Roy."

Roy Isham had performed secretarial duties for Lazorg for the past decade.

Mrs. Compton's face grew a frown more expressive of puzzlement than displeasure. "But there was one thing—"

"Yes?"

"A rather exotic foreign package with—an odd smell— Anyway, it's on the hall table."

The empty house echoed to the closing of the door behind the housekeeper, and waves of loneliness seemed to pulse through the residence, as if radiating from a central well of unsought black implacable solitude.

Lazorg fought off the sensations of being left bereft. Mildly intrigued by the thought of the delivery of something unexpected, he shuffled out to the hall.

There on a glass-topped table sat the package.

Wrapped in creased and crumpled craft paper, secured fore and aft with antique twine, grimed with the dirt of its passage and the oils of many hands, the package bore a plethora of garish foreign postage, the stamps illustrative of alien monuments, men and myths.

Big and solid as a brick, the package implied a similar weight. But when Lazorg hefted it—necessarily one-handedly, due to reliance on his cane—the package proved surprisingly light.

There was no return address; Lazorg's own information had been indicted in smearable pencil with a bold hand. A scribbled Customs form pasted to the wrapper indicated legal passage across the borders.

It was a miracle the package had even reached him.

There came a scent to Lazorg's nostrils: a dry odor akin to sun-baked rock, sterile yet somewhat organic, like formic acid. This must have been what Mrs. Compton had whiffed.

For some reason, Lazorg felt impelled to carry the package to his studio, of all rooms: a place he had visited very infrequently in the past year.

The capacious studio's glass ceiling with its adjustable shades revealed only night sky prinked with stars. Lazorg flicked on a light. A chaise lounge draped with a silk sheet spoke of past living models, the creases of the sheet almost calling forth the impress of the flesh that had molded them. In the middle of the room stood an easel bearing a large framed canvas, shrouded now with a paint-spattered cloth. Lazorg's eyes darted to the easel, then quickly away. A broad, waist-high worktable offered room for spreading out sketches, and assembling frames. He moved to a tall messy workbench where he was wont to mix his own paints: pigments, oil binders full of dopants (linseed, hemp, poppy, calendula), thinners— The colorful panoply released mingled heady scents that spoke to Lazorg of all he had once had, all he had since lost.

Lazorg rested his butt on a high stool, able thus to dispense momentarily with his cane. Irritably, his joy at receiving a surprise now diffusing, Lazorg swept aside some clutter and set the package down. He retrieved a magnifying glass from across the room and studied the postmark. The name "Santa Lucia" leaped into focus.

Santa Lucia. That visit had occurred ten years or more ago, when he had been fixated on the disturbingly lush and overripe tropical landscapes of Martin Johnson Heade. He had gone to that Central American country seeking similar founts of inspiration. But the visit had devolved to a perpetual bacchanal, native women, potent rum. And then there had been the baffling incident with the *curandero* and the thugs...

Lazorg tried to summon up the details, but found them hazy at this remove, blurred by his constant drunkenness at the time.

Could this package possibly be from the old sorcerer? What had his name been...?

Fulgencio.

Yes, Fulgencio.

Wielding scissors, Lazorg snipped the binding strings. White paste of the kind used by children sealed the seams of the craft paper. Lazorg slit along those lines. The paper came away.

Now he confronted a brick sealed with aluminum foil, inside clear plastic wrap. The aroma from the brick was more powerful, now that a layer of wrapping had been removed. It mingled with the familiar odors of the workbench in intriguing ways.

Taped to the exterior of the brick was a folded square of coarse paper.

Lazorg removed the note, opened it, and saw Spanish.

But the next moment the words resolved themselves as English. Lazorg rubbed his eyes with the backs of both hands— must be getting tired—then read the note.

Mister Frank,

You will perhaps recall how our paths crossed some years ago, and you were instrumental in saving my life. I swore then that I would repay you somehow, some day, and now I can finally make good on my debt.

You have now at your command the powder obtained from ten thousand vision scarabs, the escarabajo psicodélico, *a beetle unique to Santa Lucia. It has taken me all this time to collect and prepare this number of bugs, but I did not want to deliver to you any less than this fair amount. With what you now have, you may mix up the most beautiful crimson paint you have ever used—paint of a living sanguine hue—to paint the most wonderful scenes imaginable, and you will have enough for the rest of your life, which, Jesus and Yemaja willing, may be long indeed.*

Please accept this humble gift, the smallest repayment for the immeasureable one you gave me.

Go with God,

Fulgencio

Lazorg sat quietly for a few moments, contemplating fate and chance. Then, using the scissors, he opened up a small slit in the top of the package.

As if he had sliced into the veins of his own wrist, a seam of crimson leapt up into his vision against the surrounding dull silver of the foil, accompanied by a burst of the characteristic scent. The fine-grained powder, compacted for transit, seemed almost epidermal in its composition, the cosmetic-dusted porous skin of some exotic maiden.

Not cinnabar, nor alizarin nor vermilion, but some shade hitherto unknown.

Feeling slightly dizzy, Lazorg next did something spontaneously and almost without volition.

He dug up a few grains of the ruby powder with the tip of the scissors and placed it upon his tongue.

The taste of the powder derived from the myriad crushed bodies of the vision scarab was both metallic-mineral and citrusy-agave, like biting into a pulpy cactus covered with road dust.

The aroma-taste of the powder immediately expanded to fill Lazorg's mouth and nasal passages—and seemingly his skull and lungs—before fading away to a sharp memory. It seemed to have no other immediate perceptual effect.

Lazorg got off the stool, leaving the package where it sat. Suddenly he was sleepy.

He made it to his bedroom without trouble. He doffed his outer garments, keeping on just his underwear, and climbed into bed.

Only on the point of falling asleep, did he realize he had left his cane in the studio.

His dreams were many, and vivid, and exciting, but unrecoverable upon awakening.

After dressing his complaining, noncompliant body with the usual difficulty, Lazorg proceeded downstairs (caneless, moving precariously from one piece of furniture to another) to enjoy his bland, approved, oatmeal-and-fruit breakfast.

Thoughts of the strange powder drifted in an out of the forefront of his consciousness, but he felt no immediate compulsion to rush back to his studio to investigate further the odd gift from his past.

Instead, he spent the day with his secretary, Roy Isham, answering letters from museum curators, agents, and prospective buyers. Dark-haired, thin, and punctilious, Isham struck Lazorg as being indubitably gay, although the employer had never queried his employee. Lazorg, ever the ladies' man, had no brief against gays, regarding them in the past as simply less competition for him in the arena of sex.

Brian Foss interrupted after lunch to inquire about Lazorg's dinner preferences. Short and stout and bearded, the chef plainly indulged in more decadent fare and in greater quantities than his client was allowed. Restraining himself from ordering some of the desirable forbidden foods Foss could doubtlessly prepare, Lazorg settled on pea soup, spinach salad and poached fish.

Eventually the dull day passed, and Lazorg found himself alone again in the big empty house that his art had bought for him.

Suddenly, with nightfall and solitude, the presence of the Central American powder in the house exerted a compulsive pull. Experiencing trepidation and eagerness in equal measures, Lazorg hastened to his studio.

None of his staff were permitted entrance to this room, and so Lazorg naturally found the brick of powder exactly where he had left it the previous night.

This time, using his longish pinky fingernail, he deliberately took up a larger quantity of the granular stuff and placed it on his tongue.

The same burst of flinty odor, aloe taste—and Lazorg felt himself invigorated, his mind preternaturally clear and alert. None of the dimensions of reality appeared to alter, no phantasms manifested, but the world did acquire a luster or charm it had lacked since—since Lazorg was young and whole.

Lazorg, smiling, moved confidently about his studio, picking up with renewed interest dried crusted brushes, old sketches, various trinkets and curios and souvenirs that had formerly served as inspiration, until finally he approached the unfinished last painting on its easel.

He put his hand to the cloth covering the work, hesitated, then whisked it off.

The canvas was intended to be an homage to Courbet's *The Origin of the World*. That still-shocking canvas, as prurient as any centerfold, represented a naked woman, her head concealed by a cloth, viewed almost along the plane of her recumbent body, with her bushy crotch and quim occupying the focus of the composition.

Lazorg's version—barely begun, mostly still a sketch—distorted the female form along novel fractal dimensions, and utilized a non-representational color palette. Still, despite the unreality of the mode, the force of the woman's sexuality would be undeniable. That is, if Lazorg could ever finish it.

And surely part of the power of the finished image would derive not from Lazorg's talents, but directly from the impressive woman who served as Lazorg's model.

Velina Malaspina.

For twenty years now, since she was barely of legal age, Malaspina had served as Lazorg's primary female model. Her body and face graced dozens of book covers, CD jewel cases and movie posters, in various guises. In Lazorg's whole career, she was as close to a muse as he had ever had.

Of course they were lovers.

Or had been, before the stroke.

Sex was the only way Lazorg had been able to penetrate to Malapina's essence, to capture her in ink and paint and charcoal. He had seduced the voluptuous, willing teenager when he himself was in his still virile mid-fifties, and continued to plumb her—admittedly less and less frequently—right up till his debilitating stroke.

But the relationship between them was hardly what could be called emotionally intimate. Malaspina, although suitably athletic and aggressive in the bedroom, had always exhibited a certain coolness or reserve. She presumed nothing of her carnal connection with Lazorg, made no demands, accepted gifts dispassionately, did not cling or cajole or caress. She showed up at the assigned times, performed her duties as both model and lover, and disappeared without looking back, until the next occasion for her services arose.

At first her indifference had been galling to Lazorg, but he had come to see it as either a kind of protective armor or genuine constitutional incapacity, and grown to accept her for what she offered.

But after his stroke—

Velina Malaspina had visited Frank Lazorg precisely once in the past year, shortly after his cerebral incident, when he was still hospitalized and at his worst. She had entered his room, bearing no flowers or gifts, and strode with her lithe grace to his bedside. She had contemplated his stricken face and frame for a punishing minute, her beautiful countenance an inscrutable mask. Then she had uttered a phrase conveying more judgment and verdict than sympathy: "Too bad."

And with that she was gone from Lazorg's life, seemingly forevermore.

The blow of her cruel departure was almost more devastating than the stroke.

Now Lazorg threw the covering sloppily back over the nascent painting. An iconography of Velina Malaspina rioted through his brain. Her touch, her scent, the curvilinear lines and intersecting planes of her lush body. The neurons of his brain seemed alight with renewed desire and ambition, crimson fires flickering down his dendrites.

He must get Velina back, for his art and his personal satisfaction—

Suddenly Lazorg slumped, all energy draining from his limbs, his mind shutting down its frenetic overdrive. Ennui and drowsiness threatened to leave him zoned out on the floor of his studio. What would Mrs. Compton ever say to that self-neglect? Lazorg winced at the imagined shrill rebuke.

Lazorg tottered back to where he had propped his cane, retrieved it, and stumped toward his bedroom.

The drug. The vision scarab. Certainly that alone could explain his sudden access of energy and clear thinking, and his equally sudden crash. That substance alone held the possibility of his recovery and final triumph over fucking mortality! He would exit this life on a high note, instead of as a pitiable shadow of his best self.

But what if the drug were harmful, like cantharides, another beetle-born substance, the Spanish Fly of his youth? Fulgencio had said nothing about its properties if taken internally, but only its suitability as a pigment. Yet what further significant harm could Lazorg do to his raddled body? If he died after finishing even one more painting, then so be it. The achievement would be worth the cost. Nothing could be worse than this pointless death-in-life, without the art that had granted his existence meaning.

But he must proceed sensibly and slowly. Learn his limits, and the limit of the powder. Overdosing on the very next trial would be an ironic and futile fate.

Thus began a week of nocturnal experimentation. Flake by flake, grain by grain, mole by mole, Lazorg applied the fragrant, aluminal, cochineal-colored substance to his tongue. He discovered the various grades of increased mental discernment and bodily strength that the drug could bring, their duration and repeatability and terminal stages.

Once he pushed a little too far and entered a realm of metallic paranoia. He became convinced that Fulgencio intended him harm with this malign gift. Old memories seemed to sharpen. Had he truly rescued the ancient *curandero* from thugs, or had he, Frank Lazorg, actually been one of the party of drunken revelers who had taunted and accosted and roughed up an elderly stranger in the town square as a cruel lark? Was this the foreigner's revenge? But surely Fulgencio's friendly note had spoken of gratitude and favors…?

Lazorg tore his studio half-apart, looking for the square of coarse paper that had accompanied the brick. But it had vanished, never to be found.

(Contrariwise, the brick of powder seemed almost self-replenishing to some degree, diminishing in bulk, yes, but not commensurately with Lazorg's intake.)

At last the derangement passed, and Lazorg managed to recover by morning. Now he knew his upper bar with the organic drug.

By day he remained his old doddering self. None of his staff suspected his nightly experiments, he was certain.

But by night he rehearsed his return to potency, bolstered

by the ingestion of the scarab crumbs. He cleaned brushes and unstoppered caked-shut paint tubes, stood with dry palette and brush in hand before the *Origin of the World* canvas, trying to feel the kinesthetics of the masterpiece lying in wait at the interface of man and medium.

At last he arrived at a point of confidence where he felt equal to contacting Velina Malaspina.

That night, his voice strengthened by the drug, his nerves emboldened, Lazorg punched up the entry for Malaspina in his cell-phone and triggered the call, knowing that he would in all likelihood get her voicemail. Often quite busy socializing, Velina disdained accepting calls directly, preferring to compose her reactions ahead of time before responding to any importunings.

As expected, Malaspina's husky digitized voice recited merely her name before the chime. But even that tinny mechanical reproduction of her voice almost unnerved him. After some stuttering, he got his request across.

"Velly, my sweet, my forever girl. I need to see you. For both our sakes, for the art we made between us, please come to my home. You know the way. Tomorrow night, if you can—if I ever meant anything to you."

Lazorg terminated the call before he got maudlin, or more so.

He strode boldly to the easel holding his final canvas and unconcealed it. Under the influence of the drug, the mere penciled lines grew luminous and summoned up the tactile sensations of caressing Malaspina's curves.

She would come. Tomorrow. He knew it with certitude, before all certitude drained away for another day.

The next evening, Lazorg began consuming the drug as soon as Mrs. Compton had shut the door behind her. He knew now, he thought, how to pace himself for the optimal effect. But desirous of attaining the ultimate edge of his performance, he added a grain or two beyond the previous trials.

The extra jolt had him pacing irritably through the forequarters of the big house for hours, awaiting the inevitable ringing of the front doorbell.

Midnight came and went, and no Malaspina. Lazorg bolstered himself again and again with crumbs from the crimson cake, beyond all previous usage.

She must come! She must!

At two AM the bell sounded.

Lazorg composed himself with some effort, then went to receive his muse.

An autumnal blast sneaked past the visitor first, chilling Lazorg's old bones. Then Velina Malaspina half tumbled across the threshold, caught herself with giggles, finally straightened. Her familiar vanilla-based scent bore grace notes of metabolized booze.

The woman was bigger than Lazorg, always had been, a Juno. Masses of black curls, wide mouth, pert nose, dark eyes. Buxom, well-padded, ripe for grabbing. Tonight she spilled out of a frothy party frock and open-toed shoes, a gape-fronted abbreviated fur coat her only concession to the November chill.

Her voice when it came from her frogmouth was hoarse from smoke and liquor, her words sloppy.

"Well, well, well, the creature walks!"

In her overwhelming presence at last, Lazorg strove to ignore her insult. "Yes, Velly, I walk and talk—and even paint again!"

Malaspina dropped awkwardly into a chair, splaying her legs immodestly. Her oblate white thighs channeled Lazorg's attention to a glimpse of her bare origin of the world.

"Why'd you make me come here tonight, Frankie? I didn't really want to. After the way you looked in the hospital— But your voice— It had some of the old magic and force in it."

Lazorg stepped closer to the chair, so that he could presume to touch her bare wrist. She allowed it. "You're right, dear. I have my skills back, my strength. We can finish our last project together. It will be a masterpiece, I know it!"

Puzzlement clouded Malaspina's features. "Our last project? What was it?"

Lazorg was hurt and stunned. "You—you really don't

remember? My *Origin of the World….*"

Velina Malaspina brushed away his concern with a sloppy wave of her hand, breaking contact with Lazorg's fingers on her wrist. "Oh, that was all so long ago! And you know I could never keep all your silly titles straight."

"Well, come to the studio and I'll show you then."

With more giggles and some little effort, Malaspina managed to stand. Lazorg offered her his arm, but she jerked away.

"You're not getting back into my pants, you know. That's all over with now!"

"I'm sad, of course, but I understand. Even before my stroke, I sensed our relationship changing. But I'd be happy if you just consented to model again for me."

Malaspina began to trot in a wavery fashion on her high heels down the hall, taking the familiar path to the studio. "Let's see this unborn masterpiece!"

As she approached the studio, Malaspina said, "What's that funny smell?"

So used to the aroma of the vision scarab powder, Lazorg had to think a moment to catch her reference.

"Oh, just a new pigment I've been experimenting with."

"Smells like burnt hair and witch hazel to me."

Lazorg caught up with her at the studio door. While he fumbled with the light switch, Malaspina had already crossed the room and whisked the cloth off the easel.

Together they contemplated the embryonic painting. Lazorg hoped she would see in it all the potential he saw. But even to his eyes now, under the force of the judgmental presence of an additional witness, the barely commenced painting looked abortive. If only he dared take another flake of drug to reaffirm his vision! But he had already had too much….

Malaspina turned to confront Lazorg, her back to the canvas.

"Why do you have to paint me so—so jagged and chopped up! No one will even be able to tell it's me! You might as well be using a side of beef with a hole gouged into it for your model!"

"No, no, that's not true! Your essence will come across, your spirit, even though the outer you is distorted and deranged for a good reason—"

"Forget it, Frankie. I'm not interested in modeling for you anymore. I've got another gig. I work with someone else nowadays. Someone who makes me look beautiful in his paintings, the way you once used to. Maybe you've even heard of him. His name's Rokesby Marrs."

The name of his detested, talentless rival raised a red curtain of blood before Lazorg's eyes. His thoughts ceased to be intelligible to himself, became a chaotic whirlpool of rage and hatred. Lazorg felt himself frozen in place like one of Medusa's victims.

"You'll never paint me again, Frankie. Never."

Those brazenly merciless words shattered his immobility.

Velina Malaspina was by the studio door now, and suddenly Lazorg felt himself gripping his cane, as if it had leapt from its resting place by the workbench where the brick of powder resided, and into his hand. But he held it by its rubber foot and shaft, not its curved handle.

Malaspina's back was toward the painter. She had already dismissed him from her flighty consciousness.

A sudden access of power, a sudden impulse toward action, surged through Lazorg's arm, and he swung his cane with all possible force.

The cane connected with a sickening sound against Velina Malaspina's head, and she went down to the floor like a chainsawed tree.

In the welter of his rage, Lazorg was unsure whether she had survived the blow to her skull. But by the time his unseeing fury abated, as he sat straddling her torso, cane pressed two-handed like a bar deeply into the soft, already mottled flesh of her throat, she had definitely ceased to be alive.

Lazorg struggled weakly to his feet, employing the cane by its blood-slicked handle. He staggered back from the beautiful corpse, found the stool by his workbench. He dropped the accursed cane to the floor, and raised that hand up into his sight.

The smear of Velly's blood across his palm triggered in

him an abrupt cold epiphany whose dream logic embodied the utmost clarity—at least to Lazorg's drug-fueled reasoning.

"You'll never paint me again, Frankie. Never."

The first thing to do was regain some strength. Lazorg ingested a dram of beetle powder. Instantly he felt his world and horizons expand.

Dragging Velina Malaspina across the room to his broad, waist-high worktable, Lazorg caused her to lose both shoes. But this did not matter, as he needed her naked.

With no little effort, he contrived to get her slack body up on the hard, paint-spattered surface, scored crazily with shallow cuts from years of matting work. As if undressing a somnolent child, he stripped her of her coat and her dress, into which her bountiful breasts were merely taped.

Utterly nude, seen from an angle that concealed her wounds, Velina Malaspina looked like a dreaming goddess.

Lazorg hastened back to his high workbench. He ate more powder. Hurry, hurry! Mrs. Compton showed up precisely at eight every morning. What would happen to him then, he neither knew nor cared. But he must be finished with his task.

Assembling the necessary materials, Lazorg began to compound a special paint, finally employing the scarab pigment as Fulgencio had wished, for good or ill.

Lazorg worked the organic pigment into the raw oil base mixture with aching arms, folding it over and over itself to achieve a smooth isotropic shade, like the monochrome sunset of some far-off realm.

Gorgeous, gorgeous! Never a hue like this before. Almost not part of the spectrum.

The volatiles in the mixture disbursed the uncanny scent of the powder throughout the room. Merely inhaling this aroma gave Lazorg strength. He hardly needed to ingest the powder, which was well, since he used it all in concocting a huge tub of paint.

Lazorg paused when the compound was finished just long enough to lick the last grains of powder from the foil wrapper.

Then he grabbed a handful of brushes and the tub of paint, and moved to the corpse.

The paint clung to the brush dipped into it as if alive and eager.

The first stroke went across Velina Malaspina's open sightless eyes, sealing them behind a crimson scrim, turning eyeballs to pupil-less cherries and rendering them more artful than reality.

Lazorg painted the rest of her face with just a few confident passes. Then he went to work on her hair, plastering it with clots of paint to her skull and neck and shoulders. The effect was not ideal, but what mattered was to coat her entirely.

Down her long exquisite body, repairing the wounded neck first, then the chest, the breasts and their nipples, lifting the massive glands to get underneath. Stomach, hips, the corpse all the while assuming an enameled perfection.

He spread her cooling, stiffening legs and painted all her sex and crotch. Wherever the paint flowed, it assumed a coherent shell-like quality, as if he were not merely coating the women but embalming her like some Egyptian technician.

After Lazorg had devoted care and reverence to each toe and the soles of her feet, he realized he would have to turn Velly over to finish the job. She'd smear, but he'd repair that.

So with immense struggle, splotching his own clothing and exposed skin with paint from her body, he flipped her, and began painting her dorsal side, the well-defined blades of her shoulders, the roundels of her buttocks.

Again, the struggle, the awkward moments when she painted him with her body, and now she lay again on her back.

Lazorg fretted that now the coat of paint on her back would be mussed, but there was no getting around that. For a brief moment he contemplated flipping her in an endless loop, painting and repainting what was marred each time from his bottomless bucket until he died of inanition. But in the end he contented himself with merely touching up her front, rendering her a perfect candy-apple eidolon.

His task finished, Lazorg suddenly felt all the accumulated

weight and stress of his mad exertions. He dropped bucket and brush, staggered backwards a step or two, then sideways, then forward, to fall upon his final masterpiece in a last embrace.

Lazorg anticipated the feel of the tacky paint, beneath which rapidly coarsening flesh would resist his fall.

But he never received these sensory impressions.

Instead, he found himself dropping onto and into a woman-shaped hole, an anthropomorphic crimson portal that opened into an infinite crimson tunnel, down which he plummeted forever, too stunned even to shriek.

PART TWO

CHAPTER TWO
DWELLER IN THE BONECELLAR

Crutchsump knew that a trove of valuable fresh bones awaited her on the Shulgin Mudflats at the edge of Sidetrack City, where the metropolis met the waters of the Rodinian Sea. The myriad shimmering shifflets would have mortally spawned by now, as they did every year at this time, and their exhausted luminescent flesh would have quickly evanesced, leaving behind their delicate skeletons. These lightweight traceries of calcium and rare minerals awaited any bonepickers experienced enough to navigate the sinkholes, grapple-gnaws and mockmucks of the flats.

Normally, Crutchsump would have already shared the generous harvest with three or four other veteran bonepickers, laboriously earning a minim toward her continued sparse survival .

But not this season.

This season, the Shulgin Mudflats were haunted.

Haunted by an otherworldly monster.

Few had actually seen this beast up close. Yet its presence was incontestable.

Mournful wailings issued from the Mudflats by day and by night, solemn heart-rending ululations. From Huid Avenue, separated by a labyrinth of tall pouf-topped reeds from the Mudflats, passersby at night had witnessed the silhouette of a naked shambling figure—face-naked as well as body-naked!— crashing aimlessly through the reeds. The fruit and gorgit vendors along the Golden Boardwalk reported inexplicable thefts of their wares, victuals doubtlessly stolen by the hungry monster.

All these manifestations of something uncanny kept people away from the Mudflats—not that many had cause to trespass there in the best of times, save in search of bones or other natural materials, driftwood and miscellaneous seawrack. The Mudflats produced nothing wholesome by way of foodstuffs.

But forbidding monster or no, Crutchsump was, day by depressing day, nerving herself up to attempt the shifflet harvest.

Her expenses and her depleted savings drove her to such a risk.

Not that her lifestyle was extravagant. Far from it.

The monthly rent on her three shabby basement rooms amounted to only thirty scintillas. She subsisted contentedly on a simple diet of quorn and live water. Her clothing consisted of various ragged garments secured from several charities. She boasted only a single caul—an unfashionable model several years old, its formerly rickracked eyeholes all frayed—which she washed daily and mended as needed. As for Pirkle—well, her pet managed quite well on alley scavengings and handouts from local merchants.

Now, however, Crutchsump had reached the limits of her economy. All the bones she had of late managed to accumulate from the streets of Sidetrack City—haunting abattoirs, rummaging through mucky waste tips, cadging at back doors of diners—had been cleaned and sold to the wholesalers in the bone trade, the businessmen one level up from freelancers like Crutchsump, those who sorted and classified and packaged the osseous relics for subsequent sale to manufacturers of various stripes: the glue and gelatin factories, the corset- and button- and armor-makers, the producers of oil, char, ash and meal. The room where normally Crutchsump stored her haul was empty now, only greasy floor and walls and a fading redolence left behind to denote its function, while the tools of her trade—wire brushes, delicate picks and awls, a colony of hungry carrion ants—gathered dust.

So one bright morning with the sun Watermilk climbing the sky, when Crutchsump could no longer tolerate the rumbling and griping of her stomach, nor the unsubtle reminders from her landlord, Vannegar, about a certain approaching day of fiscal responsibility, the bone-scavenger resolved herself to attempt the Shulgin Mudflats.

Arising from her pallet, she pulled her lone caul off a peg and snugged the tailored sack over her head, pulling tight the drawstring around her neck. The jutting forefront of the caul, stretched tight over her introciptor, threatened vulgarly to split old stitches, and Crutchsump sighed. One more purchase to make....

The rags she wore in public served also as nightclothes, so no change of garments was necessary. Crutchsump slid her broad calloused feet into a pair of straw huaraches. She reached to a shelf for a flask of live water. The shallow argent contents of the flask reacted to the approach of her hand by seething. Crutchsump drained the live water flask dry, figuring that she would need the sustenance most today, and that if she met with success, she could easily replenish her larder. If not—

But that alternative did not bear contemplation.

Meanwhile, Pirkle had uncommonly roused himself. The nocturnal wurzel enjoyed his sleep, and generally spent the daylight hours, while Crutchsump was abroad, at the foot of the pallet, chirring rhythmically, the garish false eyes ringing his circumference mounting a bold bluff against antediluvian predators unseen in Sidetrack City for millennia. Now the lids of his true eyes opened, revealing bright blue orbs. Pirkle used several of his feet to scratch his rugose underbelly, flexing with pleasure the padded toes of the remaining feet as they pressed into the floor. The wurzel's mandibles clacked ecstatically.

With a hand on her door leading to a flight of steps street-ward, Crutchsump was about to order Pirkle to remain behind. But at the last moment she relented. She would appreciate the companionship of the creature while out on her scary, necessary errand. So, securing a large coarse sack used for collecting, Crutchsump set out, with Pirkle skittering along behind her.

The streets of Sidetrack City bustled with activity. Crutchsump's own ghetto neighborhood, the Telerpeton district, hosted a vibrant commercial life, although admittedly the products, vendors and customers were marginal at best. The bone-scavenger had to dodge pails of slops flung into the gutter from eel-soup booths. Late-blooming or early-rising whores monopolized a stretch of sidewalk, their cauls made of shockingly thin fabric. Crutchsump crossed the unpaved street to avoid them. She passed a pottery shop where giant ornate urns used as ghost-catchers filled a display window. Hailed by a neighbor, Grippo, she waved a pleasant hello. Grippo traded in old knives and other tools.

All the while Pirkle trotted contentedly at the heels of his mistress, darting off now and then to investigate with his delicate vibrissae one attractive bit of offal or another. Crutchsump's hunger made even the trash look appealing.

Entering the Bellefoyle district, Crutchsump experienced a grander surround. The streets became paved with broad mica-flecked stones, the pedestrians were better dressed and healthier, the stores more luxe, the civic scents pleasanter. Wagons and carriages, pulled by trundlebrumes and padlopes, racketed down the cobbles. A solemn Noetic seemed to float down the sidewalk. His long robe, woven with stylized Cosmocopian symbols, concealed his slippered feet, and a hat like a crown-dimpled loafcake perched atop his head. Feeling out of place, Crutchsump moved cautiously, sticking to walls and using alleys wherever possible. To live amidst such genteel splendor—what must it be like?

An hour later, Crutchsump reached broad, curving Huid Avenue, which followed the line of the bay. The cryptic, fecund odors of the sea dominated here. The daylight from Watermilk, reflected off the nearby waters, assumed a thicker, more penetrative aspect.

Hastening to the railing that separated the avenue from the

reedy Mudflats, Crutchsump saw that the tide was high, water lapping among the reeds just yards away from the seawall of the avenue. In her haste, she had neglected to monitor the tidal conditions at Shulgin Mudflats. Now she would have to wait for the water to retreat before she could attempt a harvest. And that circumstance would not occur, she knew, until perilously close to dark. (The second sun, Zarafa, would not fill the skies again for days.)

Return the long way home empty-handed? To an empty larder and an importunate landlord? Impossible.

Resigned to her fate, Crutchsump settled down on her haunches at the head of a ramp that led down from the avenue and into the wasteland. The ramp was flanked by heaps of trash dumped there illegally by lazy refuse carters unwilling to make the long trip out to the Kossuth Middens. Pirkle began to root among the garbage, looking for anything good to eat. For lack of a better activity, Crutchsump joined her pet.

She turned up a handleless drinking cup; a two-scintilla coin; a long scarf of cheap fabric, quite dirty of course but still useful for patching her caul; and a knife with no handle which she could sell to Grippo. All into the sack.

Then Crutchsump excavated a discarded sex toy. The rubber model of an introciptor, freakishly large, embarrassed, disgusted and compelled her. She tossed the thing away. Pirkle lunged after it across the mud, as if playing a game.

"Pirkle! Stop! Get back here!"

Obedient but unchastened, Pirkle returned to the side of his mistress. He cleaned all the mud from his legs with his strigil organ, then folded his many limbs beneath himself as he lowered his body, completely concealing them. His true eyes closed, leaving his many false ones mounting their standard protective charade. Chirring noises soon emanated from the lumpish form.

Crutchsump sat, bringing her knees up to her chin, clutching her legs and staring morosely but not unhopefully out to sea.

Watermilk was biting into the aquatic horizon, sending long shadows of the reeds across the land when Crutchsump decided it was safe to venture out onto the drained flats. She roused Pirkle and descended the ramp. At the base of the ramp she removed her huaraches, slinging them over a shoulder, and stepped barefoot onto the mud. Each step immersed her to the ankles, but no further, and so while progress was laborious, she was in no immediate danger of becoming mired.

Here and there among the reeds, Crutchsump found an occasional drifted shifflet skeleton which she promptly bagged. But she knew that the bulk of the harvest lay beyond the reeds, closer to the ocean's marge. The shifflet bones were anchored by organic threads formed during the decomposition process of the parent to the heavy, stable egg clutches, providing a protective cage for the future generation of shifflets. Removing each bone cage would doom that clutch. Nevertheless, despite the harvest, shifflets returned in force each year, so Crutchsump had no remorse.

As she forced her way through the reed jungle, Crutchsump looked warily around for signs of the monster.

She came to a dry mound, a trampled area of the reeds that might have denoted a person-sized nest elevated above the high tide. And indeed, there were discarded fruit rinds and gorgit skins there. But no monster.

Yet.

Crutchsump's steady passage through the reeds was interrupted once, when Pirkle chanced to tangle with a grapple-gnaw. The wurzel stumbled in its eager bumbling explorations on the grapple-gnaw's burrow and was instantly wrapped by three slimy ribbed and striped tentacles that shot forth from the mud. But Pirkle's stout mandibles severed those fleshy ropes easily, and in the end it was Pirkle who dined, not the grapple-gnaw.

When Crutchsump finally reached the actual beach, she was rewarded by the sight of innumerable shifflet skeletons. Scintillas practically in her pocket! She began to reap them hurriedly, discarding the worthless eggs, for only half of Watermilk remained above the horizon.

Her back sore from repetitive bending, her sack full, Crutchsump turned at last, amidst deepening twilight, toward the shore.

There at the edge of the reeds, just yards away, stood the monster, watching her.

Crutchsump let out an involuntary shriek. Pirkle, an egg clutch dangling from his mandibles, looked up. Spotting the monster, the wurzel commenced a shrill metallic keening and began to charge the apparition.

Expecting her pet to be torn in half, mutilated and tossed aside, Crutchsump cried out, "Pirkle, no!"

But the wurzel did not listen this time, and continued its charge.

The monster did something utterly unexpected then.

It collapsed in a heap to the muck, shielding its obscenely naked head with its arms, and emitting an all-too-human wail.

Realizing her golden opportunity to flee with her life and harvest intact, Crutchsump darted inland, the bag full of lightweight bones thumping against her back in encouragement.

But then she stopped, awash with anxiety.

Pirkle! She couldn't abandon her pet! Life was lonely enough with the beloved wurzel as her companion. How could she live after consigning Pirkle to such a horrid fate?

Every nerve ablaze with anguish and fear, Crutchsump turned back to face the monster and advance upon it, to rescue Pirkle. She prepared the swing her only weapon, her lightly laden sack.

What she saw utterly confounded her.

Sunk in the muck, the monster was clutching Pirkle as if for comfort, its obscenely naked face pressed against Pirkle's back. And the wurzel was licking the amniotic mud from the monster's legs with its raspy strigil.

Slowly, Crutchsump advanced on the unlikely tableau, ready to flee or defend herself at any second.

But the monster made no threatening moves, continuing instead merely to clutch Pirkle like a man adrift at sea clutching a log, all the while sobbing and wailing.

As Crutchsump got closer, she could make out words of distress and pain in the monster's unceasing lament.

"Dead! Dead! And I killed her! The bloody cane! Blood everywhere! This must be hell! Yes, hell! And I deserve it! Devil's red lacquer on her skin! The smell! The taste! Dead, my world's all dead!"

Crutchsump was hardly reassured by the tenor or content of the monster's babbling speech. But somehow, she nonetheless received the distinct impression that the monster itself intended her no harm.

Bolstered by this intuition, Crutchsump came to within inches of the monster. Tentatively, she reached out a hand to touch its arm.

Receiving the touch, the monster raised its naked face, and ceased its lamentations.

Braced for unwelcome intimacy, Crutchsump nevertheless reeled back at the proximity of horror.

The creature was a eunuch, obviously castrated sometime in the past. For where its introciptor should have jutted proudly forth was a mere blob of flesh, a cruel scarification, healed ugly long ago.

Other than that absence, however, its features were human enough, within a certain latitude: eyes, mouth, chin, ears, the whole countenance besmeared and runneled with tears.

The monster spoke, rationally this time.

"Help me. Please."

Crutchsump felt an immediate pity for the creature. She knew what it was to pass whole days in poverty, ignored by all, unspeaking.

"Help? All right. All right, I will help you. But first, we need to cover your face."

Rummaging in her sack, Crutchsump pulled out the long scarf she had earlier found in the trash. After picking tangled shifflet bones off the fabric, she wound the dirty stinking cloth around the monster's face, leaving only the creature's eyes exposed, before knotting the fabric at the back of its neck. Not a proper caul, but good enough.

"Now stand up. I don't have any clothes for you, but at least your face is decent. That's all that really matters."

The monster released Pirkle and stood.

Crutchsump received another shock.

Pegged to its groin was some kind of amorphous, bumpy tri-lobed growth, plainly a kind of goiter or cancer. Crutchsump's pity for the monster only increased, once her initial revulsion was past.

Luckily, the lashings of mud and muck across the monster's whole body blurred the anomaly, as did the oncoming night. Crutchsump prayed the smelly caked-on covering would last until they reached her home.

Now Watermilk had vanished wholly from sight, and full darkness had descended.

"Pirkle! Lead us back to the street!"

The wurzel had stood by in patient approbation of the whole process of making friends with the monster and rendering it decent. Now Pirkle proudly led his mistress and new companion through the maze of reeds and back to Huid Avenue.

Once she had attained the familiar highway, Crutchsump experienced anew the unreality of her situation: side-by-side with a creature from who-knew-where in the Cosmocopia. Oh, well, having adopted this strange refugee, she could hardly abandon it now.

"Come, let's move."

Crutchsump set off down Huid Avenue at a speedy clip—as fast at least as her tired flesh could move.

The monster followed a few paces behind.

As they approached the first of the busier districts of Sidetrack City, the monster faltered. It seemed stunned by the number and quality and hustle-bustle of the evening citizenry, reacting possibly also to that citizenry's startlement at the monster's own outrageous appearance. The sight of a majestic Noetic caused to monster to freeze completely.

Were it not for Pirkle gently nipping and chivvying with

its mandibles, the creature might have remained rooted to the sidewalk for good. But as it was, Pirkle and Crutchsump managed to guide the monster to the borders of the Telerpeton slums, and thence down the short flight of crumbling stairs into Crutchsump's apartment.

The monster quietly slumped down on Crutchsump's own pallet of shabby blankets and closed its eyes. Within minutes, a nasal burr accompanied its descent into exhausted sleep. Pirkle settled comfortably into estivation beside the monster as if nothing out of the ordinary had occurred.

Her own tired mind whirling, Crutchsump considered the exotic guest sprawled across her bed.

Did the monster eat the same food as she? How could she get some victuals at this hour? She had the two-scintilla piece she had found, but that would hardly buy a minim of live water. Perhaps she could rouse Rheaume the bone wholesaler, show him her harvest, and get an advance, even if he didn't care to process the shifflet bones at this hour. And clothes! What of clothes for the monster, and a real caul? Did anyone make prosthetics for lost introciptors? The sex toy at the Mudflats! That might've served, if only she hadn't tossed it away—

A whole catalogue of chores assembled itself in Crutchsump's brain. Many exacting tasks, not easy of accomplishment. Challenges and trials.

But somehow they seemed so very unexpectedly welcome.

CHAPTER THREE
INTERVIEW WITH A NOETIC

The monster was "he" now, just shortly after his arrival at Crutchsump's shabby basement digs.

The lonely-no-more bone-scavenger found it hard, in fact, to recall the early days when she had regarded Lazorg as a non-sentient, menacing thing.

Although he certainly did retain enough oddities of aspect, behavior and worldview to qualify as decidedly freakish, still.

But somehow his eccentricities only made Lazorg more endearing to Crutchsump, as if he were a quirky, knobby ideation—marked down for sale on a seconds shelf, malformed and inaesthetic, dusty and ignored by all the other customers of some third-rate ideatory gallery—whose odd curves and implications only she could appreciate.

Lazorg—still nameless, at this point in Crutchsump's memory of events—had slept for thirty-eight hours, nearly a whole night and day, after he had collapsed naked and muddy upon Crutchsump's sweat-redolent doss.

Crutchsump herself had passed the interminable hours of darkness until Watermilk's rising by sitting uncomfortably on a backless stool, alternately dozing lightly and jerking awake to contemplate the anomalous stranger she had taken in with a feeling of unreal anticipation. She had decided against venturing out for food until daylight, and her own stomach rumbled, engendering odd surreal dreams in her neighboring enteric cortex.

Throughout the long night, her caul—splashed with sea water from the Mudflats, and now brine-crusty—itched her, and she longed to remove it, as was common practice amongst all civilized people during their solitary moments.

But the notion of baring her private parts to even a sleeping monster left her with a mixed feeling of revulsion and illicit thrills.

When at last dim wands of daylight slid in the small windows inset high in the basement walls—windows that showcased only the hastening feet of passersby—Crutchsump roused herself fully. Pirkle, who had not abandoned his own snoozy vigil by the somnolent monster, cranked open one true eye and regarded his mistress as if to say, "Go about your business—I've got this one under watch."

Crutchsump took the wurzel at his unspoken word, and set out, clutching her bag full of shifflet bones.

Rheaume the bone wholesaler operated out of Boxall Alley, from a fairly capacious warehouse with slate floors splotched with organic matter. Beyond doors that rolled open overhead directly onto the alley, a small messy weigh station occupied the front part of the premises: bins for sorting, hand-trucks for toting, a pegboard full of differently colored and shaped discs for identifying miscellaneous lots of bones.

Luckily, Rheaume, in competition with many others in his trade, opened early.

Crutchsump found the fat ostealist ensconced behind his scales, sprawled in a spavined chair and noisily eating his breakfast, a mess of looby porridge. To accomplish this meal, of course, Rheaume had loosened the drawstring of his caul and raised the hem above his mouth, thereupon tightening the cord above his upper lip and below his jutting introciptor.

Unlike Crutchsump's unassuming caul, Rheaume's head-covering was made of luxurious fabric and tatted out with sewn-on trinkets and charms. Although the overall effect of ostentation was admittedly lessened by grease and sauce and condiment splotches, stains that also afflicted his lilac pantaloons and darker purple blouson.

Spotting Crutchsump, Rheaume licked his fingers clean, readjusted his caul, and hoisted his bulk with no small effort out of his seat.

"Ah, Crutchsump, at last! I began to think that my best freelance scavenger had given up the trade!"

"Not at all. In fact, I've got the first shifflet bones I estimate you've seen all season."

Rheaume rubbed his hands together gleefully. "If so, a bonus! Pharmacists across the city are clamoring for them!"

Powdered shifflet bones were reputed to cure many ailments, including dropsy and bale-flux.

Crutchsump upended her sack into the large dented pan of the biggest scale. Already picked clean of tissue by marine organisms, the shifflet bones gleamed white as the eyes of ghosts.

Rheaume discerned the bas-relief numbers on the scale's dial, did a mental calculation, and then moved to a lockbox. He opened the small vault and began to count out scintillas.

"Eighty, ninety, one hundred! Plus, that bonus. Ten more!"

Always deferential in her business dealings, Crutchsump never contested amounts. Until today.

"Could you possibly add five to your already generous bonus, Rheaume?"

Taken aback by this unusual self-aggrandizement, Rheaume grew flustered and irate. "Why, I never— That is, I suppose— Oh, here, just have it!"

Crutchsump caught the additional five-scintilla piece that was tossed to her. Like all the coins circulating in Sidetrack City, the unit bore no design, and was distinguished from its kin solely by color and shape and size.

Turning to leave, Crutchsump was halted by a question from Rheaume: "May I inquire as to what prompted this sudden avarice?"

"I've got two mouths to feed now," answered Crutchsump.

This reply floored Rheaume even more visibly, and Crutchsump left him shaking his head in wonderment. She was rather pleased with the effect.

The food market was lively, even at this early hour. The impoverished district of Telerpeton hardly attracted the most luxurious foodstuffs or highest-class vendors, but all the wares on display were nonetheless fresh and wholesome and nutritious, albeit the plainest varieties. The close-packed stalls and unrolled rush-mats and tiered baskets held a wide selection, all of which made Crutchsump's own empty stomach renew its gurgles.

She spent some time selecting a good mix of foodstuffs, items she seldom indulged in for her own enjoyment: lake leeks, star bread, a clutch of faufaws, some roasted medallions of clandestini. She added in some vials of livewater, the amber and teal decoctions. Then, anxious that the monster might awaken in her absence, she hurried to the adjacent district where the dry goods merchants congregated. Here she bargained for a simple taupe caul and dhoti. She also picked up a different kind of livewater, this decoction not intended for ingestion, but rather for ablutions.

Burdened with her purchases in a sling, Crutchsump hastened home.

She arrived to find the scene in her small apartment unchanged, save for brighter daylight. The monster still snored athwart her pallet, Pirkle adjacent.

The wurzel came fully alert when his mistress approached. Elevating himself, Pirkle stretched his many limbs one at a time—a long satisfying process—then shambled outside to relieve himself of aromatic waste lozenges and to seek scraps.

Crutchsump kneeled beside the monster and unwrapped the chance-found fabric from its head, without disturbing its sleep. The sight of its scarified face again, totally lacking an introciptor, caused her to quail, but only with pity.

Unstoppering the bottle of cleansing livewater, she decanted the liquid on the monster's face.

The livewater emerged as a coherent shimmering silver blob, exhibiting irregular pseudopod extensions of its body. After gauging the surface it rested upon, it began to clean, absorbing all extraneous, non-living matter into itself. Up and down and underneath the monster's body it coursed, leaving unsoiled skin in its wake.

When the livewater had finished cleaning the monster, Crutchsump allowed it to go to work on her pallet, searching for night-mites and other unwelcome visitors.

The lineaments of the monster, freed of their obscuring mud overcoat, were now plain. Its skin, marked with scratches and welts from its time in the Shulgin Mudflats, seemed normal enough. Even the bizarre growth at the crux of its legs looked oddly natural, not teratogenic or unhealthy.

Rocking back on her haunches, Crutchsump pondered the monster for a longish meditative interval. Here was someone more unfortunate than herself, without a friend in the world. The monster's condition and nature intrigued her....

At last she was distracted from her reflections by the reappearance of the livewater. The amorphous dirty blob emerged, sated, from within the rags of her pallet, and she coaxed it back into its bottle, for which it had a tropism. Later, she would return it for a partial refund good toward purchase of another such.

Crutchsump arose and laid out the food and the clothing for the monster's inspection. She took a few items for her own nourishment, and enjoyed them thoroughly. Then she commenced a long wait.

The light through the basement windows circumnavigated the rooms. Pirkle came and went on several wurzelish errands, always making sure to inspect the monster upon each return. Once an unexpected smell or motion caused the wurzel to rear up on a few of its hind legs and display its normally hidden under-beak. But when the monster offered no further challenge, Pirkle subsided.

When the quality of the light began to approach dusk, the monster at last opened its eyes in flickering stages and took cognizance of its surroundings. Looking alarmed and frightened—insofar as Crutchsump could read its mangled face—the monster spoke.

"I— But where—? How did I—?"

Crutchsump discovered that with the monster conscious, she could no longer tolerate its naked face so easily. She picked up the new caul and thrust it forward.

"Here, please—put this on."

The monster accepted the caul and donned it, aligning the eyeholes with its eyes. The monster regarded Crutchsump to make sure it had done right. The portion of the caul that would normally contain its introciptor drooped in an unintentionally comic fashion, as in some stage farce. Crutchsump found herself stifling a laugh. How could any of the shifflet harvesters have ever been scared of this creature?

Although the monster's naked body still needed covering, Crutchsump did not press the dhoti upon it right away. Other matters were more important.

"Are you hungry?"

"Yes. I think so. Yes!"

"Here. Help yourself."

The monster fell eagerly upon the buffet. It brought a crisp-skinned faufaw to its mouth, but the caul intervened.

"Like this," said Crutchsump, illustrating.

The monster ate its fill, consuming nearly everything. Crutchsump experienced a twinge when she thought of how much of her back-straining labor had gone into purchasing that meal. Could she sustain the monster for very long? But perhaps he might come to support himself somehow....

Once replete, the monster dropped back down upon the clean pallet. Crutchsump used the moment to offer the dhoti to it.

"Perhaps you'd want to wear this...?"

The monster nodded. Standing, it slipped into the loincloth. Crutchsump was impressed with its muscular agility and the obvious utility of its slightly abnormal limbs. Apparently, so too was the monster. Inexplicably, it seemed to admire its own capabilities.

Regarding itself, the monster said, "I'm—I'm different."

"Different from me?"

"No. Different from what I was."

"How so?"

"I was—"

The monster held its head in both hands for a moment. "I seem to remember being old, frail, sick...."

"That's obviously not the case now."

The monster regarded its body again. "No, it's not."

"Do you have a name?"

"Of course. Lazorg."

A perfectly acceptable name.

And with that, the monster was gone, the "it-ness" of it evaporated, and he was only Lazorg.

"My name is Crutchsump. And that's Pirkle."

Hearing his name, the wurzel began to buzz in a pleasant fashion. Pirkle rubbed against Lazorg's leg, looking to have his dorsal ridges scratched. But Lazorg recoiled in distaste.

"This—this is the kind of horror that nearly drove me mad when I first arrived here! Naked, alone, guilty, her blood on my hands— I never— What is it?"

"It's my companion, a wurzel. The wild ones of the Merhamet region are dangerous, but the domesticated ones are good, clever friends."

Lazorg crumpled back down to the pallet. He cradled his head. "These words, these things— I don't know any of them! What language are we speaking? It hurts my throat! How can I understand you? Why do you cover your face? What's the strangeness under your mask?"

The monster-who-had-been began to weep. Crutchsump felt a renewed stab of pity for Lazorg. Wherever he originated, he was plainly adrift and lost and hopeless, far from his kind.

She moved to his side, sat down on the pallet, and tentatively rested her arm over his shoulders. Lazorg did not flinch from her touch, but rather buried his face against her flat chest and continued to sob.

Crutchsump stroked the back of Lazorg's oddly contoured

head through the fabric of his caul. She considered doffing her own head-covering and disclosing herself to him in all her nudity, to satisfy his curiosity. But ultimately, she could not quite bring herself to this level of intimacy—at least, not yet.... So she resorted to words only, ones that might be used with a questioning child.

"People carry their organs of generation beneath their cauls. This organ is called an introciptor. We go face-naked only with our lovers, or during certain bathing rituals."

Lazorg ceased weeping and looked up with an astonished expression at Crutchsump. After a moment he began to laugh, softly at first, then louder and louder, till he verged on the hysterical.

"Oh, God, no, but this is—this is priceless! I'm in hell for my sins, truly I am—"

Crutchsump grew offended. She disengaged from Lazorg and stood brusquely up.

"I don't know this word 'hell,'" but it's plainly a place of disgrace. I would have you know that this world is perfect as it stands, and does not deserve your dishonor. The world arises from the Conceptus, and nothing the Conceptus does is less than ideal."

Lazorg halted his laughter. He stood up as well, and Crutchsump realized how bulky he was compared to her, how he towered above her. A momentary fright quivered through her. Pirkle stridulated a nascent warning tone.

Lazorg's demeanor was repentant, contrite. "I'm very sorry to have mocked the solemn proprieties of your kind, Crutchsump. I did not mean any disrespect, especially to the only being who's helped me so far during my troubles. It's just that everything— everything is so alien and strange to me here. For instance, you mentioned a being called the 'Conceptus' just now. I have never heard that designation before. Who or what is he?"

"Why, how can you not know of the Conceptus? The Conceptus is the origin of everything you see around you."

"The Conceptus is God?"

"What is 'God?'"

"How can I explain God?"

"How can I explain the Conceptus?"

The two fell silent. Then Crutchsump ventured: "We need to visit a noetic. They specialize in such knowledge, and possess the skillful words to convey high truths."

Lazorg's eyes brightened at the prospect of illumination. "You'd take me to such a person?"

"Yes. But let's wait until darkness. Your malformed face will attract enough attention even then. People will stare and point. Are you ready for that?"

"Nothing could be worse than being the bare-assed monster of the marshes!"

Crutchsump laughed at this description, and Lazorg chuckled too.

They passed another hour or so until full night in silence, Lazorg investigating with minute scrutiny all the common and shabby appurtenances of Crutchsump's apartment, as if they were the fixtures of a palace in the Bullacre district. Crutchsump partook of some livewater and a faufaw, and devoted some attention to a neglected Pirkle.

When darkness reigned, they set out, Pirkle too.

"The local noetic is named Palisander. He's just a hedge noetic, not a sophisticate like the ones who officiate at all the ceremonies in Liviabelle, for instance. But for simple questions like yours, he'll do just fine."

"I wish I had your faith that my questions were so simple and easy of resolution."

"Once you understand about the Conceptus, everything will be clear."

The nighted streets harbored many citizens going about their errands, legal or otherwise. Here, a slumming voluptuary, regal in striped robe and jeweled caul; there, a beggar in dhoti and dirt. True to Crutchsump's prediction, people did point and stare at the drooping, impotent introciptor pouch depending from Lazorg's caul. But the ex-monster was too intent on his destination—or too blind to propriety—to be properly ashamed of even the jeers of children.

Palisander lived in the back of a small Cosmocopian shrine on Overspan Way. The entrance from the street to the front public room of the shrine was garlanded with a curtain of beads. The clacked as Crutchsump and Lazorg stepped inside. (Pirkle, uninterested in metaphysics, had followed his vibrissae toward some tasty bit of offal.)

The windowless anteroom was lit by a bevy of candles tall as people, with heavy metal bases spiked into their bottoms to keep them upright. No one else was present to hear the droplets of melted wax as they plopped faintly to the floor. Against one wall stood a cubical altar of polished stone, nothing rare. Atop the altar resided a model of the Cosmocopia, surrounded by coils of fizzing incense. The pungent smoke from the incense subdued the light, rendering the whole room dusky.

Lazorg approached the model of the Cosmocopia and ran a hand tentatively along its length, from tip to flaring mouth.

"It's—it's a horn of plenty."

"I have never heard the Cosmocopia referred to as such. But that's a poetical description that might fit the facts."

Lazorg bent closer, to peer at the material of the model, with an artist's eye. "How was this made? I don't see any chisel marks. Was it cast? If so, what material is this? It's not a resin, or plastic. It's almost like a ceramic…."

"Again, you use words I don't recognize. That model is an ideation."

"An ideation?"

Crutchsump began to grow a tad impatient with Lazorg. Were all ex-monsters so dense? "You'll understand later. Right now, you wanted to learn about the Conceptus. It's growing late and I'm tired. I hardly slept last night, wondering and worrying about you. Let's see Palisander and then go home."

"Fine, yes, all right. I'm sorry to be a burden."

Crutchsump regretted her shortness of temper immediately, but felt too awkward to apologize. Instead, she turned toward a second portal.

This doorway likewise sported a bead curtain. The visitors pushed through it.

The inner apartment, lit by a single oil lamp, was as Spartan as Crutchsump's. A small larder, a sleeping platform, a stool. On this last piece of furniture sat Palisander the noetic. He wore the traditional robe of Cosmocopian warp and weft, and loaf-cake hat, tipped slightly askew. His caul was the color of the mingled shadows when both Watermilk and Zarafa were high.

Palisander's eyes were shut in meditation on the ineffable, and he inhaled a long plume of incense smoke.

"Palisander," called out Crutchsump mildly. "You have a questioner."

The noetic opened his eyes, which were almost the same shade as his caul, thus producing an odd effect of merged fabric and flesh.

"Ask away."

"My companion here is a being from far away, and has never heard of the Conceptus. Can you explain?"

"Of course." Palisander directed his attention to Lazorg. "Did you see the model of the Cosmocopia outside?"

"Yes."

"That is the shape of the universe."

"How so? Literally?"

"Yes. The mouth of the horn is a spreading, widening wave-front. As it sweeps out a path, new planes of existence are born, new dimensions that imagine themselves unique, whereas they are really just the latest accretions of the living eternal process that is the Cosmocopia.

"You can conceive of the Cosmocopia as a finite stack of universes, each one slightly larger and hence more attenuated than its predecessor. Working backward down the length of the Cosmocopia, the universes grow smaller and smaller, until finally we reach the endpoint—or, actually, the origin, the Omphalos, which is simultaneously without size, yet infinite, since it contains the seed of all that was to come. At this point resides the Conceptus, he who gave birth to the Cosmocopia and continues to inform it. The Conceptus manifested the Cosmocopia as an expression of his will and nature. Everything we see, everything that will be, on all the planes, is inherent in the character of the Conceptus. So, by studying his creation, we come to understand the creator. Do you comprehend?"

Lazorg was quiet for a moment. "Except for the personalization of the Monobloc, it's just like the Big Bang. The spacetime lightcone.... And your stacked universe are just parallel worlds."

"You can employ any terms you wish, but the truth is incontrovertible."

"Then I must have somehow been cast out of my own universe and wound up in this one."

"Quite likely."

"But how?"

"Please describe the circumstances attendant on your last moments in your native universe."

Lazorg winced. "I—I prefer not to. They are hazy, and I—"

"Did they involve intense emotions, and perhaps a derangement of the senses?"

"Yes, yes they did."

"These factors occasionally open up a noetic hole in the fabric of the Cosmocopia. A hole which one can easily fall through."

"Can I return the same way then?"

"Unlikely. You see, for one thing, there is a gradient to the Cosmocopia. All-that-is wishes instinctively to return to the Conceptus, to unite with its ultimate source. Therefore, travel through noetic gaps is always inward, from younger, more primitive and attenuated planes to older, more dynamic and powerful ones. Travelers are caught in an irresistible psychosomatic current. Do you note any changes in your constitution since the transition?"

"I was old and feeble before. Now I'm not."

"Certainly. Because you are now marginally closer to the Conceptus, inhabiting a plane of richer, more elemental forces. Many of your old paradigms will not apply here. You would be wise to learn the ways of your new plane, and settle down."

Crutchsump regarded Lazorg and saw his shoulders slump in defeat. "So I can never return to the plane of my birth?"

"Never. The gradient will not permit it. Even if you were able to open up another noetic gap—and such moments come rarely to anyone; once in a lifetime is the most anyone can realistically even hope for—then you would find yourself just plunging deeper into the Cosmocopian chute."

Lazorg turned wearily and wordlessly away from the noetic. Crutchsump hastened to make a proper farewell.

"Thank you, Palisander, for your teachings. May each day bring you closer to the Conceptus."

"And you also, Crutchsump."

Lazorg had stumbled out into the public anteroom, and now stood regarding the model of the Cosmocopia with an expression of numb fixity. Crutchsump laid a hand gently on his arm.

"Let's go home, Lazorg."

CHAPTER FOUR
THE VOLVOX

Whatever his hidden inner feelings, whatever tumult of despair and self-pity might be concealed in his bosom, Lazorg adapted without protest to the life of a bone-scavenger.

Crutchsump was not truly surprised.

Despite any lingering debilitating attrition of his memories, the former monster seemed a reasonable being, of above-average intelligence. He could see, like any thinking individual, that he had little choice in the matter of profession. He was a stranger in this universe, unacquainted with any of its culture or paradigms. He had to have shelter and be able to eat to survive. What could he do, other than follow in the footsteps of the only person who had so far taken his welfare to heart?

The morning after their first visit to Palisander, Crutchsump arose early. Again, she had dozed fitfully on the stool, ceding her pallet to Pirkle and Lazorg, who, in his dumbfounded daze subsequent to the noetic's revelations, seemed more in need of whatever Spartan comfort the basement apartment could afford. But Crutchsump's aching bones and muscles and unrelieved fatigue informed her that the arrangement could not persist. Although what new domestic setup could replace it, she did not know.

Also, she chafed at having to wear her caul continuously, without the relief of any naked hours.

Crutchsump hobbled wearily over to the sleeping Lazorg and shook him awake. He received the summons with equanimity, opening his eyes—Crutchsump noted for the first time their odd color, like that of a leaden sky—stretching, and saying with some small measure of enthusiasm, "Good morning, Crutchsump." Pirkle emitted a companionable chirring as well.

Crutchsump did not feel similarly civil. "We need to go to work today. The money I earned from the shifflets will not last us forever. Refresh yourself, have something to eat, and then we'll be off."

Lazorg stood and looked about. "Where, ah—where do I eliminate my wastes? It wasn't a problem yesterday, for some reason. But today—"

"The application of the cleansing livewater to your skin also attended to that inner necessity for a short time. But now we have no more such luxury."

"So, you people commonly need to void?"

"Of course! Unless one lives exclusively on oral livewater, we have to eliminate, just like you, I presume. I don't have a waste closet here. You can use the neighborhood honeyshed. It's only around the corner, once you turn left. But don't stray and get lost!"

"I won't."

Lazorg left the basement. Crutchsump immediately whipped off her caul, and used the moments of privacy to splash her face from a pot of insensate water. Scrubbing her introciptor brought muted feelings of much-missed pleasure. She was hardly a virgin, and relished intimacy with certain local bedmates as much as anyone. New living arrangements would definitely be the first order of the day....

Crutchsump just barely had time to re-don her caul when she first heard Lazorg descending the basement steps. She finished knotting the under-chin tie as he came in.

Seemingly invigorated by his short solo excursion into the streets of the Telerpeton neighborhood, Lazorg announced, "There were no signs at the honeyshed to say which closets were for males, which for females. So I just used any."

So much was confusing about Lazorg's pronouncement, that

Crutchsump hardly knew where to begin.

"What is 'signs'?"

Lazorg's eyes expressed his own bafflement. "A sign? A sign is a—" He paused. "Your language doesn't seem to have any word for it. It's a piece of writing hung for all to see."

"And what is 'writing'?"

"You don't— This world has no writing?"

"Apparently not."

Lazorg pondered long and hard upon that statement before saying: "Perhaps you're just illiterate. People who live in poverty often are. When I can ask others, surely they'll tell me what the local equivalent of writing is. Palisander will know."

Although the word "illiterate" was just gibberish, Crutchsump resented Lazorg's tone. "It's true that I live on few scintillas, but I am as smart as any rich dweller on Hedgepath Avenue! My gut brain has a deep lineage! You are the stranger in this world, not me!"

Lazorg seemed genuinely humbled. "I apologize."

Mollified, Crutchsump found herself intrigued by the way Lazorg thought. "Accepted. Now, why did you expect the closets to be separate for males and females?"

"Because that's how it works where I come from."

"Don't we all share identical organs of voiding? What would be the point of one sex concealing their equipment from the other?"

"Oh, then your—your introciptors have nothing to do with waste elimination?"

No aspect of Lazorg's looks or speech had truly disgusted Crutchsump until this moment.

"That is the most perverted thing I have ever heard of! Perhaps you *are* a monster after all!"

Sensing his mistress's dismay, Pirkle stilted himself higher in a threatening manner.

Lazorg hastened to explain himself. Crutchsump listened attentively, her ire gradually dwindling along with Pirkle's stature, then said, "Truly, the more distant a Cosmocopian plane is from the Conceptus, the more primitive life there shows itself. Well, you can thank your lucky ghosts that you have ended up one stage closer to the font of creation, where such absurd biological insults have no meaning."

Lazorg's curiosity now switched topics. "So the shape of the introciptors is what distinguishes male and female among your people?"

Putting herself in Lazorg's position—alone and bereft in a strange land, desperate for information—Crutchsump could pardon his indelicate presumption. Nonetheless, the topic was unwelcome. She felt herself flushing beneath her caul.

"Your ideas are ridiculous right down the line! Male and female introciptors are shaped identically."

"Then what—?"

"Male and female are variable roles based on size. During mating, whichever introciptor is the smaller will slip inside whichever is the larger. The smaller is considered the male."

"And at that point?"

"Well, eventually…after, ah, some activity…the male passes his gamete to the female, where it bonds with the matching gamete inside her. The fused gametes grow, and the female eventually gives birth."

"So an individual can function as male or female, all depending on their partner's size?"

"Yes."

"And do individuals exhibit preferences for performing as either sex? Do they search out partners that allow them the desired role? And what of partners with identically sized organs?"

Crutchsump regarded the packed dirt floor of her quarters. "Not so much. Occasionally. That is, attraction to one's character—"

This was ridiculous! Discussing sex with a being from another world! Crutchsump looked up with a fierce glare.

"Enough of this foolish racy talk! What does it matter to you after all? You're sexless!"

Lazorg made no reply to this rebuke, and Crutchsump felt she had effectively if harshly put an end to this unproductive line of talk.

"Pay attention now. If you're to continue living here, we have to make some alterations in this apartment. And that's going to cost money. We can spend what I have, but we'll need more for afterwards."

"I can help. I don't want to be a burden. Are we going to collect more bones from the Mudflats?"

"No. Almost as soon as I sold Rheaume the ostealist my harvest, all my peers will have learned that the Shulgin Mudflats are no longer haunted, and will have descended on the flats like a flock of minouskine. I doubt there are any shifflets left. But with your help, we can go after bigger prizes."

Crutchsump did not elaborate, and Lazorg refrained from inquiry. Just as well, since the bone scavenger was a trifle awed at her own nascent ambitions, and might have quailed stating them aloud.

"Let's go now."

"Where?"

"To Lustrum's Domestics."

Out on busy Weepmark Lane, Crutchsump led the way. Lazorg, she noted, tended to lag, fascinated by the commonplace surroundings, his gaze bouncing around excitedly from one unexceptional street tableau to another. Only Pirkle chivvying at his heels kept the fellow moving.

So intent was Lazorg on the passing parade that he failed to note or be offended by the taunts and giggles and shocked gasps elicited by his empty and flaccid introciptor pouch. But Crutchsump felt hurt and offended on his behalf. If only people knew that a stranger from another Cosmocopian plane walked among them, they'd be more respectful….

Caul-clad citizens carrying their market baskets. Mothers trundling prancer prams. Shouting children playing raggle taggle. Hawkers touting their wares, licit and illicit. A stray noetic, a brave yet circumspect uniformed member of the civil guardia, an ethical advocate proudly wearing the scarlet and gold midriff wrap of her profession....

Smells of guttermire, spices and the sea infiltrated the alleys and mews of the district. Adding to the soup of smells, Pirkle met another wurzel and exchanged aromatic scat lozenges.

Without a second look, Crutchsump passed a vendor standing beside a tray of cheap ideations, unimaginative renderings of awkward abstract shapes. The seller seemed too bored with his own wares even to praise them to potential customers.

But even without invitation, Lazorg stopped short beside the display. He picked up a palm-sized sample, all interlocking curves that frustrated intuitive vision rather than allured it.

"What is this? It's made of the same strange material as the model of the Cosmocopia at Palisander's."

"Put that down," said Crutchsump. "We have no money or time for geegaws."

Lazorg obeyed, and they moved on.

The decrepit block of conjoined buildings housing Lustrum's Domestics was composed of buttery cheesestone from the famed Boumalik quarries, legacy of the building's past fashionable existence. The combined light of Watermilk and Zarafa rendered the distressed facades luminously polychromatic, lending the tawdry street a bit of romance in Crutchsump's eyes.

The dusty interior of Lustrum's Domestics held various oddments of furniture and fabrics, most of the goods second-hand. The desultory sales staff adequately mirrored the merchandise.

Savoring this rare consumerist splurge, Crutchsump tracked down the best bargain in relatively clean bed clothes and doss pads. She selected the thickest, cheapest curtains, some rods and fittings. Lazorg did the toting. Once she had paid the toll, Crutchsump found she had just enough scintillas left for a few days' meals for the two of them.

Out on the street again, Crutchsump announced, "Back home now."

Burdened with the purchases, Lazorg still managed to dawdle

and act the lookie-loo.

Down in their basement quarters once again, Crutchsump directed her new partner. The second pallet was established as far across the room from the original as the limited dimensions of the space allowed. Standing on a wobbly crate, Lazorg erected the curtain rod up high down the middle of the room, and hung the sliding drapes on their clattering wooden rings. Retracted, the divider was hardly noticeable. But once extended, the curtains formed a seamless privacy barrier between the two sleeping pads.

Finished, they went out to shop for food.

At the market square, Lazorg became intrigued by the Belkys Tower, the time-humbled remnant of vanished Fort Verveer, which in another age had occupied the market grounds.

"Can we climb it?"

"Certainly." Crutchsump entrusted their purchases temporarily to the nearest vendor.

A circular staircase with crumbling steps clung to the exterior wall of the Belkys Tower. An iron railing on the outside edge of the steps seemed more rust than rail. Pirkle, perhaps wiser than anyone, declined to follow.

The top of the Tower afforded a small platform with waist-high crenellations. The view extended for miles in all directions, a variegated roof-scape of chimneypots, orerries, spires, windsocks, ghost-traps, beetle-browed garret windows and glass-walled penthouses of the distant rich, transected by unmappably twisting streets. Numerous birds of assorted sizes and squawks—juncos, lammergeiers and questrals, among other types—parceled the sky into avian empires.

Lazorg absorbed the view with a numb silence, pivoting slowly to take in all of Sidetrack City. Crutchsump tried to imagine his feelings and thoughts. At last the man turned to the bone scavenger. She saw tears staining his caul. Lazorg's voice was choked with emotion.

"It's real. It's all real."

Crutchsump understood the enormity of Lazorg's sudden

comprehension, and could sympathize. His transit across the membranes of the segmented Cosmocopian infundibulum constituted a monumental climacteric. But, ever practical, Crutchsump also envisioned trying to guide a big mystically bemused stumblebum down the precarious staircase, and so she sought to cast cold water on his epiphany.

"Oh, yes, it's all real—as you'll be able to ascertain as soon as your stomach starts rumbling! Let's get home and get supper on the table!"

Crutchsump's stern voice brought Lazorg's sensibilities back to earth. "Of course. I only meant— Well, never mind."

On pavement once more, they reclaimed their victuals, hailed Pirkle from his rooting in a midden—the wurzel emerged with garish dotted fruitskins draped across his brow—and headed back to the basement apartment.

Over a meal of oudknoobs and breaded, fried sea-skate, Lazorg spoke with voluntary optimism of his future.

"Back in my previous life, I was a tired, debilitated old man. My artistic impulses were all exhausted. Now I've been given youth and enthusiasm. Admittedly, at the price of losing all that was familiar and safe. But earning a living should come easy, with your help and tutelage. And once I've gotten my feet under me, I can turn my hand to my art again."

Crutchsump was intrigued. "What art was that?"

"Painting."

"What is 'painting'? Is it a kind of thing like 'writing'?"

Lazorg's voice contained a hint of hysteria. "No, don't tell me— That's impossible! I can't believe you don't know painting!"

Crutchsump yawned broadly. "I'm sure you'll discover whether your imaginary art form exists here or not. But first we have to earn some scintillas, starting bright and early tomorrow. So I'm going to sleep. I haven't rested fully for two nights now."

Lazorg stood up, making an evident effort at self-control. "I'm sorry, Crutchsump. Your unease was my fault. You were very generous to give up your bed for me. But now we have two.

Goodnight then."

Lazorg moved toward the original pallet, with its old rumpled threadbare accoutrements. Crutchsump halted him.

"No, you take the new arrangements. I'm used to that old bed."

Lazorg hesitated, then said, "Whatever you wish." He moved to his side of the room, and Crutchsump drew the thick curtains between them.

"Don't forget, you can remove your caul now. Otherwise you'll develop scaly itch."

"I'll do as you say."

Alone on her side—even Pirkle had deserted her for the allure of the fresh blankets—Crutchsump lingered a moment with her hand on the curtains. Finally though she retreated to her bed, where she removed her caul.

The bedding smelled faintly, disturbingly, of the Mudflats, from when the dirty monster had first lain there, overburdened with the odor of Lazorg's cleaner sweat. But despite the fragrances of her doss, sleep came easily, a welcome guest.

But in the middle of the long night, Crutchsump was awakened by sobs from beyond the divider, as Lazorg cried out a name over and over:

"Velina, Velina! Oh, Velina, I'm so sorry, Velina!"

* * * * * * *

The Chatterant Fields occupied a hundred acres or so outside Sidetrack City to the north. Hauling a small wain thence (borrowed from Rheaume on the promise of imminent profit for the ostealist) through the city streets starting before dawn took Crutchsump and Lazorg many hours. (Pirkle had been forced to remain home, noisily argumentative, for fear of slowing down the enterprise.) But the journey passed pleasantly enough, as Crutchsump answered Lazorg's many questions about the urban sights and activities they passed.

At last though the easygoing preliminary stage of their

workday ended, at the green margins of the place the volvox frequented.

Chatterant Fields hosted a wild monocrop of blue gasplants. At these gasplants, the volvox could oft be found, having dropped from the skies at necessary intervals to sip.

One volvox was in place now.

The volvox was an entity voluminous as the main room of Crutchsump's apartment. A symmetrically multifaceted geometrical shape, the volvox boasted a bright, slightly damp green skin whose macroscopic cellular structure was quite apparent, each cell with its own nucleus and apparatus of life. Faintly beneath the skin of the otherwise hollow being could be seen its intricate lightweight skeleton—the very prize which Crutchsump had in mind to win, with Lazorg's help.

Adhering to the trumpet of the gasplant by a suction valve, the volvox now sought to replenish its cargo of lighter-than-air lifting gases. When finished, it would detach and float away above any clouds, to absorb maximum sunlight that powered it.

Crutchsump produced a sharp knife, newly obtained on credit that morning from Grippo, the local dealer in cutlery.

"Once we rip through its skin, it will deflate and die. Then we secure the skeleton for sale!"

Lazorg studied the volvox dubiously. "Why can't one person do this?"

"The skin is tougher than it looks. It takes some sawing to get through. So: I'm alone, and I jump atop the volvox and start sawing. It panics and lifts my meager weight up into the skies. Even if I succeed in killing it, we both plummet to injury or death. But you're big and heavy, bigger than anyone else I know. You'll serve as an anchor while I stab it."

"Can't they be rushed by a group?"

"Too skittish. Even the pair of us might alarm it. So proceed delicately!"

"All right. Let's give it a try."

Lazorg and Crutchsump began stalking the blimpy creature. Whatever it used for sensory organs were not obvious, so they could not reliably select a "blind" side to focus on.

Sure enough, the volvox detected their approach, and took flight.

The scavengers retreated to the edge of the field.

"Next time I'll go alone," said Lazorg. "Then, when I've got it, you race in."

"Agreed!"

Under the shade of a geazel tree, they were just finishing the tasty cold lunch they had packed when a second volvox made its descent.

Lazorg dropped to his belly in the grass that grew around the gasplants, and began to worm toward the green faceted balloon.

Closer, closer—and a bold leap!

Even as she dashed forward, Crutchsump watched Lazorg's fingers dig into the rubbery skin of the volvox. The creature attempted to lift, but Lazorg's straining muscles and mass kept it from rising far.

Crutchsump leaped likewise through the air, landing on the upper irregular hemisphere of the volvox. She held on with one hand, while raising high the knife in the other. Down came the blade—and bounced off!

Crutchsump struck again, where skin seemed stretched thinner, over a ridge of bone.

The knife went in! She jagged the sharp side of the blade downward.

The lips of the wound vibrated with the expelled gas, making an uncanny animalistic moan that seemed to carry a freight of pain and despair.

The volvox hit the earth.

"Jump on it!" yelled Crutchsump. "Crush its bones!"

The two scavengers began to kick and mangle the relatively fragile skeleton inside the green skin. Soon the volvox had been reduced to a heap of calcific flinders, all inside a handy squishy sack much more compact than the inflated live creature.

Together, Lazorg and Crutchsump hauled the dead volvox back to the wain and heaved it aboard. They rested, panting, against the sides of the wagon, before refreshing themselves with some livewater.

"This one alone will net us a hefty sum," said Crutchsump. "Shall we call it a day?"

Shading his eyes, Lazorg looked to the sunny skies. Another volvox, only a distant dot, seemed to be heading their way.

"No, we made a long trip out here. Let's get the most for our efforts. And besides, I need my freedom as soon as possible—to paint."

CHAPTER FIVE
THE IDEATION MAKER

Pirkle rushed past and got underfoot as Crutchsump, burdened with string bags full of groceries, descended the grit-strewn stairs to her flat, nearly causing his mistress to fall. But the bone scavenger recovered herself with a natural agility, and remonstrated with the wurzel.

"Pirkle! What's the matter with you! Calm down!"

But the wurzel did not heed her words. Instead, he was capering about as if on the scent of some tasty quarry. A symphony of buzzes issued from his various diaphragms and sonic membranes.

As Crutchsump laid a hand on the doorknob, her own olfactory pits registered odd smells emanating from beyond the door. From inside the flat came explosive grunts and wordless exclamations.

Hastily, Crutchsump opened the door and entered, calling, "Lazorg! What's the trouble!"

The privacy curtain was drawn, dividing the room in half, and Lazorg's coarse cries issued from behind the drapes.

Pirkle darted below and past the barrier, buzzing furiously.

Crutchsump dropped the groceries and dashed the curtains apart.

Besieged by the jack-legged wurzel but ignoring the creature, Lazorg stood before an odd apparatus, the likes of which Crutchsump had never before seen.

A piece of cheap white shirt cloth had been stretched tight

and nailed securely across an old window-frame. That assemblage had been propped at head-height on an improvised tripod of sticks lashed together with twine.

Lazorg held a cracked dinner plate in one hand. The plate was heaped with a variety of gelatinous colored stuffs. These mixtures were the source of the odd odors. In his other hand, Lazorg flourished a stick with a clump of longish animal whiskers bound to its tip with thread.

Even as Crutchsump watched, Lazorg continued what he had been doing. He furiously scooped up portions of the colored stuffs onto his whiskery stick, then stabbed at the cloth, smearing trails across the already-clotted fabric.

Lazorgs's angry grunts cohered into words. "Damn you! Come together! Take shape! Obey me! Show yourselves! Why can't I *see!*"

Crutchsump tentatively approached Lazorg. When she laid a hand gently on his arm, he finally registered her presence, as if waking from a dream. He ceased stabbing the cloth. His eyes betrayed his immense agitation. Suddenly, he dropped his tools and clung to her, weeping.

Awkwardly, Crutchsump patted Lazorg's broad back. The big weight of him felt solid and comfortable in her arms, natural and acceptable—intimate.

This was the first time they had so embraced.

Reminded inescapably of past intimacies—mostly hurried, casual couplings with acquaintances of the Telerpeton slum at her own hardscrabble level, all now far in the past—Crutchsump half expected to feel Lazorg's throbbing introciptor resting on her shoulder, just as hers now did on his, token of intercourse to come. The lack of any such mate to her organ left her emotions feeling thwarted, prevented them from attaining a higher stage.

Gradually Lazorg ceased his tears, and Crutchsump relinquished his embrace. She felt free to question him.

"Whatever were you trying to do?"

"I was trying to paint!"

"Painting is smearing smelly stuff on cloth?"

"Not smearing. Oh, yes, I was smearing madly at the end. But that's just because I was so frustrated. Painting is carefully applying color to make a representation of something."

"A representation? You mean, the way an ideation can represent a real object? But any ideation has to have the same number of dimensions as whatever it represents. How could something flat stand for something tangible?"

"It can, it just can! At least, it can where I come from. But here—here, I can't make lines do what I want. I literally can't see shapes on the canvas. Nothing coheres in my vision. It's all just random blotches."

"There's simply no way to make something of lesser dimensions stand in for something of higher dimensions. Every child knows that."

"I'm more foolish than a child then."

"This matter is important to you? You can't be happy with our current security?"

Since the day they had captured their first volvox of many, Lazorg and Crutchsump had enjoyed a much higher standard of living—nicer clothes, better food in greater quantities—thanks to Rheaume paying them well for exclusive rights to the rare blimp bones. Crutchsump had dared to begin to imagine moving from these shabby quarters, this benighted neighborhood of her birth and childhood and maturity. Perhaps some job opportunities less rude and objectionable would even present themselves with the change of scenery, a new career before she became too old and tired to scavenge bones. Then she and Lazorg could—

Could what? She never managed to envision any aspect of their new life beyond a finer apartment.

And what guaranteed that the ex-monster would even stay with her, once he got his feet fully beneath him?

But now Crutchsump pondered instead Lazorg's obvious sincerity and puzzlement and drive to achieve his odd dreams.

"Plainly you believe in the possibility of this thing called 'painting.' But just as plainly, it doesn't exist here. So we'll have to see Palisander to solve the contradiction."

Lazorg's eyes brightened and his voice lifted. "That's a fine idea! Let's go now!"

"One moment. Let me clean up this mess."

Crutchsump bent to pick up the fragments of the plate which had shattered on the hard floor when Lazorg dropped it. Her fingers came into contact with some of the substances thereon, and she brought them to the olfactory pits under her caul and behind her ears.

"Is this fish paste? And what else?"

"Oh, various foodstuffs from the market that exhibited the colors I wanted. All blended together to make the crudest paint."

Crutchsump clucked her tongue. "Well, maybe at least we can salvage some condiments out of this art form of yours."

* * * * * * *

A poor but proud and presentable family of six occupied the anteroom of the Cosmocopian temple where Palisander reigned. The parents were dedicating several sheaves of pungent chorny-scented incense in front of the model of the Cosmocopia, while the older children hung back. Rather irreverently the kids picked at the wax drips hanging like stalactites from the candelabra, at the same time they responsibly held the hands of the younger siblings. But then a guardian child pressed a blob of warm wax against the arm of another, causing the younger one to begin crying.

Lazorg chuckled. Crutchsump kicked his ankle.

The chagrined parents turned around to hush their children and hustle them out of the shrine. On the front of one of the parents was a smallish papoose-like carrier, its hypothetical rider concealed.

After the family had departed, Lazorg said, "What did that mother have strapped to her chest?"

"That was the father. Couldn't you tell by the smaller size of his introciptor, relative to his mate's?"

"I don't have the same upbringing as you. I can't gauge such things quickly and instinctively. Besides, I didn't want to stare."

"So long as a person's caul is securely in place, there's no way to embarrass someone with a look. As for the carrier—it held a newborn."

"I would have liked to see that."

"They can't be exposed for too long during the first week after birth. They need protection."

"Oh. Well, let's go see our neighborhood noetic."

Clatter of bead curtain and scent of a more rarefied private incense preceded their entry into the back room.

Palisander was taking his midday meal, caul knotted above his upper lip. He waved a spoon at his visitors, inviting them to take a seat on the floor, then licked the utensil clean.

"Ah, such exquisite looby porridge Lindfors makes! But it's not cheap, no, not cheap at all...."

Crutchsump heeded the not-so-subtle prompting and deposited a handful of scintilla into a hammered brass plate meant for such offerings that would support Palisander and the shrine. She could hardly begrudge the noetic's abstemious needs.

"Now," said Palisander, after the coins had clinked, "what brings you two here today? Is it marital advice you need, perhaps? The whole district is buzzing about your new arrangements, Crutchsump. That Rheaume is a gossip! I know there's been no official enactment of vows between you, but as you well know, relations are naturally looser here in the Telerpeton. After all, we live far from the Grand Shrine at Shamoo, and the salons of Arcuze!"

Crutchsump tried to interrupt the mistaken flow of advice, but Palisander rushed on.

"Lazorg, pay heed! I suspect your alien trepidations are at fault here, the burr beneath the saddle. You've got a splendid mate in Crutchsump. How many beings would have taken pity on a disquietingly crippled exile from another plane and offered them shelter and a shared bed? And you physically unable to satisfy her natural desires, like any normal husband! What a paragon she is! You must cherish her and do your best to be a good spouse, despite any minor differences of temperament, any ordinary hardship which circumstances might erect in your way."

Palisander wound down his peroration and awaited a grateful word.

Crutchsump felt herself blushing beneath her caul. Lazorg exhibited only a stolid quiet, although he could be seen to fidget slightly.

"Honored Noetic," Crutchsump finally began, "while we appreciate receiving your wisdom, our actual errand is at cross-purposes to your sound advice. Lazorg, please explain…."

Lazorg began to lecture on his native-plane art form known as "painting." Palisander listened attentively, as Lazorg grew more and more animated, describing the glory of colors and lines arrayed linearly on a flat surface to simulate substantiality. When the visitor from far beyond Sidetrack City had finished, Palisander pondered his words silently for a time, then spoke.

"I can vaguely envision the technics you describe. But the physics of this world simply does not allow the creation of such representations. Or it may be that the physiology of our bodies, the capabilities of our senses, the interior conjunctions of our mind, are at fault. But in either case, your quest is a futile one, and you would be well advised to abandon it, before you bring more useless grief upon yourself."

Lazorg clutched his head. "But what shall I do instead! I've been given a second life, but for what? To collect bones in the street?"

Crutchsump felt a brief flare of guilt and indignation at Lazorg's demeaning of her profession. But she released the irksome emotion before it could fester.

Lazorg released his grip on his skull. "Maybe I could sculpt! That's it! I'll sculpt!"

Crutchsump eyed Palisander, who returned her baffled gaze.

"'Sculpt?' What is it, to 'sculpt?'"

Lazorg jumped up and loosed a wordless howl before recovering himself. "Don't tell me you don't know sculpting! I've seen sculptures everywhere. You've got one right outside your doorway here. The model of the Cosmocopia—"

"Oh, you mean ideations. Do you not know how ideations are produced?"

Lazorg sunk back down to the floor. "Not another quirky aspect of this place. Please, I can't take it...."

Palisander had reached around and was rummaging under his bed. He pulled out a long wooden wand with an obvious hand-grip at one end and a set of curious irregular protuberances near the pointed tip.

"This is a tranche. It's not a very good one, I'm afraid, because I'm not a very good ideator. Strictly an amateur. Watch."

Palisander lofted the tranche and began poking at the empty air. The tranche met no obvious resistance to its prodding—until Palisander hit a certain spot. There, the tranche seemed to catch and hang.

"An interstitial node. They're everywhere, really."

The tip of the tranche disappeared into some subtle flaw newly opened up in spacetime. Palisander worked the invisible tip about for a time, then withdrew it.

Attached to the tip of the tranche was a sizable blob of glowing ivory stuff.

"Cosmocopian nacre. Now, watch!"

Palisander continued to maneuver the tranche with blob attached in a circuitous path through the air: dipping, weaving, bobbing.

Lazorg appeared fascinated. The performance, thought Crutchsump, who had not often enjoyed the leisure time to watch ideators publicly create since the days when she was a carefree child, had something of a dance about it, something of a glassblower's actions, and something of the drunken flight of a swamp bee.

"This is the stage where skill and artistry are most involved. The physical dexterity of the ideator must be matched and complemented by his mental acuity and emotional sensitivities, projected through the tranche, as he imposes his vision on the nacre."

The blob gradually began to take on an altered shape and coloration. The conclusion to the process was signaled by the completed object detaching itself from the now-clean tranche and falling to the floor, where it clunked and bounced but did not break.

Lazorg shifted his rump to reach and claim the ideation. He held it in his palm, and Crutchsump could discern that it was a crude model of the Cosmocopia, like the grander one out front.

"You can see that I was not being merely self-effacing when I claimed amateur status. Compared to the genuine Arbogast creation out front, this trinket is a muddy lump. But you may feel free to take it with you, as an expression of my concern for you. Now, if there's nothing else troubling you...?"

Lazorg said, "This fellow Arbogast— He lives locally?"

"Yes. He's Telerpeton's most famous ideator. He could certainly afford to make his lodgings in a more exclusive neighborhood, but he retains an affection for the district of his birth. He donated the ideation up front out of the goodness of his heart!"

"Can you arrange for me to meet him?"

"Well, I don't see why not...."

Lazorg jumped up, grabbed Crutchsump's hand, as well as the noetic's, and pulled both to their feet.

"Quick! Let's go!"

* * * * * * *

Arbogast lived on the top floor of a sprawling, solid but battered copper-roofed tenement, its stucco walls stained with verdigris streaks, the whole structured around an immense courtyard attained through a tall wide portal in the building's north side. The courtyard teemed with the quotidian life of its inhabitants: children playing, domestic washing of both clothing and bodies being undertaken at a soapy stone trough fed by a fountain, a cook cart sending up charcoal smoke and the odor of clandestini meat on skewers.

Crutchsump imagined how splendid it would be to live in such luxury.

Upon being dragged from his shrine, Palisander had moved very slowly through the streets, reluctant to dispense with a noetic's traditional decorum, and now Lazorg was fuming with impatience. He hustled Crutchsump and the noetic across the courtyard and up an indicated set of stairs.

"Slow down," said Palisander. "There will be just as much interstitial nacre available an hour or a year from now as there will be in the next few seconds. The supply is, for all purposes, infinite."

Lazorg paid little heed to the injunction, but took the stairs two at a time, leaving his companions to hasten after him.

On the top floor a wide corridor faced with numerous humble side doors terminated at a grander entrance to what was plainly a more impressive apartment. Palisander led them to this doorway, and knocked.

Arbogast himself opened the door before too long.

The master ideator was a burly fellow with a game leg. His sleeveless leather-and-fur jerkin revealed impressive arm muscles and a barrel torso. Wrestling with the nacre had evidently built his biceps and forearms up. He radiated a certain brusqueness not untempered by curiosity and a childlike vivacity and interest in whatever life presented him. His caul was studded with abstract trinkets.

"Palisander," Arbogast said, "what draws you out of your meditative cubbyhole?"

"I'd like to present this fellow named Lazorg to you. He's a curious case, a wanderer across the dimensions, and I thought you might find his story lively."

Lazorg pushed forward. "Arbogast, I'd like to apprentice myself to you. I want to make ideations."

Holding up a hand, Arbogast said, "Hold on one moment! Who says I'm taking any apprentices?"

"But you must!"

"Well, let's discuss this inside."

Arbogast's apartment was a huge unwalled studio featuring broad skylights, with all the domestic furniture pushed into a corner. The rest of the space held shelving, and on these shelves rested a wide assortment of ideations of all types: figures of animals and buildings, as well as sensual sinuosities with no common referents.

But none of sentients such as Arbogast and Palisander and Crutchsump themselves.

In the middle of the space was a rack full of tranches of distinct shapes, a cushion for sitting and several other pillows meant to catch finished ideations safely as they fell like fruit from the tranche.

Arbogast led them to this work zone. He picked up rudimentary tranche of low complexity and handed it to Lazorg.

"Here, let's see if you have any natural facility."

Lazorg attempted to mimic what Palisander had done. Crutchsump watched with sympathy and hope.

Probing the air, Lazorg eventually encountered an interstital node, but was unprepared for resistance. The tranche was almost jerked out of his grip. He managed to maintain his hold, however, and began to reel nacre out of the rift. But when he attempted to disengage, the lump of nacre did not sever, but pulled back like rubber, yanking the tranche out of Lazorg's hand and snapping the bulbous wand in half against the edges of the rift.

Lazorg looked at Arbogast with despair in his eyes and stance. Arbogast regarded his broken tool for a moment, then said:

"It took me three days with my master before I could even sense a node. Perhaps your passage across the dimensions has endowed you with a certain intuition. But whatever the case, you may consider yourself my pupil from this moment forth."

CHAPTER SIX
ARTISTS AND MODELS

Climbing the cooking-redolent stairs to Arbogast's apartment, Crutchsump vented an unusually self-indulgent expression of her weariness in the form of a deep trembling sigh. Her feet ached from tromping all about Sidetrack City in search of bones. (Today she had been as far as the Zolah stockyards, seeking whatever bones might be cadged from backdoor transactions with shifty employees.) Her hands still smelled faintly but distinctly of carnal muck and rot, although she had indulged in a bath of livewater before venturing here. And she had sprained her left wrist pulling the carcass of a guyan from a ditch.

But, she reminded herself, all her daily labors would be repaid once more in full, as they had been daily for the past six months, when she opened the door to Arbogast's studio.

Two noisy children, their cauls colored in the bright shades favored by the young, rushed past Crutchsump on the stairs, and, avoiding them, she banged her sore wrist against a railing.

"Ow! Watch out!"

The unrepentant children laughed and raced on. Crutchsump vowed that if she ever had children, she'd be a better mother—or, less probably, father—than the parents who had failed to instill respect in these urchins.

At Arbogast's door, Crutchsump knocked out of courtesy, but then let herself in. Had she waited, the preoccupied master and apprentice inside might have taken forever to answer.

Beneath grimy skylights that dimmed the twinned sunlight,

the central workspace now boasted a second cushion for apprentice ideator, next to the master's seat. Both cushions were occupied.

Arbogast held his tranche high, wielding it deftly, as Lazorg managed with a fair degree of success to mimic the master's movements. On the tip of each tool, a sizable blob of nacre was assuming the unmistakeable shape of a clandestini, from the points of its horns to the barbs of its tail. The little models were more or less evenly matched in fineness of detail, albeit exhibiting differences of style.

"That's right," urged Arbogast, "impress your will upon it! Every ounce of recollection and sympathy and zeal! And listen to your gut brain!"

Lazorg faltered in his making. "You keep saying that, but I still don't know what you mean!"

"Your gut brain, your gut brain! What kind of infant are you?"

Suddenly the incomplete ideation fell, abortive, from Lazorg's tranche. He dropped his tool on the cushions and angrily jumped up.

"I'm not an infant, damn you, Arbogast! In my own world, I'm a master! There's no one more accomplished at my style of painting! Not even that pretender, Rokesby Marrs!"

Imperturbable, Arbogast unhurriedly completed his own ideation, and the perfect image of a clandestini fell to the receptive pillows, bearing the unmistakable Arobgast imprimatur. Only then did the master stand.

Rather than take umbrage at Lazorg's impatience and bad temper, Arbogast laid a friendly hand on his pupil's shoulder.

"I acknowledge your past, Lazorg. You've shared with me a fascinating story, these past six months. You've almost succeeded in making me imagine what 'painting' could be. But you have to face the reality of your current situation. Here, in this world, you're not a master, you're a student. Very much a natural adept, I admit, but still with a fair amount to learn. You have no reputation, no following, no patrons. Those are yet to be earned."

Lazorg appeared mollified but still somewhat grumpy. "Well, how can I earn those things, if I never show my work to the public?"

Arbogast did not immediately answer that question, instead saying, "Repeat that last exercise for me, please."

Lazorg picked up his tranche and began again.

Arbogast turned his back on Lazorg and finally spotted Crutchsump.

"Ah, here's my pupil's first and truest patron! Welcome, Crutchsump!"

Deeply focused on his task, Lazorg himself did not greet Crutchsump. Her heart sank a little, but she bucked herself up.

"I trust today was not completely enervating for you," said Arbogast pleasantly.

"I did work very hard, as always. Supporting two alone is not easy, even with our simple needs. But I know that Lazorg needs to spend all his time practicing. And it won't be forever."

Arbogast turned again to watch his pupil intently. "No, no, it certainly won't be forever...."

A muffled thump signaled the completion of Lazorg's ideation of the clandestini. Arbogast bent to pick it up for close inspection. Crutchsump hastened over to look.

The little animal formed of nacre shared the exact coloration of the living species. Crutchsump could see the perfect compound pupils in its minute eyes. At the same time, it displayed a larger-than-life element of caricature, as if its creator had been unable completely to endorse its existence, and the ideation differed in that regard from Arbogast's own personally stamped version.

"It's beautiful," said Crutchsump.

Lazorg surprised Crutchsump with a quick hug, and all her weariness dissipated.

Arbogast continued to study the creation from all angles. Finally he looked up to regard both Crutchsump and Lazorg.

"If, over the next week, you can produce a dozen ideations of equal quality, following the templates of Standard Series Six, then I will arrange a show at my gallery, the Jutesuitor, to introduce you to the right crowd."

Lazorg gripped Arbogast by both shoulders. "A dozen! I'll produce ten times that many!"

"Don't overdo it. Quality over quantity should be our motto. And remember: always follow the archetypes. Now go home and rest—with your friend."

Lazorg took Crutchsump's hand, and she thrilled. "Yes, she's been the best of friends."

The two headed for the door of the studio, but stopped when Arbogast hailed them again. Crutchsump turned and saw the ideation maker removing a leather poke from a trunk.

"Here are a few extra scintilla. Go out for a meal, and then both of you buy some better clothes. Although ideally an artist should be judged exclusively by his creations, not his appearance, this is not the reality. And an artist's date for the evening must look her best as well."

* * * * * * *

That night, lying on her pallet, Pirkle thrumming at her feet, Crutchsump, watching the curtain dividing the room, waited with anticipation, imagining that Lazorg might silently breach the barrier and come to her.

But he did not, and she passed into exhaustion's arms.

* * * * * * *

The Jutesuitor gallery lay outside the Telerpeton district. Palisander the noetic had explained to Crutchsump that Arbogast's birth and continuing residence in the slums lent a certain enviable lowbrow cachet to his art and reputation. But actually to display at some amateur venue within the mirey, dangerous alleys and lanes, requiring buyers to visit the benighted ghetto—well, that would have been asking too much of his rich and exclusive patrons.

And so on the night of Lazorg's debut as a publicly commod-ified ideator offering his wares to collectors—an "artist," in short—Crutchsump found herself in a hired shay pulled by a matched pair of diaverdes, their six tails braided with colorful ribbons, entering the lovely district of mansions and carriage-trade shops known as the Passacantado.

The driver paused the shay a moment, so that he might get down and light the fore and rear lamps subsequent to dusk's overtaking them a few blocks from the gallery. Crutchsump used the moment to glance at Lazorg beside her on the padded bench.

The alien visitor wore a sharp brocaded suit, leaf-green, and new caul of silky red material. Lazorg's introciptor pouch was defiantly left empty, despite the socially prestigious occasion. Despite Crutchsump's nervous advice to remedy his lack with a prosthetic, both Lazorg and even Arbogast had demurred.

"Your unique origin," said Arbogast, "is already dissemi-nated and impossible to hide. By now, the brutish 'Monster from the Mudflats' who became an ideator is a small and growing legend in the city. So you might as well flaunt your past. It could very well add to your selling power. Egregious and extraneous and reprehensible as it may be, collectors appreciate a story they can attach to an artwork, and will always favor an object with an anecdote appended over one without."

For her own part, Crutchsump had splurged on satiny blue pantaloons and blouse, a small capelet and a caul featuring daring eyelets punched at random. She felt almost brazen, nearly drunk.

Lazorg had been fingering something in a pocket all during the ride, and Crutchsump could no longer contain her curiosity.

"Lazorg, what is that object? A lucky talisman of some sort?"

"Huh? Oh, this? I suppose you could call it a touchstone of sorts. It's an ideation I created. One that I hope will send this show of mine over the top."

"Can I see it?"

"Well…. Sure."

Lazorg took out the object and handed it to Crutchsump.

The ideation retained, presumably by artist's choice, the primal color of the nacre. It depicted two monsters—aliens of Lazorg's species—locked in some kind of struggle, their bare limbs intertwined, their groins butting against each other, so as to conceal that bizarre excrescence sported by Lazorg down there, and, in all likelihood, by the other monster as well.

As the shay got underway once more, Crutchsump pondered the aberrant ideation intently. The obscenity of the uncovered faces of the protagonists in the static eternal tussle was alleviated slightly by the fact that they lacked introciptors. But still, the overall impression conveyed by the little "sculpture" was one of transgression against some ineffable set of proprieties.

Crutchsump sought to remember Lazorg's features from that long-gone day when she had rescued him from the Mudflats, taken him home, cleansed the mud from his face.

Yes, yes, the features of the large figure were the same!

"One of these figures is you."

"True."

"And this other, with the deformed chest?"

"My old lover, Velina."

Crutchsump remained silent, restraining any inquiry as to why they wrestled thus.

Lazorg seemed to radiate a measure of guilt. "She's dead now."

Crutchsump shoved the ideation toward Lazorg. "It doesn't matter to me."

Lazorg took back the ideation and repocketed it. He paused, then spoke with feeling.

"Standard Series Six! What a bore! I can stamp those predictable archetypes with a little of my personal flair. But the subjects are identical to what every other artist is attempting. How will my work ever stand out? I have to be recognized as unique! As a master! And quickly! The only way to do that is to shock!"

"What do you plan to do?"

"Arbogast wouldn't let me display this non-standard piece

when we were setting up the show. But when he's not looking tonight, I'll set it out in an empty niche."

"Surely he knows best. You risk everything!"

"Risk, yes—for a bigger reward!"

"I—I can't object. It's your show."

"Our show, Crutchsump! Without your support, I never could have attained this moment!"

This acknowledgement of her contributions melted Crutchsump's resistance. "All right, take your chances."

They arrived at the Jutesuitor gallery with half an hour to spare before the opening time. The tasteful display windows hosted Arbogast creations against velvet backdrops. The gilded, leaded-glass door had to be unlocked for them personally by the gallery's owner, a slim and elegant fellow named Gaddis.

Gaddis ignored Crutchsump, but embraced Lazorg fulsomely. "Ah, my newest discovery! I predict a wonderful career for you, my friend! Your interpretation of a dwindle bush is beyond compare! I can practically smell the peppery sap! We both stand to make a handsome profit tonight, I'm certain!"

"Is Arbogast here yet?"

"No, but he always shows up late for these affairs—even his own. Don't worry, your mentor won't desert you. Meanwhile, please indulge in some punch and brochettes and comfits."

Gaddis led them to a long table covered with a damask cloth, atop which the refreshments sat. Besides the punch, there were shashliks, mushroom tartlets, cubeb pasties and candied ants.

"You'll excuse me," Gaddis said, "but I've got to attend to a dozen last-minute matters."

Left alone, Lazorg ignored the refreshments. Fearing to appear greedy or uncultured, Crutchsump followed his lead, although the smells of the spread were enticing. She did take a cup of heavily spiked punch, though, to soothe her nerves.

From her empty stomach the liquor spread throughout her limbs and gut brain, rendering the scene about her even more dreamlike than it had been upon sober arrival.

Soon the doors were thrown open for those with invitations,

and a parade of smartly dressed connoisseurs entered, babbling happily of trivialities and gossip.

Crutchsump conjured up a counterbalancing mental image for her own amusement: the whole lot of privileged wastrels digging for shifflets, their fine clothes smeared with mud. She had to suppress giggles.

Watching Lazorg, Crutchsump hung apart, her back against a pillar.

Although this was his first show in Sidetrack City, Lazorg had no problem knowing how to act, how to meet and greet the wealthy patrons, put them at their ease, flatter their opinions, modestly accept compliments. He gave an impressive performance, which seemed to please Gaddis.

For the first time, the reality of Lazorg's past life struck Crutchsump. Any lingering conceptions of him as a naïve foundling, a helpless unworldly immigrant, dissipated.

She wondered how much longer he would deign to associate with her.

Arbogast showed up an hour or so into the reception, greeting his pupil heartily, and boosting the level of excitement in the gallery.

Finally, after the buffet had been decimated by the patrons, Crutchsump gathered together a few tidbits for herself.

As she was munching, she witnessed Lazorg sneakily insert his rogue ideation into an empty niche. No one else saw.

Lazorg noted Crutchsump's attention, and winked broadly at her.

Unwitting of the insertion of a new item, Gaddis approached Lazorg and spoke softly into the artist's encauled ear. Nonetheless, Crutchsump overheard.

"We've had a few tentative feints, but no one's committed yet to a purchase. No reflection on your art, Lazorg. It's just the way these affairs build from a slow start. I'm sure that in a few weeks, sales will take off—"

And then a commotion at the door drew everyone's gaze.

A tall, regal figure clad in a fur-trimmed gown had appeared.

Her understated yet stylish caul was fashioned from fabric sporting expensive metallic threading, gold and silver. Her introciptor was so large, almost freakishly so, that in all imaginable couplings, she must necessarily play the engulfing female.

The newcomer's name circulated sibilantly among the crowd like wildfire.

"Serrapane, Serrapane, Serrapane…."

One of the gallery's employees hastened to bring Serrapane a drink. She unknotted her caul and lifted the veil above her lips with a slow and calculated sensuality that thrilled along the nerves of every person present. She sipped, lowered her drink, then let the hem of her caul fall down, remaining loosely unsecured in an alluring manner.

Gaddis greeted Serrapane, but she ignored him. Crutchsump approved of the fact that Lazorg hung back, and did not thrust himself obsequiously upon the obviously influential collector.

Serrapane began to circulate among the offered ideations, examining each one with expert appraisal. She exhibited no outward signs of interest.

But then she came upon the rogue item.

Serrapane deposited her drink carelessly on the edge of the niche, and it fell to the floor. Paralyzed by the concentrated deliberateness of Serrapane's motions, no servitor moved to pick it up. She reached out and grasped the "sculpture" of Lazorg and Velina wrestling.

Across the room Arbogast assumed a startled stance, his attention focusing for the first time on the novelty item.

Serrapane revolved the vaguely obscene oddity a dozen ways, held it afar and up close, ran a fingertip along all its surfaces and curves, cupped it in both hands so as to nearly conceal it. Then she returned it to its niche.

"Gaddis."

The gallery owner was instantly by Serrapane's side. "Yes, Serrapane?"

"Whatever the cost, this one is mine. Now, introduce me to the creator."

Gaddis brought Serrapane and Lazorg together. The woman loomed nearly as tall as Lazorg. She offered her hand, and he took it. But Crutchsump was unable to overhear whatever words they exchanged, since an immense hubbub arose, as all the other collectors besieged Gaddis with bids for the remaining ideations of the Standard Series Six.

* * * * * *

Long after midnight, the shay discharged Lazorg and Crutchsump outside their cellar apartment, which looked at once both homey and more dismal than ever, after the splendors of Passacantado. With the shay sounding a hoof beat retreat, the whole night assumed a phantasmal semblance in Crutchsump's tired brains. Were it not for the fancy clothes she wore, she could have mistaken this moment for the end of a long commonplace workday of luring volvox to their doom.

Maintaining the pleasant tired silence shared during their trip back, the two descended the stairs somewhat wobbly and entered the small quarters. The dividing curtain remained in its daytime configuration, bunched against the wall, secured with a makeshift cord.

Pirkle, registering their return, readjusted himself drowsily upon Lazorg's bed, then went back to sleep.

Lazorg swept his arm in a grandiose gesture to encompass the whole space.

"Take a good look around you, Crutchsump. Fix this dingy place in your memory. Oh, not that it hasn't served us well enough. But in a short while, you and I will be ensconced in much grander quarters!"

"What—? But how—?"

Lazorg began unbuttoning his jacket. "Serrapane has commissioned an extensive series of sculptures from me—so long as they're all as unique as the one she bought tonight! Even Arbogast finally had to concede the rightness of my gamble. We're rich, Crutchsump! Rich, even with Gaddis's outrageous agent fees! And this is just the start!"

"I don't— I don't know what to think…."

Lazorg threw his jacket atop Pirkle, who didn't even stir. He hugged Crutchsump to his chest.

"Don't think! Just be glad!"

"Oh, I am! I am!"

Lazorg released her, and moved to the curtain, speaking as he fussed with its fastenings. "Well, it's been a long day. Time for rest."

All the while, Crutchsump, obeying impulses she could not have put into words, was mirroring Lazorg's actions with the curtain fastenings by undoing the knotted string of her caul. Her breath came fast and seemed to burn her throat.

She had her caul fully off when Lazorg turned, pulling the curtain after himself, the pouch for her introciptor having inverted like a sock during the hasty removal.

He stopped dead. She eyed him boldly, face-naked before him at last, feeling the rings of muscles banding her introciptor clenching and releasing, clenching and releasing. The long organ throbbed and juddered. The delicate palps surrounding the opening at the end flexed and spread wider, assuming the female configuration that invited entrance, not the cone-like formation of a male that preceded penetration.

Lazorg did not utter a word. But he dropped the curtain and came to her. He removed his own caul, and Crutchsump discovered that his uncanny features no longer inspired the unease they had upon that long-ago day, but only affection.

"Oh, Lazorg, I know you're crippled, and that we can never mate! I hope seeing me this way isn't too painful. But despite that sadness, I want to be all yours! And this is how I can show it!"

Very gently and tentatively, Lazorg reached up to Crutchsump's face to grip her generative organ. He squeezed it, ran his curled hand up and down its length. The familiar foreplay evoked a moan from her.

"It's—it's beautiful. So soft and warm and velvety—but

strong. And these little fingers at the tip—like what I saw once on a star-nosed mole—"

Crutchsump's introciptor dripped clear liquid on Lazorg's palm. Inquiringly, he put a finger inside. The outer palps caressed his digit.

Crutchsump moaned again. "Oh, that's so pleasant, so nice! But you—you're getting nothing in return."

Lazorg removed his finger and licked it. "It's honey." Then he started to remove his trousers. Crutchsump undressed as well, and soon they were both completely naked.

Lazorg cupped the weird growth at his crotch. "Crutchsump, look close. This is my sex."

Crutchsump kneeled down and peered at the alien organ. It bore a superficial resemblance to an introciptor, but one permanently in the male configuration. And as she watched, it lengthened and stiffened and jutted out from Lazorg's loins.

Lazorg said nothing, made no demands. He held his organ in one hand, rubbed it once, twice—

Her face at his groin, Crutchsump brought the tip of her larger female introciptor up against the head of his sex. The palps embraced it, drew it into the wet tunnel.

Now Lazorg groaned. He cupped the back of Crutchsump's head and slowly delivered his whole length into her. They rested a moment, with locked gazes, one up, one down, then Lazorg made to withdraw, as if for some inexplicable reason to repeat the process of insertion. But Crutchsump gripped his sex implacably, so that to withdraw would require jarring effort.

"No, you do nothing now. Let me."

Complex waves of peristalsis traversed Crutchsump's introciptor, annular muscles milking Lazorg's sex without gross exterior movements. He gripped the sides of her face, covering her olfactory pits, so that all she could smell was his skin. She clamped her hands on his backside, so as never to let him go.

Lazorg began to rock on his heels, his pelvis pumping in a short arc, as much as she allowed.

Crutchsump felt filled, replete. Milking the strange organ

within her was bringing her to climax.

Lazorg bellowed, and flooded the upper reaches of her uterine tract with his spend. Crutchsump climaxed as well, slicking his loins with the female's exudation.

Lazorg collapsed to the floor, drawing Crutchsump semi-awkwardly down as well. His breath came ragged, as did hers. They said nothing for a time. Lazorg gradually shrunk free of her.

When they moved to Lazorg's pallet, Pirkle grudgingly made room.

CHAPTER SEVEN
MANSION IN THE CLOUDS

During the year since Lazorg's spectacular and triumphant debut into the rarefied art world, Crutchsump had discovered that she excelled at maintaining a home: particularly, at cooking. She had a positive talent for transforming raw ingredients into sophisticated meals. All her former life, an existence now removed into half-painful, half-nostalgic insubstantiality, she had subsisted on the cheapest of foodstuffs. Oftentimes live-water had been all she could afford. She had never possessed enough money to lay in and continually replenish a rich larder, full of choice meats, fresh vegetables, beans and tubers and grains, spices and dried roots and herbs. A nicely equipped kitchen, with a self-regulating sea-coal stove and plenty of cookware, had also been absent. And time, or lack of same, had played its role as well. Often, while out scavenging during the day or finally at home, weary to her last blood cell at night, she had defaulted to the cheap prepared food from vendors.

But no longer. Now, she was mistress of a fine, well-stocked galley and pantry that funneled its delicious creations into a large dining room that was often filled with guests—guests who praised Crutchsump inordinately.

But praise for her culinary creations, or because she was the mate of an ideation maker whose works they coveted at bargain prices?

No matter, and nothing she could do about the impulses behind the flattery. Despite any doubtful praise, this discovery of her innate skills gave her immense pleasure. Meal preparation was her sole way these days of contributing to the household economy—of sustaining Lazorg in his work.

Well, perhaps not the *sole* way—

Crutchsump reddened now beneath her caul, and momentarily froze while reaching into her wallet. The delivery boy from Knollypop's Provender asked, "Is anything the matter? Old Knollypop added up the total twice. See?"

The boy took out a handful of colorful enumerative tokens, each with a different mathematical figure in bas-relief on its face.

"One hundred-and-twenty-six scintilla. It's right there."

Recovering her aplomb, Crutchsump fetched out the requisite amount of money from her wallet, the smallest part of its contents, and handed it over. "No, no, everything's fine. I was just taken by a passing fancy."

The small boy grew a little nervous. He made the sign of the Cosmocopia, bunching all his fingertips together and aiming them at the floor. "Not a passing ghost, I hope."

"Not at all. All our ghost-catchers are in fine shape. Thank you for running this order over at the last minute. An unexpected dinner tonight. And please ask Knollypop if he'll have any soutines in stock next week."

Crutchsump added in a generous tip.

"Sure thing!"

The boy left, and Crutchsump began unpacking the hinge-topped wooden boxes he had left behind, each bearing a raised tradesman's seal indicating their origin with Knollypop, and their expected return. She shelved pots and crocks and boxes, net bags of onions and tarbix, a carton of the brand of looby flakes that Lazorg liked best for his morning porridge....

By the time she was done arranging things to her satisfaction, the hour was nearly noon. She'd have to begin working on the dinner preparations soon. When Lazorg had ordained tonight's banquet, over their breakfast table this very morning, he had been insistent on its importance to his career, and Crutchsump intended to outdo herself.

But first, given that there was still plenty of time until guests arrived at eight, she'd treat herself to a visit with Lazorg himself. He should be in his studio.

There might even be time for a quick, exciting coupling. Crutchsump felt her introciptor tingling; her gut brain conjured up quick vivid flashes of past sexual storms. She hoped that such a spontaneous emotional and physical union might occur today. Lazorg had been working so hard of late, that they hadn't had sex for nearly two weeks. Crutchsump missed the closeness, felt such a sensual drought could not be good for Lazorg either.

She pulled a bell to summon one of the servants. Flumareen showed up, a very smart and obedient girl from the Telerpeton district, whom Crutchsump had known since Flumareen was an orphaned child.

"Thank you for taking that order to Knollypop's, Fluma. Now I need you to fire up the stove and get some of the basic sauces simmering."

"Yes, Crutchsump."

Leaving the girl shoveling sea-coal with a wooden scuttle, Crutchsump walked down lush carpets through the dining room, the front parlor, the games room and the rear parlor, until she reached a wide ascending staircase. Every spotless, well-furnished inch of the apartment's first floor brought her immense pleasure and pride.

For the past eight months, Lazorg and Crutchsump had occupied three rented, high-ceilinged levels—the fourth, fifth and sixth—in an exclusive residential building in the Stallkamp district. They had moved out of the squalor of Telerpeton within a week of Lazorg's gallery debut (within a week of the thrilling consummation of their passions for each other, thought Crutchsump), but only into modestly better lodgings just a mile or so away, in the Ubiwerke district, home to middle-class merchants and skilled workers. But as soon as Lazorg had amassed a fair amount of money, as soon as his continued sales seemed assured, and not a passing fad among collectors, he had determined to splurge on what Crutchsump could only regard as a mansion in the clouds.

"We need a residence befitting our dreams, Crutchsump. A reward for all your hard work—for my genius. And we cannot command the highest prices for my creations if we don't represent ourselves as quality. So this expenditure is really in the nature of an investment, you see, that will repay itself a hundredfold!"

Leery of spending anything above the bare necessities, already feeling guiltily self-indulgent in their Ubiwerke lodgings, Crutchsump had grudgingly consented.

What surprised her, once they were ensconced in the Stallkamp quarters and the money continued to flow in reassuring freshets much larger than their expenses, was how quickly she had gotten used to the new mode of living.

The second floor of their rental quarters hosted their private rooms, bed, bath, wardrobes full of new clothes and cauls. An entire suite for Pirkle!

One room remained empty. Crutchsump had a dream for this space—but more and more, that dream seemed fated never to materialize.

The ascent from fifth to sixth floor consisted of a spiral staircase that debouched directly in the middle of Lazorg's wide-open studio space. This penthouse with its glass roof echoed but outdid Arbogast's atelier, and had been outfitted similarly.

As Crutchsump spiraled round the stairs, closer and closer to poking her head into the studio, she could hear two voices raised in argument. She recognized the speakers as Lazorg and Arbogast. While she was always pleased to see the stern but enthusiastic ex-teacher who had set their feet on the path to such prosperity, Crutchsump could not help feeling a bit disappointed at not having Lazorg all to herself.

Lazorg and Arbogast stood near a rack of ideations. Arbogast held one in his hand.

"But why? Why can't you be content with producing small

items like this? If I could summon up such outré imagery from my brains, I'd regard myself as blessed!"

Lazorg took the ideation from Arbogast. Crutchsump saw that it was one of the series Lazorg called "Cars." The four-wheeled object was plainly meant to represent some kind of enclosed vehicle. But its bizarre lines, its lack of any attachment for motivating beasts of burden, its weird interior accoutrements, all radiated a fascinating sense of alienness.

"This damn 'Tonka toy'!" exclaimed Lazorg. "It's nothing, just a straight reproduction of something I would see every day back home in my world."

Lazorg chucked the ideation—for which any collector in Sidetrack City would have gratefully paid a large sum—across the room, where it struck a wall and shattered. Although cured nacre was strong, it wasn't indestructible.

Lazorg's voice reeked of rue, but not at the destruction of the ideation. "It's so ironic! These mimetic reproductions from my old world are the stuff of high fantasy here. They shock and intrigue your jaded collectors. And if I could ever somehow smuggle your Standard Series Six back to my plane, they'd have the same effect. Our two worlds are each the other's dream and nightmare!"

Arbogast pondered this seeming paradox for a moment, then said, "But that's only a natural reciprocity, it seems to me. What's your problem?"

"The relationship between our worlds locks me and my art in a double bind."

"How so?"

"Well, for most of my career back home, I traded in fantastical imagery, but longed to 'paint' naturalistically. I was working on such a 'canvas' at the end. 'The Origin of the World.' But if I were to take up that subject matter here, as an ideation, it would come across as purest fantasy, just like my 'Cars' series or my 'Dogs' series or my 'House' series."

"True."

"Yet at the same time, if I attempt to work in a similar 'realistic' mode here, I can't escape the feeling that I'm creating fantasy again—because the things of this world are so alien to me."

"What would you like to do then? What can you do?"

Lazorg mulled this question for a while. His answer surprised Crutchsump.

"The most real 'objects' to me here are the people. The individuals in my life. I want to do 'portraits.' But your race has no tradition of portraiture!"

"We've discussed this before," Arbogast said with some small exasperation. "You've tried to tell me about 'mirrors,' and how they can reveal one's likeness to oneself in a flat surface. But without them, portraiture was never born here. For while it's true that we might theoretically like to hold and admire and cherish the ideation of a loved one, the prime mover in that hypothetical mode is ego, seeing the representation of oneself. And without the initial seed of that idea, your 'portraiture' mode died aborning—"

Lazorg interrupted with a wave of his hand. "Whatever the reason for this lack, I'm determined to pioneer the mode. That's the reason for my dinner tonight. I'll introduce the concept at table."

"I doubt you'll find many patrons for this odd conceit."

"We'll see. But now, another matter. I want to determine if you can help me increase the amount of nacre I can pull. Eventually, I want my portraits to be life-sized."

"You know that's impossible. Wrestling that amount of nacre would result in you yourself being dragged into the interstices."

"But with two of us?"

"Coordinating the wills of two ideation makers is problematical...."

"Let's try."

Still unwitting of Crutchsump's silent presence, Lazorg and Arbogast took up tranches and proceeded to rip a slit in the continuum. Soon they began to pull a massive blob of nacre, doubly pierced and snaffled, like taffy from out of the air.

Arcane coiling motions by the tranches caused more and more of the pliable substance to be accreted. But the strain began to show on the quivering arms of the makers, and sweat stained their cauls.

Crutchsump found herself holding her breath.

"Detach! Detach!" yelled Arbogast.

"No! Just a while longer—!"

But Arbogast had already released his grapple, and Lazorg could not maintain the person-sized mass on his own. He was forced also to relinquish his hold, and the nacre snapped back into its lair.

Panting, the makers dropped down among the cushions.

Crutchsump hastened to their side.

Lazorg saw her first. "Ah, little Moley! Did you witness our heroic struggle?"

Hugging Lazorg, Crutchsump said, "Yes, yes I did! And it looked very dangerous! Please don't try that again!"

Lazorg disengaged himself from Crutchsump's embrace and stood up with the decisive air of a man of action, committed to his art. "I can't promise that, little Moley. But I do promise I'll be as careful as possible. Now, tell me what you've got planned for our menu tonight."

Crutchsump outlined the exotic dishes they would enjoy, with Lazorg nodding approvingly and Arbogast chiming in with his own delight and anticipation. Then she left the two makers, to begin her own work with Flumareen's help.

Descending, she thought, *"Little Moley!" How sweet it sounds, every time he says it—whatever a "mole" is. But if only we could have a moment's privacy these days, like when we were poor....*

* * * * * *

Lazorg sat at one end of the long table, spiked with flickering candles amidst the shining cutlery and plates, and Crutchsump, as mistress of the house, occupied the other end, with guests ranked between them.

But that left the closest seats to Lazorg, at either hand, to be apportioned to Arbogast—and Serrapane.

When the latter had swept into their apartments that evening, Crutchsump had been nearly overwhelmed by the intoxicating and domineering female aura of the rich, high-status, famous and extraordinarily endowed woman. She had felt her own introciptor adopting a male configuration, even though there was no overt emotional attraction between her and her guest. Quite the opposite, in fact.

Following behind Serrapane, other guests trailed like so many Pirkles on the scent trail of a particularly ripe midden.

Or so Crutchsump uncharitably thought. And she was chiding herself for the mean comparison when Serrapane handed Crutchsump her shawl and said, "Here, you, please find a hook for this."

"I beg your pardon!"

Serrapane looked down on Crutchsump from her superior height. "Oh, it's you, dear. I mistook you for one of the servants. How foolish of me! Please forgive."

Crutchsump thought to hear a few stifled sniggers from the other guests, but chose to ignore them. She handed off the shawl to Dunt, the house's second servant.

"An easy enough mistake—if one's poorly tailored caul slips and slides all about and interferes with one's vision. I'll give you the name of the place where I shop."

Not easily disconcerted, Serrapane replied, "Oh, please do. It's so hard these days to find good solid everyday wear for doing housework and other chores."

Appetizers and drinks were served in the main parlor. Crutchsump received many compliments, as usual, particularly for her breaded land-shrimp. Lazorg circulated with good humor and witty remarks.

For a moment, memories of their earliest days of poverty together washed over Crutchsump, and she experienced a curious doubling and disorientation that, luckily, soon passed.

The meal went well, with each perfect and surprising course meriting oohs and aahs. But Crutchsump resented how Serrapane monopolized Lazorg. The only time the woman paid any heed to her hostess was when she took a moment to say, "Oh, Crutchsump, how clever—you've taken all the *bones* out of the clandestini!"

Crutchsump felt mortified down to the soles of feet.

Eventually, Lazorg made a public announcement of his "portraiture" series. As usual, the collectors all deferred to Serrapane's initial reaction. The woman paused for a dramatic interval, then said, "I will be the first to sit for our genius! A new history of ideations begins with me!"

After that, the commissions flowed fast and deep.

But Serrapane could not be content with deserting center-stage so soon, and chose that moment to make an announcement of her own.

"I'm holding a séance next week, and you're all invited. It's been too long since anyone has dared to visit with our local ghosts, and they've all probably grown quite lonely!"

The notion of a séance disturbed and frightened Crutchsump, but she held her tongue. Perhaps there would be some way to talk Lazorg out of going.

A problem with dessert necessitated Crutchsump visiting the kitchen.

When she returned to the dining room, both Lazorg and Serrapane were missing.

"Where have they gone?" she demanded of Arbogast.

Arbogast had the grace to look chagrinned on Crutchsump's behalf. "Serrapane insisted on seeing what Lazorg was currently working on."

Crutchsump practically ran through the house, toward the studio.

The penthouse was mostly dark, with just a single handheld candle lighting a small sphere of space: Lazorg and Serrapane standing close to each other, near cushions, not inspecting the rack of finished ideations.

Crutchsump cleared her throat noisily, and the two turned to face her.

The strings of Serrapane's caul dangled loose.

And at that exact moment, Crutchsump knew what she must do to keep Lazorg.

CHAPTER EIGHT
LOVE AND GHOSTS

The shrine run by Palisander hadn't changed in any objectively discernible manner in the past year, but to Crutchsump's eyes the two-room ghetto outpost of the Cosmocopian teachings appeared to have shrunken and acquired new layers of grime, poverty and despair. She marveled at how the ineffable majesty of the Cosmocopia could be contained in such a humble hole. (And the visit here certainly dissuaded her immediately from seeking out the old apartment she had shared with Lazorg, where their romance had first been consummated, for fear of experiencing a similar dreary disillusionment.)

Behind Crutchsump, entering the shrine through its clattering curtain, Lazorg said, "I can't believe I let you drag me here. Don't you know I should be home doing studies? I'm using Dunt as a model for small busts. He'll do well enough, until I feel confident in having Serrapane sit for me."

"I know your work is important, Lazorg. But this visit is too."

"I'm not making the progress I thought I would. It's these damn cauls. They hide so much that's distinctive to an individual. Mouth, cheekbones, jaw line— I know the veils are socially necessary, but still…. If only I could convince Serrapane to sit face-naked—what a triumph! I know I'd craft a masterpiece then! Although how could she possibly show the portrait off to anyone afterwards!"

Crutchsump bit the inside of her cheek to keep from replying to this bold effrontery. How could Lazorg dare to display his infidelity and lust so openly, masquerading as artistic ambition?

Or did his alien origin innocently betray propriety?

She couldn't decide.

But given what she had witnessed, she knew she couldn't risk not acting on her worst suspicions.

Confronted in the penthouse on the night of the dinner, both Serrapane and Lazorg had cavalierly shrugged off Crutchsump's polite but brittle insistence on knowing what they were about. Serrapane casually securing her caul as if it had come undone in a wind, the trio had rejoined the dinner party amidst a politely suppressed air of general curiosity. And the next day, Crutchsump had chosen not to trouble Lazorg with any further accusations or imputations.

Argument or threats or recriminations were all beside the point anyway: she possessed ultimate confidence in her instantly inspired plan to retain Lazorg's affections forever.

A plan which would utilize Serrapane's own grandiose séance, and which first involved a visit to Palisander.

Crutchsump advanced to the altar. "I know your work is very important, dear. But so is this visit. And it won't take long. You need to understand about ghosts, and I don't have the words. They're dangerous, and you're not familiar with them, being from another plane."

Lazorg seemed to take these words to heart. "Well, all right. I admit that much about this plane is still foreign to me."

Crutchsump grabbed a handful of incense sticks and began arranging them in the sand-filled pot set before the Cosmocopian model. "I only have your safety at heart, Lazorg."

The incense smoldering, they ventured into Palisander's private quarters.

The noetic had removed his traditional loaf of a hat and was furiously scratching his scalp through his caul. He replaced the hat with whatever dignity remained to him, exclaiming, "Conceptus blast this case of scaly itch! Not even Hackberry's Salve works! Now, how can I help you, children?"

Crutchsump laid a hefty sum of scintilla into a brazen bowl, and Palisander assumed an attentive pose.

"I'd like you to explain ghosts to Lazorg."

Lazorg preempted Palisander. "I never believed in ghosts back home. But I'm willing to admit they exist here. Still, what real harm can the dead do to the living? Spirits are by definition immaterial. They can only affect weak psyches."

Palisander looked at Crutchsump, who returned his gaze and shrugged.

"What are you talking about?" the noetic asked Lazorg.

"Ghosts. The uneasy souls of the dead."

"That may be what ghosts are on your plane, but such is not the case here."

"What are your ghosts then?"

"Ghosts, insofar as long experience with them over millennia have taught us, are direct sendings from the Conceptus, his agents."

Lazorg blithely waved off the mention of that distant demiurge. "That grain of sand at the heart of the Cosmocopian pearl? How can anyone know anything definite about the doings of such an enigma?"

"This is the job of a noetic, to assimilate all the lore and wisdom relating to the Conceptus, cadged one iota at a time from the grudging multiverse. You may trust what I tell you as being the most expert knowledge available."

"All right, all right, then. The Conceptus sends out his ghosts. Why? What are they? And what do they accomplish?"

"Like your ghosts, ours are immaterial but visible. Ghosts roam our world indiscriminately, seeking receptive minds to fasten upon. The kind of mind they look for is one possessed of a deep yearning ache, an emotional and spiritual wound. We hypothesize that ghosts are a mechanism engineered by the Conceptus to remedy any innate defects in his creation. The ghost seeks to supply whatever the person feels they must have to fill their void."

"Seeks to supply? How?"

"By reifying the wish."

Lazorg contemplated this momentarily. "You get whatever you wish for from a ghost? Why avoid them?"

"Wishes are dangerous. Everyone knows that."

"Why have I never seen a ghost?"

"Sidetrack City is entirely protected against them. Surely you've noted ghost catchers everywhere, inside and out."

Crutchsump chimed in. "That's one reason hunting the volvox was so dangerous, Lazorg, why so few attempted it. I never mentioned it at the time. I was afraid you wouldn't risk it with me then, and we needed the money so badly. But we were outside the city, unprotected. I just prayed neither one of us were in such a state as to attract a ghost."

Lazorg tugged irritably at his caul. "Let's assume all that you tell me is true. Why do I need to know this?"

"Because," said Crutchsump, "we're going to a séance. Serrapane is going to bring down a ghost. And you have to be mentally prepared."

"The point of séance," added Palisander, "is to converse with a ghost, tease it, seek to learn mystical tidbits, yet not invite or succumb to its blandishments. It's foolish, almost like racing your flumerfelt mount to the edge of a high cliff and hoping you can pull up short in time. But people do it regardless."

"Well, if that's all the two of you are worried about, then have no fear. I've currently got everything I desire. A loving mate, my art, wealth— No ghost is going to fasten on me."

No indeed, thought Crutchsump. *Any ghost will be drawn to me, and me alone.*

* * * * * * *

Beneath an ebony-lilac night sky shot through with looping filamentary walls of polychromatic stars, the lead carriage in a long parade pulled up at Serrapane's doorstep. The driver, high atop his perch, worked a lever, and the curbside carriage door swung open. Out stepped Crutchsump and Lazorg.

Crutchsump stopped a moment to marvel, her arm entwined

with Lazorg's.

Whereas she and Lazorg lived in expansive comfort on three floors, Serrapane resided in sheer opulence. Her home, an ancestral manse, squatted on an entire city block, bounded by streets denominated Stanch, Greenwallet, Blackseep and Gandy. The family's wealth derived from mercantile trade with other regions and cities such as Lyndtorke, East Pitchblende, Fazzbazz and distant Tarsialand, beyond the Rapeseed Mountains.

Now the palazzo shone with the light of torches along its first-floor façade. Candlelight poured forth from the windows. Music drifted out: sackbut, hautboy, kora and thumb piano.

Crutchsump stood in awe of the manse, with its walls of amber sandstone, lintels of travertine, and stained glass windows exhibiting the ideational family crest: a trader's barquentine with sails bellied out in an imaginary wind. At five stories, the building was the tallest in the whole district.

Every moment new guests arrived, being discharged from their carriages and pushing past Lazorg and Crutchsump.

Finally Lazorg grew impatient. "Enough gawping. Let's go inside."

Crutchsump regarded Lazorg, big and handsome in his suit of lisle and swallows-silk. By now, his cruel lack of an introciptor hardly registered on her apprehension of his innate selfhood. Especially since she knew his secret virility.

She tugged nervously at the hem of her own maroon trapunto jacket, thinking of the fateful séance that lay ahead. "All right, I'm ready."

They climbed a broad set of steps and were ushered by liveried servants into a capacious ballroom already half-filled with partygoers. They found their hands almost immediately occupied with drinks and finger foods.

Across the wide room their hostess, domineering and impressive in an exotic caftan and caul adorned with gemstones, presided over an adoring claque.

Lazorg's gaze went to Serrapane, but then jagged off. "There's Arbogast," he said. "I need to ask him why my Brumidi tranche is giving me resistance along the fourth integral. You feel free to mingle, little Moley."

Lazorg patted her shoulder affectionately, then stepped off.

Crutchsump meandered slowly through the crowd, listening to snatches of conversation, admiring the clothes, saying hello to and chatting with the minority of people she recognized from among Lazorg's clients. The necessity for partially unfastened cauls to accommodate eating gave the whole evening a louche cast.

Her gut brain fluttered nervously, anticipating the séance.

That risky recreation, she knew, would not be open to the masses, but only to a select coterie. Crutchsump had no intention of being excluded, and so stayed always in sight of Serrapane. She did not try to track Lazorg's path through the crowd, certain that he would soon affix himself to his patron. And without fail, before too long he validated her instincts, stationing himself at Serrapane's elbow.

As the hour approached midnight, Crutchsump, in the midst of a yawn, noted Serrapane, Lazorg and several others trending slyly toward an exit from the ballroom. She hastened to attach herself to the elite subset.

Serrapane grudgingly acknowledged Crutchsump's arrival with a slight nod.

"Ah, dear Crutchsump. We couldn't spot you anywhere, you blend into the background so demurely. Thank goodness you found us. The ghosts would have lamented your absence, I'm sure."

"They would have been alone in that emotion, I fear."

Lazorg had the good graces to look guilty. He took Crutchsump by the arm. "Don't feel bad, I wouldn't have left you behind."

Crutchsump squeezed his bicep. "I'll always be by your side, Lazorg, no matter what happens."

Serrapane partially suppressed a rude noise. "Follow me, everyone. The night is ripe for our taunting of the ghosts—and, by proxy, the Conceptus himself!"

Led by Serrapane, the party went down a long corridor that terminated in a lesser staircase seemingly devoted to the use of servants. Ascending, the guests nervously chattered among themselves about the upcoming brush with the ghosts.

The long staircase finally debouched on a portion of the manse's rooftop that stretched flat across many square yards. The only illumination came from the starry weft overhead. A squad of servants awaited instructions.

As on every rooftop across the entire city, ghost traps— ornate pots and vases and basins with intricate topologies—were mounted here and there. But unlike elsewhere, these particular ghost catchers on the Serrapane roof were about to be nullified by canvas coverings pooled at their bases.

Serrapane gave a hand signal, and the servants hastened to cover the ghost traps.

A chill seemed to pass across the roof. The guests had fallen silent, their brave boasts and satirical quips now extinguished. They shifted nervously from foot to foot, eyes raised to the skies.

Suddenly a voice rang out. "There, I see one!"

Crutchsump spotted the ghost, high up, a blot against the starscape. It was dropping rapidly.

"Steel yourself against melancholy and morbidity!" exhorted their hostess. "Prepare your questions and bring them to the forefront of your mind. The pallid, timorous noetics will pay handsomely for any data we learn tonight!"

Shortly the lineaments of the ghost became discernible.

The ghost's translucent body was amorphous and constantly in flux, like jelly shaken on a plate. Large as a carriage, its features erupted and were reabsorbed every minute: horns, fins, lobes, fans, tendrils, maws. The only constant: two white, saucer-like, pupil-less eyes. Faintly luminescent, it changed colors in subtle gradations: pastel blue to rose pink to flower yellow to smaragdine.

The ghost halted about ten feet above the people, as if probing their mentalities and choosing the recipient of its miraculous benefactions, determining if any needs were great enough to draw it down the final distance to the messy mortal sphere.

Stunned by the living cubic aurora, Serrapane and her guests were initially silent, despite all their prior determination to extract secrets. But then Serrapane called out boldly.

"Ghost! Tell us what the Conceptus has planned for our world!"

A gelatinous voice resonated from above. "Marvels and illuminations. Strange conceptions and uncanny births...."

Along with the rest, Crutchsump had felt herself frozen, mentally and physically. But the voice of the ghost reawakened her to her purpose.

With the totality of her being, she projected forth her desires, her lack, her needs.

Ghost, help me—please! Conceptus, lift my burdens! Grant me my wish!

At first, there was no response from the ghost. Crutchsump began to despair.

And then, as if the despair itself had provided the missing essential strong flavor of her request, the ghost began to descend upon her.

All the other frightened séance-goers scurried away from the ghost's target, tripping and falling over each other in their haste to vacate a circle of space around Crutchsump. Even Lazorg, despite his fine bold talk in Palisander's, reacted at first with mindless fear.

In a moment, Crutchsump was completely enveloped in ghost flesh.

The cool tissues of the hollowed-out ghost allowed her to breathe, but tinted her vision in rainbow hues. She felt enwrapped in a sentient fog that permeated her every fiber. She witnessed all the fellow guests recoiling from her. Lazorg, recovering his nerve, extended a sympathetic arm toward her, but was pulled back by others.

Her envelopment seemed to last forever. Crutchsump could feel changes within her.

Then the ghost was gone, retreating skyward.

Crutchsump staggered. Lazorg shook off the cautious hands and raced to her side, catching her before she could fall.

"Lazorg—please—take me home—"

Serrapane radiated irritation. "Go! The séance is over. Activate the traps once more!"

In the carriage, huddled in Lazorg's arms, Crutchsump began to regain her strength and confidence. She knew her wish had been granted.

Once home, she fell with fervid desire upon Lazorg. She ripped off her caul, burst the snaps of his pants, worked his alien sex rigorously with her hands until he was soon erect, and then socketed him down the wet channel of her introciptor.

He burst inside her with a howl, spraying his seed deep within her womb.

Her womb. Infertile for the past year when receiving the seed of this monster from another plane.

But no longer.

CHAPTER NINE
FATHER AND SLUG

Crutchsump paused outside the door to the chirurgeon's office in Humble Alley, her hand on the brass latch, undecided.

Despite the warmth of the day, a long blue swallow-silk scarf enwrapped her neck, from collarbones up to just beneath her jaw.

Pedestrians passed by without paying any particular notice to her hesitancy. A blood-linnet landed on a ledge and began to sing its curdled song. Two suns shone down merrily, as if intent on illuminating only paradisiacal scenes.

Did she want to spoil the immense happiness she had experienced over the past three months since the evening of the séance? Her gravid days and nights spent managing her household, companioning an unsuspecting Lazorg at his work, and cultivating her surprise inside herself had been a timeless vista of contentment, pride, and expectation for even greater future happiness. She knew her courting and acceptance of the ghost had been the lone and best way of cementing her relationship with Lazorg, of ensuring that he remained forever hers. Still, a small doubt troubled her. Had there been any selfishness in her actions? What if Lazorg didn't belong with her? What if Serrapane could provide better for him, make him happier?

No! Since that day she had rescued the unloved, troubled monster from the Shulgin Mudflats, their fates had been linked. No one could be allowed to intervene between them. The new life being nurtured within her womb would be the final capstone to their relationship.

But her condition had become so troubling of late. Not normal. And if anything should go really wrong, Lazorg would be deeply impacted. After all, it was his child as well as hers....

A small stabbing pain behind her eyes interrupted Crutchsump's deliberations, settling the issue once and for all.

Pressing the handle of the latch down, she entered the chirurgeon's office.

Moffoletto had been recommended to Crutchsump by Linosariat, the wife of one of Lazorg's clients. Linosariat had always been one of the few among the rich and mighty who treated Crutchsump with respect and genuine fellow-feeling.

"He's very discrete," the other woman said. "Gentle and quite expert. His services aren't cheap, you understand, but you can rely on him absolutely."

Moffoletto's elegant office bespoke his stature, outfitted tastefully with fine furniture and ideations (but none originating with Lazorg, Crutchsump noted critically). Even the examining table resembled a luxurious couch rather than a clinical apparatus, despite the halo frame at its head.

Moffoletto sat behind his desk. Beneath his plain professional's caul, his unusually small introciptor rendered him male vis-à-vis most everyone else he might meet, and Crutchsump felt an instinctive trust toward him.

"Welcome," said the chirurgeon. "You are Crutchsump?"

"Yes. Thank you for making time to see me."

"This is my work. Now, what seems to be the problem?"

"My—my pregnancy. Within the past few weeks, it seems to have gone wrong somehow."

"Off with that scarf, please, and your caul as well."

Crutchsump unwound the scarf reluctantly, revealing her irregularly swollen neck. No preganancy she had ever seen had ever resulted in this degree of engorgement. She took off her caul next, and her introciptor showed distended and tight-skinned.

Moffoletto came to her and began gently to palpitate her face and neck and organ.

"Does this hurt?"

"Not really. But I do have some small pains—inside me."

"Come to the couch, please."

Once stretched out, with her head immobilized in the rigid halo frame, Crutchsump could only stare at the ceiling, while Moffoletto busied himself elsewhere. But he soon returned to her field of vision, bearing a small ceramic lidded container. From within the container he withdrew a mucousy flatworm.

"The harmless planarian will travel down your birth canal and trace the outlines of your womb, all without disturbing the fetus. When it emerges, it will convey the memorized information to me by replicating its uterine path in a bowl filled with a livewater tracing medium. Do you understand?"

Crutchsump felt scared, but tried not to show her feelings. "Yes—yes, I understand. What do I have to do?"

"Nothing. Simply try to relax."

Moffoletto introduced the small planarian into the opening of her introciptor. There was no sexual thrill involved, given the implications of the examination, just an odd interior tickling which ceased when the worm passed deeper within.

Crutchsump waited patiently for minutes, her mind blank of either hope or fear.

Moffoletto produced a small cube of aromatic herbs and touched it to the opening of her introciptor.

"This is the cue for our little friend to make his exit."

A short time thereafter, the worm emerged from Crutchsump. Moffoletto handled it tenderly and stepped away. Crutchsump heard the planarian plop into liquid. Moffoletto returned and freed her. She redonned her caul and scarf.

Using its cilia to swim about, the worm was carving stable lines in the transparent liquid, lines that glowed enduringly white.

Soon the deep glass bowl contained an intricate three-dimensional representation of Crutchsump's charted interior.

Moffoletto studied the liquid schematic from every angle.

Crutchsump wanted to question him, but remained silent.

At last he ceased his examination, and returned to his seat behind his desk. Crutchsump took a seat as well.

"Are you prepared? The news is not good. This pregnancy is like none I have ever seen. The fetus is excessively large, much bigger than the typical fingerling that can be easily accommodated by the sinusoid womb. As a result, your womb has thrust out extra lymphatic extensions for support. That explains your neck swelling."

Crutchsump felt tentative relief. "That's not so bad then...."

"No. But the other developments are. The grasping womb is impinging on various arteries and veins. And it is even trespassing on your brain. These irruptions are the source of your internal distress, and they are bound to get worse. I am afraid that if you do not terminate this pregnancy, your life will be in danger. Even if you carry to term, the delivery will be inescapably traumatic."

Crutchsump's mind went blank for an eternal moment. But then she was filled with a serene certainty.

"That's impossible. I must have this child. Too much depends on it."

Moffoletto was taken aback. "But your health, your very life—"

"I am doing what I want with my life, what has to be done."

Standing, Crutchsump said, "If you could help with the birth, I'd be very appreciative. Now, how much do I owe you for today?"

* * * * * * *

The hour was past ten o'clock at night. Lazorg had not attended dinner at home with Crutchsump—no entertaining was scheduled this evening—being busy in his studio for many hours, and she had eaten alone, meditating as positively as possible on the day's bad news. But Crutchsump had kept a plate warm for the artist atop the stove. She sat now in the kitchen, awaiting his hungry arrival.

She could hear him now tromping down the hall, muttering to himself.

"Pull smarter—smarter, not harder...."

He entered the kitchen and was taken aback at Crutchsump's presence.

"I thought you'd be asleep."

"No, dear, I was waiting for you. We have to talk."

"Talk? About what? Have the household expenses gone up again? I can afford to give you more money, you know. Just ask. You shouldn't have to stint. Those days are over forever."

"No, nothing like that. It's this."

Crutchsump undid her scarf. Lazorg jumped. They had not been intimate for weeks, and he was seeing her disfiguration for the first time.

"What—what is it? What's happened to you?"

For one brief moment, Crutchsump wanted to accuse, to say, *If you had paid more attention to me of late, you'd already know.* But then affection supplanted recrimination. She explained everything, calmly, all secrets revealed.

Lazorg dropped down heavily into a chair. "But this—this is a tragedy. You can't go on with the pregnancy. It's absurd. I don't want to lose you for some—some monster child!"

"Our child won't be a monster. He'll be ours, the symbol of our linked destinies. I believe this is what the ghost referred to, when he said the future would contain 'marvels and illuminations.' Our child will astonish the world."

Lazorg jumped up. "No! I won't let you!"

"You can't stop me. It's my choice, my body, my sacrifice."

Lazorg looked at her imploringly, then rushed from the room, overcome by his emotions.

Crutchsump picked up his plate of food and followed him.

He would need to keep up his strength to be a good father.

* * * * * * *

That night in bed, Lazorg held Crutchsump tightly, and they wept together.

* * * * * * *

The full term for a pregnancy was, of course, four months. And the final month after Crutchsump's visit to the chirurgeon passed all too quickly.

Lazorg had insisted on further immediate medical consultations, once he knew the truth. Various high-priced experts were brought onto the case, but all eventually concurred with Moffoletto's initial diagnosis: the invasive womb and its unseen occupant's metabolism were now too intricately entwined with Crutchsump's physiology to permit severing. Any attempt at excision would be fatal to the mother, as fatal as giving birth would be. But allowing the fetus to mature would at least preserve one life out of the inexorably linked pairing of mother and child.

Crutchsump had accepted the latest findings calmly. Nothing she heard changed her certitude about the rightness of her actions. She felt radiant, blessed.

Lazorg, however, raged like a madman in the privacy of their home.

"It's not fair! Not fair to anyone! I lost my woman once already, paid the highest price! Why again! Why me!"

He berated himself for infidelity.

"If only I hadn't frightened you with my attentions to Serrapane. None of this would have happened! How I detest her now!"

Crutchsump said nothing, but was quietly pleased.

The artist was not totally egocentric, though.

"You don't deserve this, Moley! Not at all. You saved me when I was lost and friendless, and this is your reward. It's too cruel, too mean! Just when we had a good life together, after all your suffering in poverty. Why? Why! Maybe you're just too fine for this world. That's how it often worked in mine."

Crutchsump would hold Lazorg's hand and stroke his arm, or his naked face. "No one's to blame, Lazorg. We fashion our own destinies. I invited the ghost to descend on me. I alone am to blame, if there is any blame at all. You never thought you could impregnate me after a barren year. And no one knew our child would be so vigorous in the womb. But that's all good! He'll be a sturdy youth."

Lazorg failed to take solace from this line of reasoning.

The only time he troubled Crutchsump was when he delved into blasphemy.

"I curse the Conceptus! Goddamn him! Worm in the rose, he is! Hiding at the nub of creation. All this is his fault! He made the universe, he sent the ghost. I hold him responsible, for all our suffering! If I could, I'd kill him!"

"No, no, Lazorg, you mustn't say that. Promise me you'll forget such thoughts. They do you no honor."

But Lazorg would make no such promise.

* * * * * * *

In the final week of her fourth month, her neck and introciptor grossly enlarged and "teratological," according to Moffoletto, Crutchsump had to take permanently to bed.

She had a momentary pang about her appearance. She had never been a beauty like Serrapane, but her average features had been familiar and attractive enough to satisfy herself. But when she weighed the loss of her modest beauty against the nurturing of her child, she didn't really mind. And Lazorg did not seem to be repulsed.

(Were all the inhabitants of this plane, she wondered, still so alien to him that even major abnormalities were elided in his vision?)

Pirkle responded to his mistress's dilemma with utmost devotion. He climbed into bed with her and simply refused to leave, except to deposit his scat lozenges in a nearby sand box. He began to emit a constant, plangent, wavering, almost subliminal drone that had a soothing effect on all who heard it.

Crutchsump remained fairly robust physically. But her mind was going, as the rogue womb expanded inward into her brain.

Her powers of speech left her before her rationality departed, trapping her in noncommunicativeness. But she didn't really mind, as she was still able to clutch Lazorg's hand as he sat for hours beside her, and she could still listen to his voice, even if she didn't always comprehend him anymore.

Livewater sustained her, and the child, and that was good.

Then, in her final days, a strange thing happened.

As her rational brain lost its functions one by one, in the face of colonizing extensions by the womb, her gut brain began to assume a new prominence, a leading role in her minute-by-minute awareness and stream of quasi-consciousness. Her distributed enteric neurons rose to the challenge, and assumed new roles different from the gut brain's traditional function of subconscious guidance and inspiration.

This novel form of sentience did not exactly mirror her old awareness, but it was an intriguing substitute. Crutchsump still had access to many of her memories, and these continuing connections allowed her to appreciate people and her situation, such as when Palisander or Arbogast came to visit.

Moreover, she began to experience a new talent, that of remote viewing. With physical eyes closed, she could direct her mind's eye and mind's ear to roam at will, disclosing happenings anywhere she wished.

Perhaps this ability was latent in everyone, but was generally subsumed and squelched in the workings of the higher brain, and only emerged now in her unique case, as her higher brain relinquished dominance. Perhaps it was an incidental ghost-given talent. Perhaps she was only hallucinating.

But whatever the explanation, Crutchsump enjoyed the freedom afforded by these audiovisual panorama.

Not that every moment of eavesdropping was reassuring.

One such unsettling moment concerned a conversation between Lazorg and Palisander, at the latter's shrine.

"Is it possible to reach the Conceptus physically?" asked Lazorg. "To confront that demiurge directly?"

"He resides so deep within the Cosmocopia, beyond so many multiple universes, that if you could traverse one universe a day, it would take you millennia to reach him. And how can you punch through the skin of each plane? You saw what was necessary to bring you from your home to here. Absolute mental derangement and chemical enhancement. You could not induce multiple thousands of such incidents of such magnitude and survive."

Lazorg pondered this response. Back in her bed, Crutchsump felt glad that any insane plans of Lazorg's to wreak vengeance on the Conceptus were doomed to failure.

But then Palisander, intellectually bemused, offered this: "You know the interstitial realm, of course, from which you draw the nacre for your ideations. Well, some say that this realm connects every plane intimately, a kind of rat's maze between all the walls of the Cosmocopia, and that travel through it is possible, and less time-consuming than a blunt path across every intervening dimension. But what its features are, or how one would traverse it— Well, even legends don't offer much advice."

Lazorg nodded sagely, and Crutchsump, watching from afar, was dismayed.

Another interview, this time with Arbogast, did nothing to alleviate her trepidations.

The two ideation makers were speaking in Lazorg's studio, just a floor away from where Crutchsump lay, both men thinking her unwitting of their conversation.

"If I disappear one day after Crutchsump dies," said Lazorg, "I want you to assume control of all our properties. Do whatever you wish with them. I doubt I'll ever be back."

"Where are you going? What do you intend?"

"I can't say. You'll think me mad."

Arbogast didn't press the matter. "As you wish."

Lazorg made one final stipulation. "If I succeed at one final ideation, you'll recognize that I've done something grand and unprecedented. I'd like you to honor my last artistic accomplishment as you think best."

"Of course."

Lazorg's nebulous plans raised a diffuse alarm in Crutchsump's gut brain. But it was overwhelmed by other, more urgent sensations.

She knew herself ready to deliver their child.

* * * * * * *

Pirkle was the one who brought Lazorg running into Crutchsump's bedroom. The wurzel had dashed into the studio and dragged him with mandibles until he got the message. Both Lazorg and Arbogast hastened downstairs, and arrived just in time to witness the delivery.

No time to fetch Moffoletto. But his professional obstetric experience would have availed naught.

Crutchsump felt massive contractions inside her sinusoidal womb that sent the flesh of her face quivering. Her introciptor began to pulse and throb, seeking to eject what should have been a tiny fingerling. But the hybrid child conceived by Crutchsump and Lazorg was ten times bigger. It stalled at the inner mouth of the birth canal. Pressure mounted.

Her gut brain autonomously pumped out endogenous opiate chemicals that muted any pain. *Oh, please, let my child be born safely!*

The stressed flesh of Crutchsump's face could no longer hold.

In an explosion of blood and fluids, her whole rotted countenance sloughed off, revealing her cratered insides, and the child sluiced out from the cranial womb and down her chest in a gush.

Blinded, dying, Crutchsump nonetheless looked down on herself from a ghostly vantage near the ceiling, thanks to her odd new talent.

The abnormally large fingerling possessed the immature features and form of all babies, still more a larva than a true imago. But this was as it should be, and Crutchsump had innate, immense, intuitive confidence that her child would grow up whole and healthy.

Her life force ebbing, she watched as Lazorg bent down and picked up the baby. He brought it to his bosom, and began to weep.

Then Crutchsump performed her final action. Out of her ruined lipless mouth she forced a last message, ingrained in her gut brain by days of silent repetition and practice, to be triggered by this final carnal sprint.

"Lazorg, I love you. Take care of our son. His name is Slug."

PART THREE

CHAPTER TEN
INTO THE NACRE

Stepping inside, Lazorg swung shut the front door to his home.

He was alone.

Alone and awakened.

Awakened to the foundational reality of his situation, the bedrock ontological substratum of his current existence.

Since his primitive existence in the Shulgin Mudflats, he had been operating within the mental paradigm of this alien gyre of the Cosmocopia.

But now, as if a dream had shattered, Crutchsump's death had remade Lazorg's consciousness. Jerked his mentality out of its domestic, art-obsessed, ego-boosting groove, a rut that had bred in him an acceptance of his surroundings.

He had truly come back to himself and his larger responsibilities, he felt, for the first time since he had been propelled into this mad world adjacent to his own.

And he knew what constituted his ultimate goal, after the disposition of a few more mundane tasks here.

An explanation, and revenge.

Revenge on the Conceptus, author of all the troubles heaped on the backs of innumerable sentients across the Cosmocopia.

* * * * * * *

The funeral for his strange lover was over.

Crutchsump's body had been consigned to the Pools of Forgetting and the Flowers of Oblivion, that swampy, primeval region on the outskirts of Sidetrack City whose subtle brines and acid-chromatic flora dissolved all that which lacked the spark of life. The entourage that had accompanied her to her boggy interment would have pleased her, Lazorg speculated, consisting as it had of scores of rich and important people; in attendance, if truth be told, more to honor a well-known artist than his meek, undistinguished concubine of lowly origins.

Concubine, and fearless birther of his child.

Lazorg could not yet parse the depths of what Crutchsump had done, and generally held the memories of her final month of life at sanity-preserving mental arm's length.

After the disposal of Crutchsump's corpse, wrapped completely from ruined head to strong feet in pastel swallow-silks, the funeral attendees had repaired to a memorial banquet held at Spurback's Rotunda. Lazorg had not the least interest any longer in cultivating these people, but had bowed to this final conventional ceremonial gathering, partly to extend the honor paid to Crutchsump, partly to preserve his (posthumous?) reputation, so that Arbogast could ultimately benefit as Lazorg's heir. He endured the elegaic banquet stoically, with no little boredom.

But now all social duties were behind him, and he could concentrate on immediately fulfilling his heart's quest.

Now that the fateful moment was here, Lazorg experienced some slight trepidations. But any unease was vastly counterbalanced by a mix of despair, determination, disgust and deranged, demanding anger.

A sudden firm but bloodless pincering of Lazorg's left ankle caused him to look down.

Pirkle was demanding his attention, and for an obvious reason.

The wurzel wanted Lazorg to visit Slug.

Fingerlings in this world emerged paradoxically both more self-sufficient than infants in Lazorg's home plane, and yet more undeveloped. That is, the form they exhibited upon birth possessed superior powers of survival, but did not yet fully reflect the mature adult.

Therefore, Lazorg had not bothered to hire a nurse or nanny for his son. Fitted immediately to eat many common foodstuffs, Slug could best and most safely feed himself from a large sippy flask of livewater. Unable to escape his cradle, he could not get into trouble. (Placed on the floor, Slug could maintain a fairly swift pace by a kind of inchworm-like behavior.) Thus Lazorg felt justified in leaving him alone for long intervals.

Not precisely alone. Pirkle had appointed himself the child's guardian, as if honoring the legacy of his mistress in the only way he knew how. Except for his own necessities, the wurzel stationed himself by the cradle, alert for any disaster. Lazorg was certain that if, say, fire struck, Pirkle would have Slug out of the house faster than Lazorg could manage.

But sensing the return of Lazorg, the wurzel deemed some fatherly attention in order.

"All right, all right, I'm coming. Let go of me."

In his recently altered consciousness, the words he spoke sounded immeasurably foreign compared to English. Yet on another level, they came as instinctively as that old natal tongue.

Pirkle released his grip, and the two went upstairs to the nursery.

Although Slug could not see over the edge of his cradle, lying on his back and staring at the ceiling, he sensed Lazorg's arrival and called out, "Poppa!"

Lazorg came up to the cradle and regarded its contents.

When Slug had been born three days ago, he had fit inside Lazorg's two scooped hands.

(So big for a fingerling! No wonder Crutchsump's cranial womb had exploded. The miracle was that she had been able to carry to term. Lazorg knew only her devotion to him had sustained her. The knowledge pierced him.)

Now Slug was as long and wide as Lazorg's forearm.

Slug possessed only nubbins appropriately sited where his

four limbs would eventually appear. His face was a cartoon: eyes twice as big as an adult's, large rubbery gash of a mouth. Where his nose or introciptor should be was a mere bud. The crown of his head showed a row of bumps whose ultimate function Lazorg was unsure of.

Slug began to squirm with excitement and utter small yelps. He managed to upset his sippy cup and dribble livewater in his bedding.

Lazorg swore. "Damn it! Calm down! Now I've got to change you *and* your bed."

Lazorg picked up his son. The muscular squirmy body settled contentedly into the crook of one arm.

"Poppa."

With his free hand Lazorg stripped the bedding and dumped it on the floor. Pirkle gathered it up and dragged it to the laundry.

As Lazorg unbuttoned Slug's onesie, he wondered why he was even bothering. Let Arbogast handle the child's wants and needs when he dropped by tonight and thereafter, once he found Slug an orphan.

But some wordless impulse to honor Crutchsump's sacrifice would not let Lazorg leave Slug dirty.

With only livewater input, the infant made very little waste, just a slight pasty film from his defecatory organ. Lazorg cleaned the boy and dressed him. He refashioned the bedding of the cradle. He placed Slug in it.

Slug began to wail. "Poppa, poppa, poppa!"

Pirkle came running, stridulating with alarm.

Lazorg made it as far as the doorway before the intensity of both summoners drew him back.

He picked up Slug and carried him to his studio, Pirkle following. Let both of them watch his mad assault on the Cosmocopia. What did it matter?

Lazorg set Slug down on the cushions where, normally, finished ideations dropped from the tranche.

Defiantly, he ripped off his caul, crumpled it and flung it to the floor, exposing his face to the world. No more cloaking of his true nature.

Then he went to his rack of tranches and selected his two largest and most powerful, a Jakbrite and a Pompion.

Moving to the center of the large room, Lazorg hefted both tranches high. He paused a moment.

This was farewell.

Then he ripped the biggest slit in the fabric of the continuum he had yet essayed, a veritable door.

Plunging the tips of the tranches in, he hauled out an enormous mass of nacre.

The effort corded his muscles, bulged his veins, drew sweat from his skin. He bellowed with the strain. The nacre fought back, but Lazorg didn't relent. Muscles toughened by much prior ideational work now fulfilled their role. He pulled and pulled, using finesse as well as brute strength.

Soon he had detached a mass of nacre large as a person. On this he began to impose his will and imagination.

Finally the finished effigy thudded to the floorboards, big and solid enough not to be harmed by its uncushioned impact.

Lazorg dropped his tranches and himself fell to the floor in exhaustion.

As he had hoped, the seeping, radiant interstitial doorway remained open, so vast was the nacreous wound and withdrawal of plastic matter.

Lazorg pushed himself up and began to wrestle with the statue he had created, until he managed by superhuman effort to stand it up on its base.

Here was his dead wife, all in nacre.

Face-naked, Crutchsump directed a tender frozen smile on her family. This world had its first portrait. Let Arbogast and society make of it what they would.

Lazorg approached the interstitial wound. He poked a foot over the threshold and into the nacre. There was some resistance, but not insurmountable. No evil sensations threatened his bodily integrity.

The wound was closing. He gripped both edges and held it

apart by main force, just wide enough to squeeze through.

Something bulled past him, into the nacre.

Pirkle and Slug!

Lazorg hurled himself after them, disappearing into the pearly billows.

The wound cemented its edges invisibly together, and the studio was empty of life.

Crutchsump's statue continued to beam beatifically.

* * * * * * *

Light. Unbearable light filled all his senses. He could taste and smell and hear the seductive nacreous light. He breathed it, and it breathed him. Now the radiance threatened to drown him as if in numinous sperm, swallow him whole, dissolve his identity.

But Lazorg summoned up all the experience he had garnered as an ideator, bending the nacre to his will. He pushed against the omnipresence, sought to disentangle himself from the interstitial medium.

Pirkle? Slug? No time to worry about them now!

Slowly, the nacre retreated, Lazorg's will pushing it back in all directions, so that after an immeasurable time he found himself floating at the center of an egg-shaped vacuity not much bigger than himself.

He paused at that time, and the glowing walls of the hollow stayed constant. He corralled all his strength and purposefulness, building up his interior vibrational prana until he felt nearly ready to explode.

At the point of intense painfulness, he thrust out his arms in a broad gesture of defiance and cried out, "Let there *not* be light!"

Instant and total transfiguration!

Born from his seed syllables, a nearly infinite landscape prevailed, of varying shades of non-blinding whiteness, with enough tonality to define transition between its parts.

Beneath Lazorg's feet stretched a perfectly flat ivory plane. Above his head curved a pearly sky. The two met at the distant horizon.

Slowly Lazorg spun about. Sameness, sameness, jagged color—

Pirkle and Slug!

The wurzel, infant clasped to its flat back, was already moving toward him. Lazorg trotted forward to meet them.

"Poppa!"

Lazorg bent down and relieved Pirkle of his burden. He made no useless chastisements. In truth, he was rather glad not to be alone in this wan, white desert. He took off his shirt and fashioned a sling out of it. Now Slug rested secure against his bare bosom.

Motion beneath his feet snagged Lazorg's attention.

The impenetrable plastic floor of this interstitial world had gone translucent, revealing that the cubic volumes below it were stuffed with vague shapes: men, beasts, artifacts, structures, plants—all lazily swimming as if moved by currents or tides through a subterranean ocean, so that some objects gained more distinction as they approached nearer to the surface, while others drifted downward, deeper into obscurity. A million different incompatible paradigms informed them.

Recognizing little, Lazorg watched the kaleidoscopic show with deep fascination, as if creation were offering him a revue of its fecundity, and daring him to match it.

Was this a natural phenomenon, or some willful boast by the Conceptus? Lazorg did not want to encourage his enemy by bestowing admiration....

The ground tremored beneath Lazorg's feet, nearly toppling man and wurzel. More judders followed. Lazorg threw himself down onto his back, arms folded around Slug, while Pirkle hunkered down with limbs tucked inside.

Multiple eruptions everywhere!

Many of the things seen below the crust were manifesting, as the land itself assumed a complex topography!

Grass peppered the friable soil of a moderate slope beneath his back. Fully mature trees shot up around him, a veritable instant forest. Lazorg prayed no sharp object would rise up from directly below and impale him.

After some duration, the remaking of the world ceased.

Shakily, Lazorg got to his feet.

A million shades of white and grey colored the objects that had manifested.

Lazorg and Pirkle stood in a thick forest devoid of underbrush, all its odd herbaceous and barked trees as pale as mushrooms. Bloodless birds fluttered from limb to limb. Rodent-like animals of milky coloration scurried, bearing blanched nuts.

Only the three intruders retained any hues.

Now that the interstitial world had assumed what appeared to be its stable semblance, Lazorg could focus again on his quest.

To reach the murderous, reckless, heedless Conceptus and demand justice and payment for the insults associated with life.

But how?

Probably not by simply standing here.

Lazorg took a step in a random direction. "Let's go, Pirkle. We are walking to the Cosmocopia's end."

Pirkle seemed agreeable.

* * * * * * *

The large graceful house loomed in the middle of a clearing, a beacon of security and welcome and companionship. Lazorg paused at the edge of the forest to observe it. The residence looked familiar, but he could not place its provenance within his memories at first. This uncertainty irked him.

Beside him, standing as tall as Lazorg's waist, Slug, neatly formed now along anthropic lines, reached up timorously for the man's hand.

"What is it, Poppa? I've never seen anything like it…."

"It's a house, Slug, a place to live."

"Does anyone live in it now?"

"That's the question, isn't it?"

Both man and boy—and wurzel—had been bleached as pallid as the rest of the environment, due to ingestion of the interstitial food and water over the indeterminate weeks and months they had traveled the world. During all that time there had been no signs of higher intelligence or civilization, just wildlife and variable geography: savannah, mountains, valleys, seacoast. The climate across these multifarious terrains remained temperate.

Lazorg had almost forgotten why he traveled. The speedy maturation of his smart and inquisitive son demanded much of his attention and resources.

As a hybrid child, blended of maternal and paternal genomes, Slug possessed a nose that was not an introciptor, but not precisely a normal human nose either, more like a tapir's snout. He also had male genitals, like his father. Lazorg thought him rather handsome, but that might have been parental prejudice.

Lazorg had had to impart Slug's whole biography to the boy. He tried to give an accurate portrait of Crutchsump and her sacrifice. He wasn't sure how much Slug comprehended. The youth seemed content with the world at hand. After all, it was all he knew. Lazorg wished he could feel the same. But the goad of his losses still drove him.

The bipeds survived in large part only thanks to Pirkle's hunting abilities. The wurzel bagged plentiful small game, which they learned to savor raw and bloody. Additionally, Pirkle could sniff out plants and roots, berries and nuts that were safely edible.

Life in the interstitial realm had assumed a certain monotonous, organic self-sufficiency.

Until this moment, when the house intruded.

Lazorg studied the structure for a time. No inhabitants emerged, no activity could be seen through the windows. Why was this place so familiar...?

A millipede big as a vacuum cleaner ran harmlessly over Lazorg's bare foot. Pirkle set off after it.

Slug exhibited restlessness. "Are we going to stand here all day, Poppa? Shouldn't we be moving on?"

Slug's philosophy seemed to be travel for travel's sake, letting the unrolling of the land beneath their feet carry them effortlessly. Lazorg had tried to instill larger goals in the boy, but without much success.

"Hold on just a little longer, son. This place could provide us with some useful tools. Maybe clothes too."

Lazorg's trousers were ragged. Slug, having long ago outgrown his onesie, wore Lazorg's ripped adult-sized shirt like a gown.

Lazorg studied the house another minute, then announced, "You wait right here. Pirkle should be back soon to companion you. I'm going to scout."

There was no cover in the clearing, so Lazorg, crouching, ran a zigzag course to the front door of the house. Why he suspected danger, he couldn't say. He looked back to make sure Slug was doing as he had been instructed. The boy crouched behind a shrub, plainly enjoying this silly game.

Keeping below the level of the windows, Lazorg circled the house to the back. Less chance of being seen there, perhaps....

At a rear window, Lazorg cautiously raised his head to peer inside.

He regarded a kitchen. Inside, an older human woman talked to a man fussing at a stove.

Lazorg thought he knew these people. But from where?

Of course!

This was his house! His employees!

Lazorg tapped on the window and called out in low tones: "Anna! Brian!"

The people inside jumped, startled expressions on their faces, then looked at the window. The older woman put a hand to her mouth, then raced to open the window.

"Mister Lazorg! What are you doing here! Do you want him to catch you!"

"Who? Who's going to catch me?"

The chef, Brian, had come up to the window. "Rokesby

Marrs. He owns this place, ever since you left. We're all his servants now. Me, Anna, Dean and Roy. He drives us hard, Frank—hard."

The chef lifted his shirt and turned, to reveal fresh welts and scars on his back.

At the sound of his hated rival's name, Lazorg experienced a seething in his blood.

"I'll kill him!"

"Oh, no, Mister Lazorg, you couldn't! He's a giant."

"A giant?"

"Twice as big as you or I. Strong, and mean, too."

Lazorg felt a sense of helplessness. "What can I do? This is my house! I want it back!"

His housekeeper studied the situation a moment before answering thoughtfully. "You might visit the witch. She's very smart."

"A witch? Where?"

"Not far from here, just follow that trail over there. She might be inclined to help."

"All right, I'll do it! Don't despair, I'll be back…."

Lazorg rejoined Slug. Pirkle was feasting on the millipede with a joyous crunching.

"Son, we have to visit someone now. Come along."

Slug seemed slightly disconcerted by this announcement. "Another person? I've never met another person before."

"It'll be fun, you'll see. C'mon now!"

Father and son circled the clearing's perimeter inside the tree line, the contented wurzel following, until they reached the path indicated by the housekeeper. They set off down the trail.

Before too long, insofar as could be measured amidst the constant illumination from the whitely smoldering sky, they came upon a small cottage, snug and well-kept.

Lazorg strode right up to the front door with Slug in tow, and knocked. He was answered shortly.

In the open doorway stood a slim young woman whose hair was the darkest shade found in this land, and whose complexion was the palest. Her face tickled Lazorg's memories.

That student journalist—

"You—you're Nia—Nia Hemphill."

The woman smiled. "That's correct. And you are Lazorg. Come in."

Lazorg entered with Slug, while Pirkle chose to remain outside. That the wurzel seemed trusting of the witch reassured Lazorg.

The interior of the cottage featured plain and simple accoutrements. Nia had them pull up cane-bottomed chairs to a wooden table. Slug seemed unable to take his wide eyes off this woman, only the third person beside himself and his father whom he had ever seen.

"What can I do for you, Lazorg?"

Lazorg explained his dilemma.

"So you wish to be big as the giant then?"

"I suppose so."

"You'd fight him, and kill him, and regain your estate?"

"That is what I intend."

Nia smiled coyly. "How will I benefit?"

"I don't know how right this minute. But if you help me, I won't forget you. I promise."

"Fair enough. Come with me. then. Slug, have this bun and wait, please."

Nia gave the boy a roll hot from the oven. Slug seemed entranced by the hot, refined food. Its aroma tantalized Lazorg as well.

Nia conducted Lazorg to a back room and shut the door. She began to disrobe. Her body was boyish, slim, muscular and tight, but still quintessentially female. Lazorg felt himself becoming aroused.

"Don't dally!"

Lazorg hastily stripped.

A big bed received them somehow.

Lazorg found himself between Nia's alabaster thighs, his rigid penis like a stick of chalk.

Sex enveloped him. Her cunt, so different from Crutchsump's introciptor—yet somehow akin. It seemed eons since he had last savored the familiar thumping coitus. He had been old and feeble in one universe, then lost amidst strangeness in another. But now he was almost home—

Lazorg climaxed, then flopped insensate.

Waking, he found himself alone in the bed. His feet and arms hung over the edges. He stood up, and his head bumped the rafters. He had almost to double over to get out the door. Naked, since his old clothes were like doll clothes now to him.

In the front room where the oven loomed, Nia and Slug were playing with manikins, making them enact adventures on the tabletop. Slug seemed to be fully at ease, and thoroughly enjoying himself.

Lazorg thought, *What a fine mother she'd make.*

Nia interrupted her play. Slug looked around and saw his father. The boy's eyes widened.

The witch's bold gaze carried frank admiration. "You're certainly big enough now to meet your enemy. But build up your strength first with something to eat."

Nia produced a seemingly limitless supply of hot rolls from the oven, and colorless sweet butter. Lazorg wolfed them down. When he felt replete, he announced, "Now I'll set out."

"And we'll come with you, of course."

Lazorg had to squeeze and twist to get out the front door. When Pirkle saw him, he stilted up comically with startlement, like a jack-in-the-box.

Lazorg, naked, set off down the path back to his house, his huge strides causing the others to hurry behind him. Eventually, he lost sight of them in his haste to confront his foe.

Lazorg entered the clearing surrounding his rightful home. He came close to the house and bellowed out his challenge.

"Rokesby! Come out and fight!"

The frightened yet hopeful faces of the help appeared around the edges of curtains. From the window of an upper story roared an answer.

"Go away, old man, I'm busy painting! I have to satisfy all your old clients!"

Lazorg let out a wordless howl. He raced to the front door and burst it down. He dashed upstairs, elbows and knees smashing furniture along his path, and into his studio.

There stood the detested Rokesby Marrs, naked also. The man wore a foolish-looking goatee. His hair was long and secured in a ponytail. An earring glimmered in one earlobe.

The studio was filled with Rokesby's putrid imitations of genuine Lazorg creations—and he was in the process of covering over one of Lazorg's original canvases with gesso!

"Get out—now!" yelled Lazorg.

"You're already dead, old man. You should be the one to leave!"

Lazorg wasted no more words, but hurled himself at Rokesby.

The two nude titans grappled like Olympian wrestlers. They staggered around the room, sending easels crashing down, toppling plinths that held statues, smashing their feet and elbows into canvases.

They each lost their balance at the same time and went down, still locked in battle. Writhing and searching for winning holds, their huge muscles straining, they rolled across the floorboards until they slammed against a wall with tremendous force, Rokesby's body interposed between Lazorg and impact.

Rokesby's grip necessarily loosened. Lazorg managed to slither away and get to his feet. He picked up Rokesby around the waist in a surprise maneuver, and threw him out a wide window whose twin panes of hinged glass were already opened outward.

Rokesby landed with a muffled thud on the grass, and lay still. Lazorg raced downstairs and outside.

Rokesby Marrs was dead, his neck snapped, his head twisted at an unnatural angle.

Lazorg found himself surrounded by his staff, as well as Nia, Slug and Pirkle. They awaited his victory speech.

Lazorg grinned. "Now we begin to live properly."

* * * * * * *

Lazorg lay dying in his bed, somehow older than he had ever been, his body withered, his mind dull and querulous. Nia and Slug stood by him.

Slug was a man now. Nia the witch remained as young as she had always been.

Lazorg's stature had diminished to normal the very next day after he had vanquished Rokesby Marrs, and subsequent sex with Nia Hemphill did not result in future incidents of gigantism. And there were many such occasions, since Nia moved into Lazorg's home, and became a wife to Lazorg and a mother to Slug.

Lazorg did not resume painting. He found he had no taste for that art form any longer, especially when limited to shades of grey. The pure power and control he had experienced when creating ideations had spoiled him for the cruder technics of paint on canvas.

He had not in fact pursued any art all these long years in this interstitial land, but been content to live out his daily life in enjoyment of food and drink, the raising of his and Crutchsump's child, and the company of those few souls around him.

Pirkle died five years after the defeat of Rokesby Marrs. Some unknown bestial opponent assailed the wurzel after darkness one white "night." Sounds of a tremendous battle, featuring Pirkle's trademark stridulations, awoke everyone in the house, but no rescue could be attempted for fear of injury to the humans. When silence fell and they finally ventured outside, amidst torn turf and felled saplings only bits and pieces of Pirkle's carcass could be found.

Slug cried. So did Lazorg.

And then somehow he was aged and at death's door.

Lazorg gazed through rheumy eyes at his wife. The scene seemed familiar somehow, as if he had encountered her under these circumstances before.

Nia reached down to stroke his parchment brow. Slug held

Lazorg's hand.

Suddenly he recalled what had brought him to this house.

"I—I was searching for the Conceptus. I wanted to confront him, tell him something. But I quit walking, quit traveling, and now it's too late."

"No," said Nia. "It's not. You've been moving toward him all along. Because time and space are equivalent. The sheer passage of all these years has brought you to the origin point of the Cosmocopia. In fact, the Conceptus awaits you right through that door."

Lazorg painfully turned his head. A door had opened in the wall where formerly there was none.

"Slug, will you take your father to complete his journey?"

"Of course."

Slug bent down and lifted Lazorg's frail, wasted body up with ease. Lazorg was reminded of how he had picked up Rokesby Marrs so long ago and flung him to his doom.

"Goodbye," said Nia. "I loved you for many reasons."

"I loved you too."

Slug carried him through the door.

* * * * * * *

Lazorg had forgotten what color was. He had even lost the words for it. Now all the hues of a rainbow seemed to assail him, as he found himself facing the Conceptus, the demiurge at the heart of the Cosmocopia.

Beneath a dome of lilac sky, against a backdrop of bright green foliage and garish flowers, the Conceptus presented himself now in what might or might not have been his one true guise: in the form of a crimson beetle large as a man: *el escarabajo psicodélico*. The beetle stood improbably upright on two lowermost legs of many, showing his ventral side, plates of bright chitin overlapping.

Slug set his father down and Lazorg was surprised to discover that he could stand up. He looked down at himself and found he was young again, as young as when he first encountered his old home in the nacre. But Slug remained an adult.

The beetle's face seemed to flow back and forth between its insect appearance and that of an old Indian man, like water over a streambed.

Fulgencio?

"You—you are the Conceptus?"

The beetle spoke out of its pincered mouth with a buzzy voice. Its many legs twitched in cryptic mudras.

"Yes."

"Then I have to kill you, for what you've done to me, and to those I loved."

"I've done nothing except set worlds in motion. You and your kind have done all the rest to yourselves."

"You could have stopped all the tragedies."

"What tragedies?"

"My wife's death, for one."

"She's still alive, in all the days she lived. Those days exist eternally."

"But they came to an end so cruelly."

"Only if you think so."

Lazorg tried to rekindle all his old hatreds. But he was too far removed, he found, from the incidents and days that had engendered those puerile grudges.

"What now? What now for me and my son?"

"I am generous. What do you want?"

Lazorg considered. "To go back, I guess. Back to Crutchsump's world."

"Very good."

But then Lazorg considered his debts, and said, "No. Not back to that place. It was never really home. I left behind a mess in my first existence. Maybe I should go settle accounts there. Yes. Send my son to the world of his birth, and send me back to mine, to make redress."

"As you wish."

Lazorg turned to Slug and they embraced.

"Poppa."

"Do good, boy."

Slug was gone.

Lazorg faced the Conceptus again. "All right, I'm ready."

"So you say."

CHAPTER ELEVEN
CODA

In Frank Lazorg's studio, upon the paint-splattered work-table, the dead woman was stretched out, her naked body covered with pungent red enamel that had dried to a hard insectoid shell. Outside the studio windows, the sun was just coming up. Blood on the floor was just congealing. The gore-clotted cane leaned precariously against a stool.

Suddenly the dead woman's crushed skull recohered, brains re-gelling, bones re-knitting. She experienced a tremendous galvanic convulsion as life retook her, and all the enamel shattered into a crazy paving that began to flake off her as she writhed.

Her legs splayed open involuntarily as her eyes rolled back and showed their whites.

Her vagina dilated instantly, and the crown of a child's head showed, although her flat, toned midriff exhibited no signs of pregnancy. It was as if her sex were a mere gateway to the origin of all worlds.

The child plopped effortlessly out amidst womb-blood and amniotic fluids. Afterbirth soon followed.

Velina Malapsina seemed to come to her senses then. She pushed herself up on the worktable with a bewildered expression upon her face, raising her hand up to brush off a few last red flakes, and regarded the squalling infant between her legs.

She reached down tentatively to touch the grey-eyed baby, and, for no good reason she could immediately offer, said:

"Frank?"

ABOUT THE AUTHOR

PAUL DI FILIPPO'S fiction has been appearing in print for over thirty years now. He's aiming to beat Jack Williamson's career record, but is counting on medical science to help. He lives in Providence, Rhode Island, amidst daily reminders of Lovecraft's tenure in that town. His mate of nearly forty years is Deborah Newton, and their companions at the moment are Penny Century, a calico cat, and Brownie, a chocolate-colored cocker spaniel.

AFTER THE COLLAPSE

From the swarming, last-redoubt towers of the polar regions, where humanity huddles from the savage heat of Greenhouse Earth, to the dusty refugee camps of a shattered America; from the virtual reality landscape where teenagers seek to repair a wounded planet, to the post-human globe populated by wily transgenic heirs to mankind; and, lastly, across the ideology-splintered ruins of the USA...a cast of dedicated survivors tries to make the best of what's left behind, picking up the pieces of their lives and arranging them in new patterns of hope and dreaming.

Here are six riveting tales of life during the hard-luck times of a post-holocaust planet.

Borgo Press Books by PAUL DI FILIPPO

After the Collapse: Stories from Greenhouse Earth
Cosmocopia: A Science Fiction Novel

AFTER THE COLLAPSE

STORIES FROM GREENHOUSE EARTH

PAUL DI FILIPPO

THE BORGO PRESS

MMXI

AFTER THE COLLAPSE

FIRST EDITION

Published by Wildside Press LLC

www.wildsidebooks.com

DEDICATION

To **Deborah**,

Who persists through all calamities,

And to my Mother,

Claire Louise,

Who never stops trying.

CONTENTS

ACKNOWLEDGMENTS

These stories have been previously published as follows:

"Life in the Anthropocene" was originally published in *The Mammoth Book of Apocalypse Science Fiction*, ed. by Mike Ashley, Robinson Publishing, 2010. Copyright © 2010, 2011 by Paul Di Filippo.

"Clouds and Cold Fires" was originally published in *Live Without a Net*, ed. by Lou Anders, Roc Books, 2003. Copyright © 2003, 2011 by Paul Di Filippo.

"Waves and Smart Magma" was originally published in *The Mammoth Book of Mindblowing Science Fiction*, ed. by Mike Ashley, Robinson Publishing, 2009. Copyright © 2009, 2011 by Paul Di Filippo.

"FarmEarth" was originally published in *Welcome to the Greenhouse*, ed. by Gordon Van Gelder, OR Books, 2011. Copyright © 2011 by Paul Di Filippo.

"Escape from New Austin" was originally published in *Jigsaw Nation: Science Fiction Stories of Secession*, ed. by Edward J. McFadden III and E. Sedia, Wilder Publications, 2006. Copyright © 2006, 2011 by Paul Di Filippo.

"Femaville 29" was originally published in *Salon Fantastique: Fifteen Original Tales of Fantasy*, ed. by Ellen Datlow and Terri Windling, Running Press, 2006. Copyright © 2006, 2011 by Paul Di Filippo.

INTRODUCTION

Life goes on.

Along with the sentence "This too shall pass," the line above is simultaneously the most pessimistic formulation of the way the universe works, and the most optimistic one. On the one hand, "Life goes on" indicates that we are capable of picking ourselves up after any tragedy and continuing with some kind of meaningful and useful existence, no matter how damaged we might be from our experiences. There's always tomorrow for dreams to come true. On the other hand, "Life goes on" does seem in our blackest hours to imply one dreary, torturous day after another, with no surcease till death, and an uncaring response from a heartless creation.

I tend, in my writings and personal life, to favor the upbeat interpretation of the motto. We can recover from anything short of death, finding hope and victory and love in the ruins. That's the message these stories are meant to convey, beneath what I hope are some surface thrills and excitement and neat ideas.

As the Buddhists tell us, life is continuously collapsing from one millisecond to the next. That's just the nature of creation. Stability and consistency are illusions. All is a froth of chaotic activity below the Planck level. The universe is like a human being walking: managing to move forward through a series of barely averted falls.

So please take heart by also recalling the words of some western sages, Steely Dan: "Any major dude with half a heart surely will tell you my friend/Any minor world that breaks

apart falls together again/When the demon is at your door/In the morning it won't be there no more/Any major dude will tell you."

—Paul Di Filippo
Providence, Rhode Island
11 July 2011

LIFE IN THE ANTHROPOCENE

1.
Solar Girdle Emergency

Aurobindo Bandjalang got the emergency twing through his vib on the morning of August 8, 2121, while still at home in his expansive bachelor's digs. At 1LDK, his living space was three times larger than most unmarried individuals enjoyed, but his high-status job as a Power Jockey for New Perthpatna earned him extra perks.

While a short-lived infinitesimal flock of beard clippers grazed his face, A.B. had been showering and vibbing the weather feed for Reboot City Twelve: the more formal name for New Perthpatna.

Sharing his shower stall but untouched by the water, beautiful weather idol Midori Mimosa delivered the feed.

"Sunrise occurred this morning at three-oh-two AM. Max temp projected to be a comfortable, shirtsleeves thirty degrees by noon. Sunset at ten-twenty-nine PM this evening. Cee-oh-two at four-hundred-and-fifty parts per million, a significant drop from levels at this time last year. Good work, Rebooters!"

The new tweet/twinge/ping interrupted both the weather and A.B.'s ablutions. His vision grayed out for a few milliseconds as if a sheet of smoked glass had been slid in front of his MEMS contacts, and both his left palm and the sole of his left foot

itched: Attention Demand 5.

A.B.'s boss, Jeetu Kissoon, replaced Midori Mimosa under the sparsely downfalling water: a dismaying and disinvigorating substitution. But A.B.'s virt-in-body operating system allowed for no squelching of twings tagged AD4 and up. Departmental policy.

Kissoon grinned and said, "Scrub faster, A.B. We need you here yesterday. I've got news of face-to-face magnitude."

"What's the basic quench?"

"Power transmission from the French farms is down by one percent. Sat photos show some kind of strange dust accumulation on a portion of the collectors. The on-site kybes can't respond to the stuff with any positive remediation. Where's it from, why now, and how do we stop it? We've got to send a human team down there, and you're heading it."

Busy listening intently to the bad news, A.B. had neglected to rinse properly. Now the water from the low-flow showerhead ceased, its legally mandated interval over. He'd get no more from that particular spigot till the evening. Kissoon disappeared from A.B.'s augmented reality, chuckling.

A.B. cursed with mild vehemence and stepped out of the stall. He had to use a sponge at the sink to finish rinsing, and then he had no sink water left for brushing his teeth. Such a hygienic practice was extremely old-fashioned, given self-replenishing colonies of germ-policing mouth microbes, but A.B. relished the fresh taste of toothpaste and the sense of righteous manual self-improvement. Something of a twentieth-century recreationist, Aurobindo. But not this morning.

Outside A.B.'s 1LDK: his home corridor, part of a well-planned, spacious, senses-delighting labyrinth featuring several public spaces, constituting the one-hundred-and-fiftieth floor of his urbmon.

His urbmon, affectionately dubbed "The Big Stink": one of over a hundred colossal, densely situated high-rise habitats that amalgamated into New Perthpatna.

New Perthpatna: one of over a hundred such Reboot Cities

sited across the habitable zone of Earth, about twenty-five percent of the planet's landmass, collectively home to nine billion souls.

A.B. immediately ran into one of those half-million souls of The Big Stink: Zulqamain Safranski.

Zulqamain Safranski was the last person A.B. wanted to see.

Six months ago, A.B. had logged an ASBO against the man.

Safranski was a parkour. Harmless hobby—if conducted in the approved sports areas of the urbmon. But Safranski blithely parkour'd his ass all over the common spaces, often bumping into or startling people as he ricocheted from ledge to bench. After a bruising encounter with the aggressive urban bounder, A.B. had filed his protest, attaching AD tags to already filed but overlooked video footage of the offenses. Not altogether improbably, A.B.'s complaint had been the one to tip the scales against Safranski, sending him via police trundlebug to the nearest Sin Bin, for a punitively educational stay.

But now, all too undeniably, Safranski was back in New Perthpatna, and instantly in A.B.'s chance-met (?) face.

The buff, choleric, but laughably diminutive fellow glared at A.B., then said, spraying spittle upward, "You just better watch your ass night and day, Bang-a-gong, or you might find yourself doing a *lâché* from the roof without really meaning to."

A.B. tapped his ear and, implicity, his implanted vib audio pickup. "Threats go from your lips to the ears of the wrathful Ekh Dagina—and to the ASBO Squad as well."

Safranski glared with wild-eyed malice at A.B., then stalked off, his planar butt muscles, outlined beneath the tight fabric of his mango-colored plugsuit, somehow conveying further ire by their natural contortions.

A.B. smiled. Amazing how often people still forgot the panopticon nature of life nowadays, even after a century of increasing immersion in and extension of null-privacy. Familiarity bred forgetfulness. But it was best to always recall, at least subliminally, that everyone heard and saw everything equally these days. Just part of the Reboot Charter, allowing a society to func-

tion in which people could feel universally violated, universally empowered.

At the elevator banks closest to home, A.B. rode up to the two-hundred-and-first floor, home to the assigned space for the urbmon's Power Administration Corps. Past the big active mural depicting drowned Perth, fishes swimming round the BHP Tower. Tags in the air led him to the workpod that Jeetu Kissoon had chosen for the time being.

Kissoon looked good for ninety-seven years old: he could have passed for A.B.'s slightly older brother, but not his father. Coffee-bean skin, snowy temples, laugh lines cut deep, only slightly counterbalanced by somber eyes.

When Kissoon had been born, all the old cities still existed, and many, many animals other than goats and chickens flourished. Kissoon had seen the cities abandoned, and the Big Biota Crash, as well as the whole Reboot. Hard for young A.B. to conceive. The man was a walking history lesson. A.B. tried to honor that.

But Kissoon's next actions soon evoked a yawp of disrespectful protest from the younger man.

"Here are the two other Jocks I've assigned to accompany you."

Interactive dossiers hung before A.B.'s gaze. He two-fingered through them swiftly, growing more stunned by the second. Finally he burst out: "You're giving me a furry and a keek as helpers?"

"Tigerishka and Gershon Thales. They're the best available. Live with them, and fix this glitch."

Kissoon stabbed A.B. with a piercing stare, and A.B. realized this meatspace proximity had been demanded precisely to convey the intensity of Kissoon's next words.

"Without power, we're doomed."

2.
45th Parallel Blues

Jet-assisted flight was globally interdicted. Not enough resources left to support regular commercial or recreational aviation. No military anywhere with a need to muster its own air force. Jet engines too harmful to a stressed atmosphere.

And besides, why travel?

Everywhere was the same. Vib served fine for most needs.

The habitable zone of Earth consisted of those lands—both historically familiar and newly disclosed from beneath vanished icepack—above the 45th parallel north, and below the 45th parallel south. The rest of the Earth's landmass had been decertified or drowned: sand or surf.

The immemorial ecosystems of the remaining climactically tolerable territories had been devastated by Greenhouse change, then, ultimately and purposefully, wiped clean. Die-offs, migratory invaders, a fast-forward churn culminating in an engineered ecosphere. The new conditions supported no animals larger than mice, and only a monoculture of GM plants.

Giant aggressive hissing cockroaches, of course, still thrived.

A portion of humanity's reduced domain hosted forests specially designed for maximum carbon uptake and sequestration. These fast-growing, long-lived hybrid trees blended the genomes of eucalyptus, loblolly pine and poplar, and had been dubbed "eulollypops."

The bulk of the rest of the land was devoted to the crops necessary and sufficient to feed nine billion people: mainly quinoa, kale and soy, fertilized by human wastes. Sugarbeet plantations provided feedstock for bio-polymer production.

And then, on their compact footprints, the hundred-plus Reboot Cities, ringed by small but efficient goat and chicken farms.

Not a world conducive to sightseeing Grand Tours.

On each continent, a simple network of maglev trains, delib-

erately held to a sparse schedule, linked the Reboot Cities (except for the Sin Bins, which were sanitarily excluded from easy access to the network). Slow but luxurious aerostats serviced officials and businessmen. Travel between continents occurred on SkySail-equipped water ships. All travel was predicated on state-certified need.

And when anyone had to deviate from standard routes—such as a trio of Power Jockeys following the superconducting transmission lines south to France—they employed a trundlebug.

Peugeot had designed the first trundlebugs over a century ago, the Ozones. Picture a large rolling drum fashioned of electrochromic biopoly, featuring slight catenaries in the lines of its body from end to end. A barrel-shaped compartment suspended between two enormous wheels large as the cabin itself. Solid-state battery packs channeled power to separate electric motors. A curving door spanned the entire width of the vehicle, sliding upward.

Inside, three seats in a row, the center one commanding the failsafe manual controls. Storage behind the seats.

And in those seats:

Aurobindo Bandjalang working the joystick with primitive recreationist glee and vigor, rather than vibbing the trundlebug.

Tigerishka on his right and Gershon Thales on his left.

A tense silence reigned.

Tigerishka exuded a bored professionalism only slightly belied by a gently twitching tailtip and alertly cocked tufted ears. Her tigrine pelt poked out from the edges of her plugsuit, pretty furred face and graceful neck the largest bare expanse.

A.B. thought she smelled like a sexy stuffed toy. Disturbing.

She turned her slit-pupiled eyes away from the monotonous racing landscape for a while to gnaw delicately with sharp teeth at a wayward cuticle around one claw.

Furries chose to express non-inheritable parts of the genome of various extinct species within their own bodies, as a simultaneous expiation of guilt and celebration of lost diversity. Although the Vaults at Reboot City Twenty-nine (formerly

Svalbard, Norway) safely held samples of all the vanished species that had been foolish enough to compete with humanity during this Anthropocene Age, their non-human genomes awaiting some far-off day of re-instantiation, that sterile custody did not sit well with some. The furries wanted other species to walk the earth again, if only by partial proxy.

In contrast to Tigerishka's stolid boredom, Gershon Thales manifested a frenetic desire to maximize demands on his attention. Judging by the swallow-flight motions of his hands, he had half a dozen virtual windows open, upon what landscapes of information A.B. could only conjecture. (He had tried vibbing into Gershon's eyes, but had encountered a pirate privacy wall. Hard to build team camaraderie with that barrier in place, but A.B. had chosen not to call out the man on the matter just yet.)

No doubt Gershon was hanging out on keek fora. The keeks loved to indulge in endless talk.

Originally calling themselves the "punctuated equilibrium-ists," the cult had swiftly shortened their awkward name to the "punk eeks," and then to the "keeks."

The keeks believed that after a long period of stasis, the human species had reached one of those pivotal Darwinian climacterics that would launch the race along exciting if unpre-dictable new vectors. What everyone else viewed as a grand tragedy—implacable and deadly climate change leading to the Big Biota Crash—they interpreted as a useful kick in human-ity's collective pants. They discussed a thousand, thousand schemes intended to further this leap, most of them just so much mad vaporware.

A.B. clucked his tongue softly as he drove. Such were the assistants he had been handed, to solve a crisis of unknown magnitude.

Tigerishka suddenly spoke, her voice a velvet growl. "Can't you push this bug any faster? The cabin's starting to stink like simians already."

New Perthpatna occupied the site that had once hosted the Russian city of Arkhangelsk, torn down during the Reboot. The

closest malfunctioning solar collectors in what had once been France loomed 2,800 kilometers distant. Mission transit time: an estimated thirty-six hours, including overnight rest.

"No, I can't. As it is, we're going to have to camp at least eight hours for the batteries recharge. The faster I push us, the more power we expend, and the longer we'll have to sit idle. It's a calculated tradeoff. Look at the math."

A.B. vibbed Tigerishka a presentation. She studied it, then growled in frustration.

"I need to run! I can't sit cooped up in a smelly can like this for hours at a stretch! At home, I hit the track every hour."

A.B. wanted to say, *I'm not the one who stuck those big-cat codons in you, so don't yell at me!* But instead he notched up the cabin's HVAC and chose a polite response. "Right now, all I can do is save your nose some grief. We'll stop for lunch, and you can get some exercise then. Can't you vib out like old Gershon there?"

Gerson Thales stopped his air haptics to glare at A.B. His lugubrious voice resembled wet cement plopping from a trough. "What's that comment supposed to imply? That I'm wasting my time? Well, I'm not. I'm engaged in posthuman dialectics at Saltation Central. Very stimulating. You two should try to expand your minds in a similar fashion."

Tigerishka hissed. A.B. ran an app that counted to ten for him using gently breaking waves to time the calming sequence.

"As mission leader, I don't really care how anyone passes the travel time. Just so long as you all perform when it matters. Now how about letting me enjoy the drive."

The "road" actually required little of A.B.'s attention. A wide border of rammed earth, kept free of weeds by cousins to A.B. beard removers, the road paralleled the surprisingly dainty superconducting transmission line that powered a whole city. It ran straight as modern justice toward the solar collectors that fed it. Shade from the rows of eulollypops planted alongside cut down any glare and added coolness to their passage.

Coolness was a desideratum. The further south they trav-

eled, the hotter things would get. Until, finally, temperatures would approach fifty degrees at many points of the Solar Girdle. Only their plugsuits would allow the Power Jockeys to function outside under those conditions.

A.B. tried to enjoy the sensations of driving, a recreationist pastime he seldom got to indulge. Most of his work day consisted of indoor maintenance and monitoring, optimization of supply and demand, the occasional high-level debugging. Humans possessed a fluidity of response and insight no kybes could yet match. A field expedition marked a welcome change of pace from this indoor work. Or would have, with comrades more congenial.

A.B. sighed, and kicked up their speed just a notch.

After traveling for nearly five hours, they stopped for lunch, just a bit north of where Moscow had once loomed. No Reboot City had ever been erected in its place, more northerly locations being preferred.

As soon as the wide door slid upward, Tigerishka bolted from the cabin. She raced laterally off into the endless eulollypop forest, faster than a baseline human. Thirty seconds later, a rich, resonant, hair-raising caterwaul of triumph made both A.B. and Gershon Thales jump.

Thales said drily, "Caught a mouse, I suppose."

A.B. laughed. Maybe Thales wasn't such a stiff.

A.B. jacked the trundlebug into one of the convenient step-down charging nodes in the transmission cable designed for just such a purpose. Even an hour's topping up would help. Then he broke out sandwiches of curried goat salad. He and Thales ate companionably. Tigerishka returned with a dab of overlooked murine blood at the corner of her lips, and declined any human food.

Back in the moving vehicle, Thales and Tigerishka reclined their seats and settled down to a nap after lunch, and their drowsiness soon infected A.B. He put the trundlebug on auto-pilot, reclined his own seat, and soon was fast asleep as well.

Awaking several hours later, A.B. discovered their location

to be nearly atop the 54th parallel, in the vicinity of pre-Crash Minsk.

The temperature outside their cozy cab registered a sizzling thirty-five, despite the declining sun.

"We'll push on toward Old Warsaw, then call it a day. That'll leave just a little over eleven hundred klicks to cover tomorrow."

Thales objected. "We'll get to the farms late in the day tomorrow—too late for any useful investigation. Why not run all night on autopilot?"

"I want us to get a good night's rest without jouncing around. And besides, all it would take is a tree freshly down across the road, or a new sinkhole to ruin us. The autopilot's not infallible."

Tigerishka's sultry purr sent tingles through A.B.'s scrotum. "I need to work out some kinks myself."

Night halted the trundlebug. When the door slid up, furnace air blasted the trio, automatically activating their plugsuits. Sad old fevered planet. They pulled up their cowls and felt relief.

Three personal homeostatic pods were decanted, and popped open upon vibbed command beneath the allée. They crawled inside separately to eat and drop off quickly to sleep.

Stimulating caresses awakened A.B. Hazily uncertain what hour this was that witnessed Tigerishka's trespass upon his homeopod, or whether she had visited Thales first, he could decisively report in the morning, had such a report been required by Jeetu Kissoon and the Power Administration Corps, that she retained enough energy to wear him out.

3.
The Sands of Paris

The vast, forbidding, globe-encircling desert south of the 45th parallel depressed everyone in the trundlebug. A.B. ran his tongue around lips that felt impossibly cracked and parched, no matter how much water he sucked from his plugsuit's kamelbak.

All greenery gone, the uniform trackless and silent wastes baking under the implacable sun brought to mind some alien world that had never known human tread. No signs of the mighty cities that had once reared their proud towers remained, nor any traces of the sprawling suburbs, the surging highways. What had not been disassembled for re-use elsewhere had been buried.

On and on the trundlebug rolled, following the superconductor line, its enormous wheels operating as well on loose sand as on rammed earth.

A.B. felt anew the grievous historical impact of humanity's folly upon the planet, and he did not relish the emotions. He generally devoted little thought to that sad topic.

An utterly modern product of his age, a hardcore Rebooter through and through, Aurobindo Bandjalang was generally happy with his civilization. Its contorted features, its limitations and constraints, its precariousness, and its default settings he accepted implicitly, just as a child of trolls believes its troll mother to be utterly beautiful.

He knew pride in how the human race had managed to build a hundred new cities from scratch and shift billions of people north and south in only half a century, outracing the spreading blight and killer weather. He enjoyed the hybrid multicultural *mélange* that had replaced old divisions and rivalries, the new blended mankind. The nostalgic stories told by Jeetu Kissoon and others of his generation were entertaining fairytales, not the chronicle of any lost Golden Age. He could not lament what he had never known. He was too busy keeping the delicate structures of the present day up and running, and happy to be so occupied.

Trying to express these sentiments and lift the spirits of his comrades, A.B. found that his evaluation of Reboot civilization was not universal.

"Every human of this fallen Anthropocene age is shadowed by the myriad ghosts of all the other creatures they drove extinct," said Tigerishka, in a surprisingly poetic and somber manner,

given her usual blunt and unsentimental earthiness. "Whales and dolphins, cats and dogs, cows and horses—they all peer into and out of our sinful souls. Our only shot at redemption is that some day, when the planet is restored, our coevolved partners might be re-embodied."

Thales uttered a scoffing grunt. "Good riddance to all that nonsapient genetic trash! *Homo sapiens* is the only desirable endpoint of all evolutionary lines. But right now, the dictatorial Reboot has our species locked down in a dead end. We can't make the final leap to our next level until we get rid of the chaff."

Tigerishka spat, and made a taunting feint toward her co-worker across A.B.s chest, causing A.B. to swerve the car and Thales to recoil. When the keek realized he hadn't actually been hurt, he grinned with a sickly superciliousness.

"Hold on one minute," said A.B. "Do you mean that you and the other keeks want to see another Crash?"

"It's more complex than that. You see—"

But A.B.'s attention was diverted that moment from Thales's explanation. His vib interrupted with a Demand Four call from his apartment.

Vib nodes dotted the power transmission network, keeping people online just like at home. Plenty of dead zones existed elsewhere, but not here, adjacent to the line.

A.B. had just enough time to place the trundlebug on autopilot before his vision was overlaid with a feed from home.

The security system on his apartment had registered an unauthorized entry.

Inside his 1LDK, an optical distortion the size of a small human moved around, spraying something similar to used cooking oil on A.B.s furniture. The hands holding the sprayer disappeared inside the whorl of distortion.

A.B. vibbed his avatar into his home system. "Hey, you! What the fuck are you doing!"

The person wearing the invisibility cape laughed, and A.B. recognized the distinctive crude chortle of Zulqamain Safranski.

"Safranski! Your ass is grass! The ASBO's are on their way!"

Unable to stand the sight of his lovely apartment being desecrated, frustrated by his inability to take direct action himself, A.B. vibbed off.

Tigerishka and Thales had shared the feed, and commiserated with their fellow Power Jock. But the experience soured the rest of the trip for A.B., and he stewed silently until they reached the first of the extensive constructions upon which the Reboot Cities relied for their very existence.

The Solar Girdle featured a tripartite setup, for the sake of security of supply.

First came the extensive farms of solar updraft towers: giant chimneys that fostered wind flow from base to top, thus powering their turbines.

Then came parabolic mirrored troughs that followed the sun and pumped heat into special sinks, lakes of molten salts, which in turn ran different turbines after sunset.

Finally, serried ranks of photovoltaic panels generated electricity directly. These structures, in principle the simplest and least likely to fail, were the ones experiencing difficulties from some kind of dust accretion.

Vibbing GPS coordinates for the troublespot, A.B. brought the trundlebug up to the infected photovoltaics. Paradoxically, the steady omnipresent whine of the car's motors registered on his attention only when he had powered them down.

Outside the vehicle's polarized plastic shell, the sinking sun glared like the malign orb of a Cyclops bent on mankind's destruction.

When the bug-wide door slid up, dragon's breath assailed the Power Jocks. Their plugsuits strained to shield them from the hostile environment.

Surprisingly, a subdued and pensive Tigerishka volunteered for camp duty. As dusk descended, she attended to erecting their intelligent shelters and getting a meal ready: chicken croquettes with roasted edamame.

A.B. and Thales sluffed through the sand for a dozen yards to the nearest infected solarcell platform. The keek held his pocket

lab in gloved hand.

A little maintenance kybe, scuffed and scorched, perched on the high trellis, valiantly but fruitlessly chipping with its multi-tool at a hard siliceous shell irregularly encrusting the photovoltaic surface.

Thales caught a few flakes of the unknown substance as they fell, and inserted them into the analysis chamber of the pocket lab.

"We should have a complete readout of the composition of this stuff by morning."

"No sooner?"

"Well, actually, by midnight. But I don't intend to stay up. I've done nothing except sit on my ass for two days, yet I'm still exhausted. It's this oppressive place—"

"Okay," A.B. replied. The first stars had begun to prinkle the sky. "Let's call it a day."

They ate in the bug, in a silent atmosphere of forced companionability, then retired to their separate shelters.

A.B. hoped with mild lust for another nocturnal visit from a prowling Tigerishka, but was not greatly disappointed when she never showed to interrupt his intermittent drowsing. Truly, the desert sands of Paris sapped all his usual joie de vivre.

Finally falling fast asleep, he dreamed of the ghostly waters of the vanished Seine, impossibly flowing deep beneath his tent. Somehow, Zulqamain Safranski was diverting them to flood A.B.'s apartment....

4.

The Red Queen's Triathalon

In the morning, after breakfast, A.B. approached Gershon Thales, who stood apart near the trundlebug. Already the sun thundered down its oppressive cargo of photons, so necessary for the survival of the Reboot Cities, yet, conversely, just one more burden for the overstressed Greenhouse ecosphere.

Feeling irritable and impatient, anxious to be back home, A.B. dispensed with pleasantries.

"I've tried vibbing your pocket lab for the results, but you've got it offline, behind that pirate software you're running. Open up, now."

The keek stared at A.B. with mournful stolidity. "One minute, I need something from my pod."

Thales ducked into his tent. A.B. turned to Tigerishka. "What do you make—"

Blinding light shattered A.B.'s vision for a millisecond in a painful nova, before his MEMS contacts could react protectively by going opaque. Tigerishka vented a stifled yelp of surprise and shock, showing she had gotten the same actinic eyekick.

A.B. immediately thought of vib malfunction, some misdirected feed from a solar observatory, say. But then, as his lenses de-opaqued, he realized the stimulus had to have been external.

When he could see again, he confronted Gershon Thales holding a pain gun whose wide bell muzzle covered both of the keek's fellow Power Jocks. At the feet of the keek rested an exploded spaser grenade.

A.B. tried to vib, but got nowhere.

"Yes," Thales said, "we're in a dead zone now. I fried all the optical circuits of the vib nodes with the grenade."

A large enough burst of surface plasmons could do that? Who knew? "But why?"

With his free hand, keeping the pain gun unwavering, Thales reached into a plugsuit pocket and took out his lab. "These results. They're only the divine sign we've been waiting for. Reboot civilization is on the way out now. I couldn't let anyone in the PAC find out. The longer they stay in the dark, the more irreversible the changes will be."

"You're claiming this creeping crud is that dangerous?"

"Did you ever hear of ADRECS?"

A.B. instinctively tried to vib for the info and hit the blank frustrating walls of the newly created dead zone. Trapped in the twentieth century! Recreationist passions only went so far.

Where was the panopticon when you needed it!?!

"Aerially Delivered Re-forestation and Erosion Control System," continued Thales. "A package of geoengineering schemes meant to stabilize the spread of deserts. Abandoned decades ago. But apparently, one scheme's come alive again on its own. Mutant instruction drift is my best guess. Or Darwin's invisible hand."

"What's come alive then?"

"Nanosand. Meant to catalyze the formation of macroscale walls that would block the flow of normal sands."

"And that's the stuff afflicting the solar cells?"

"Absolutely. Has an affinity for bonding with the surface of the cells and can't be removed with destroying them. Self-replicating. Best estimates are that the nanosand will take out thirty percent of production in just a month, if left unchecked. Might start to affect the turbines too."

Tigerishka asked, in an intellectually curious tone of voice that A.B. found disconcerting, "But what good does going offline do? When PAC can't vib us, they'll just send another crew."

"I'll wait here and put them out of commission too. I only have to hang in for a month."

"What about food?" said Tigerishka. "We don't have enough provisions for a month, even for one person."

"I'll raid the fish farms on the coast. Desalinate my drinking water. It's just a short round trip by bug."

A.B. could hardly contain his disgust. "You're fucking crazy, Thales. Dropping the power supply by thirty percent won't kill the cities."

"Oh, but we keeks think it will. You see, Reboot civilization is a wobbly three-legged stool, hammered together in a mad rush. We're not in the Red Queen's Race, but the Red Queen's Triathalon. Power, food and social networks. Take out any one leg, and it all goes down. And we're sawing at the other two legs as well. Look at that guy who vandalized your apartment. Behavior like that is on the rise. The urbmons are driving people

crazy. Humans weren't meant to live in hives."

Tigerishka stepped forward, and Thales swung the gun more towards her unprotected face. A blast of high-intensity micro-waves would leave her screaming, writhing and puking on the sands.

"I want in," she said, and A.B.'s heart sank through his boots. "The only way other species will ever get to share this planet is when most of mankind is gone."

Regarding the furry speculatively and clinically, Thales said, "I could use your help. But you'll have to prove yourself. First, tie up Bandjalang."

Tigerishka grinned vilely at A.B. "Sorry, ape boy."

Using biopoly cords from the bug, she soon had A.B. trussed with circulation-deadening bonds, and stashed in his homeopod.

What were they doing out there!?! A.B. squirmed futilely. He banged around so much, he began to fear he was damaging the life-preserving tent, and he stopped. Wiped out after hours of struggle, he fell into a stupor made more enervating by the suddenly less-than-ideal heat inside the homeopod, whose compromised systems strained to deal with the desert condi-tions. He began to hallucinate about the subterranean Seine again, and realized he was very, very thirsty. His kamelbak was dry when he sipped at its straw.

At some point, Tigerishka appeared and gave him some water. Or did she? Maybe it was all just another dream.

Outside the smart tent, night came down. A.B. heard wolves howling, just like they did on archived documentaries. Wolves? No wolves existed. But someone was howling.

Tigerishka having sex. Sex with Thales. Bastard. Bad guy not only won the battle, but got the girl as well....

A.B. awoke to the pins and needles of returning circulation: discomfort of a magnitude unfelt by anyone before or after the Lilliputians tethered Gulliver.

Tigerishka was bending over him, freeing him.

"Sorry again, ape boy, that took longer than I thought. He even kept his hand on the gun right up until he climaxed."

Something warm was dripping on A.B.'s face. Was his rescuer crying? Her voice belied any such emotion. A.B. raised a hand that felt like a block of wood to his own face, and clumsily smeared the liquid around, until some entered his mouth.

He imagined that this forbidden taste was equally as satisfying to Tigerishka as mouse fluids.

Heading north, the trundlebug seemed much more spacious with just two passengers. The corpse of Gershon Thales had been left behind, for eventual recovery by experts. Dessication and cooking would make it a fine mummy.

Once out of the dead zone, A.B. vibbed everything back to Jeetu Kissoon, and got a shared commendation that made Tigerishka purr. Then he turned his attention to his personal queue of messages.

The ASBO Squad had bagged Safranski. But they apologized for some delay in his sentencing hearing. Their caseload was enormous these days.

Way down at the bottom of his queue was an agricultural newsfeed. An unprecedented kind of black rot fungus had made inroads into the kale crop on the farms supplying Reboot City Twelve.

Calories would be tight in New Perthpatna, but only for a while.

Or so they hoped.

—This story is indebted to Gaia Vince and her article in *New Scientist*, "Surviving in a Warmer World."

CLOUDS AND COLD FIRES

Out of a clear sky on a fine summer morning, a buckshot rattle of hailstones across the living pangolin plates of Pertinax's rooftop announced the arrival of some mail.

Inside his cozy, low-ceilinged hutch, with its corner devoted to an easel and canvases and art supplies, its shelves full of burl sculptures, its workbench that hosted bubbling retorts and alembics and a universal proseity device, Pertinax paused in the feeding of his parrot tulips. Setting down the wooden tray of raw meat chunks, he turned away from the colorfully enameled soil-filled pots arrayed on his bright windowsill. The parrot tulips squawked at this interruption of their lunch, bobbing their feathery heads angrily on their long succulent neck stalks. Pertinax chided them lovingly, stroking their crests while avoiding their sharp beaks. Then, hoisting the hem of his long striped robe to expose his broad naked paw-feet, he hurried outdoors.

Fallen to the earth after bouncing from the imbricated roof, the hailstones were already nearly melted away to invisibility beneath the temperate sunlight, damp spots on the undulant greensward upon which Pertinax's small but comfortable dwelling sat. Pertinax wetted a finger, raised it to gauge the wind's direction, then directed his vision upward and to the north, anticipating the direction from which his mail would arrive. Sure enough, within a minute a lofty cloud had begun to form, a flocculent painterly smudge on the monochrome canvas of the turquoise sky.

The cloud assumed coherence and substance, drawing into itself its necessary share of virgula and sublimula omnipresent within the upper atmosphere. After another minute or two, the cloud possessed a highly regular oval outline and had descended to within five meters of the ground. Large as one of the windows in Pertinax's hutch, the cloud halted its progress at this level, and its surface began to acquire a sheen. The sheen took on the qualities of an ancient piece of translucent plastic, such as the Overclockers might cherish. Then Pertinax's animated mail appeared across the cloud's surface, as the invisible components of the cloud churned in coordinated fashion.

Sylvanus's snouty whiskered face smiled, but the smile was grim, as was his voice resonating from the cloud's fine-grain speakers.

"Pertinax my friend, I regret this interruption of your studies and recreations, but I have some dramatic news requiring our attention. It appears that the Overclockers at their small settlement known as 'Chicago' are about to launch an assault on the tropospherical mind. Given their primitive methods, I doubt that they can inflict permanent damage. But their mean-spirited sabotage might very well cause local disruptions before the mind repairs itself. I know you have several projects running currently, and I would hate to see you lose any data during a period of limited chaos. I would certainly regret any setbacks to my ongoing modeling of accelerated hopper embryogenesis. Therefore, I propose that a group of those wardens most concerned form a delegation to visit the Overclockers and attempt to dissuade them from such malicious tampering. Mumbaugh has declined to participate—he's busy dealing with an infestation of hemlock mites attacking the forests of his region—but I have firm commitments from Cimabue, Tanselle and Chellapilla. I realize that it is irksome to leave behind the comforts of your home to make such a trip. But I am hoping that I may count on your participation as well. Please reply quickly, as time is of the essence."

Its mail delivered, the cloud wisped away into its mesoscopic

constituent parts. A light misty drizzle refreshed Pertinax's face. But otherwise he was left with only the uneasy feelings occasioned by the message.

Of course he would help Sylvanus. Interference with the tropospherical mind could not be tolerated. The nerve of those Overclockers!

Not for the first time, nor probably the last, Pertinax ruefully contemplated the dubious charity of the long-departed Upflowered.

When ninety-nine-point-nine percent of humanity had abandoned the Earth for greener intergalactic pastures during the Upflowering, the leavetakers had performed several final tasks. They had re-arcadized the whole globe, wiping away nearly every vestige of mankind's crude twenty-second-century proto-civilization, and restocked the seas and plains with many beasts. They had established Pertinax and his fellows—a small corps of ensouled, spliced and redacted domestic animals—as caretakers of the restored Earth. They had charitably set up a few agrarian reservations for the small number of dissidents and malfunctioning humans who chose to remain behind, stubbornly unaltered in their basic capabilities from their archaic genetic baseline. And they had uploaded every vestige of existing machine intelligence and their knowledge bases to a new platform: an airborne network of miniscule, self-replenishing components, integrated with the planet's meteorological systems.

During the intervening centuries, the remaining archaic humans—dubbed the Overclockers for their uncanny devotion to both speed and the false quantization of holistic imponderables—had gradually dragged themselves back up to a certain level of technological achievement. Now, it seemed, they were on the point of making a nuisance of themselves. This could not be tolerated.

Hurrying back into his compact domicile, Pertinax readied his reply to Sylvanus. From a small door inset in one wall, which opened onto a coop fixed to the outside wall, Pertinax

retrieved a mail pigeon. He placed the docile murmuring bird on a tabletop and fed it some special seed, scooped from one compartment of a feed bin. While he waited for the virgula and sublimula within the seed to take effect, Pertinax supplied his own lunch: a plate of carrots and celery, the latter smeared with delicious bean paste. By the time Pertinax had finished his repast, cleaning his fur with the side of one paw-hand all the way from muzzle to tufted ear tips, the pigeon was locked into recording mode, staring ahead fixedly, as if hypnotized by a predator.

Pertinax positioned himself within the bird's field of vision. "Sylvanus my peer, I enlist wholeheartedly in your mission! Although my use of the tropospheric mind is negligible compared to your own employment of the system, I do have all my statistics and observations from a century of avian migrations stored there. Should the data and its backups be corrupted, the loss of such a record would be disastrous! I propose to set out immediately by hopper for 'Chicago.' Should you likewise leave upon receipt of this message, I believe our paths will intersect somewhere around these coordinates." Pertinax recited latitude and longitude figures. "Simply ping my hopper when you get close enough, and we'll meet to continue the rest of our journey together. Travel safely."

Pertinax recited the verbal tag that brought the pigeon out of its trance. The bird resumed its lively attitude, plainly ready to perform its share of the mail delivery. Pertinax cradled the bird against his oddly muscled chest and stepped outside. He lofted the pigeon upwards, and it began to stroke the sky bravely.

Once within the lowest layers of the tropospheric mind, the bird would have its brain states recorded by an ethereal cap of spontaneously congregating virgula and sublimula, and the bird would be free to return to its coop.

Pertinax's message would thus enter the meterological medium and be propagated across the intervening leagues to Sylvanus. Like a wave in the ocean, the information was not dependent upon any unique set of entities to constitute its iden-

tity, and so could travel faster than simple forward motion of particles might suggest. To span the globe from Pertinax to the antipodes took approximately twelve hours, and Sylvanus lived much closer. Not as fast as the ancient quantum-entanglement methods extant in the days before the Upflowering. But then again, the pace of life among the stewards was much less frenzied than it had been among the ancestors of the Overclockers.

Having seen his mail on its way, Pertinax commenced the rest of his preparations for his trip. He finished feeding his parrot tulips, giving them a little extra to see them through his time away from home. If delayed overlong, Pertinax knew they would estivate safely till his return. Then from a cupboard he took a set of large saddlebags. Into these pouches he placed victuals for himself and several packets of multipurpose pigeon seed, as well as a few treats and vitamin pills to supplement the forage which his hopper would subsist on during the journey. He looked fondly at his neat, comfortable bed, whose familiar refuge he would miss. No taking that of course! But the hopper would provide a decent alternative. Pertinax added a few other miscellaneous items to his pack, then deemed his provisions complete.

Stepping outside, Pertinax took one fond look back inside before shutting and latching his door. He went around shuttering all the windows as a precaution against the storms that sometimes accompanied the more demanding calculations of the tropospheric mind. From the pigeon coop he withdrew three birds and placed them in a loosely woven wicker carrier. Then he took a few dozen strides to the hopper corral, formed of high walls of living ironthorn bush.

Pertinax's hopper was named Flossy, a fine mare. The redacted Kodiak Kangemu stood three meters tall at its shoulders. Its pelt was a curious blend of chestnut fur and gray feathers, its fast-twitch-muscled legs banded with bright yellow scales along the lower third above its enormous feet. A thick strong tail jutted backward for almost half Flossy's length.

Pertinax tossed Flossy a treat, which she snapped from the air

with her long jaws. In the stable attached to the corral, Pertinax secured a saddle. This seat resembled a papoose or backpack, with two shoulder straps. Outside again, Pertinax opened the corral gate—formed of conventional timbers—and beckoned to Flossy, who obediently came out and hunkered down. Holding the saddle up above his head, Pertinax aided Flossy in shrugging into the seat. He cinched the straps, then hung his saddlebags from one lower side of the seat and the wicker basket containing the pigeons from the other. Deftly Pertinax scrambled up, employing handholds of Flossy's fur, and ensconced himself comfortably, the seat leaving his arms free but cradling his back and neck. His head was now positioned above Flossy's, giving him a clear view of his path. He gripped Flossy's big upright ears firmly yet not harshly, and urged his mount around to face northeast.

"Gee up, Flossy," said Pertinax, and they were off.

Flossy's gait was the queerest mixture of hopping, vaulting, running and lumbering, a mode of locomotion unknown to baseline creation. But Pertinax found it soothing, and his steed certainly ate up the kilometers.

For the first few hours, Pertinax enjoyed surveying his immediate territory, quite familiar and beloved, noting subtle changes in the fauna and flora of the prairie that distance brought. In early afternoon he stopped for a meal, allowing Flossy to forage. Taking out a pigeon and prepping the bird, Pertinax recited his morning's scientific observations to be uploaded to the tropospheric mind. Its data delivered, the bird homed back to Pertinax rather than the cottage. In less than an hour, the warden was underway again.

Pertinax fell asleep in the saddle and awoke at dusk. He halted Flossy and dismounted to make camp. With the saddle off, Flossy cropped wearily nearby. The first thing Pertinax attended to was the establishment of a security zone. A pheromonal broadcaster would disseminate the warden's exaggerated chemical signature for kilometers in every direction, a note that all of wild creation was primed by the Upflowered to respond

to. Avoidance of the distinctive trace had been built into their ancestors' genes. (The bodily signature had to be masked for upclose work with animals.) Pertinax had no desire to be trampled in the night by a herd of bison, or attacked by any of the region's many predators. Sentient enemies were nonexistent, with the nearest Overclockers confined by their limited capacities nearly one thousand kilometers away in "Chicago."

After setting up the small scent broadcast unit, Pertinax contemplated summoning forth some entertainment. But in the end he decided he was just too tired to enjoy any of the many offerings of the tropospheric mind, and that he would rather simply go to sleep.

The upright Flossy, balanced tripodally on her long tail, was already herself half a-drowse, and she made only the softest of burblings when Pertinax clambered into her capacious marsupial pouch. Dry and lined with a soft down, the pouch smelled like the nest of some woodland creature, and Pertinax fell asleep feeling safe and cherished.

The morning dawned like the first day of the world, crisp and inviting. Emerging from his nocturnal pouch, Pertinax noted that night had brought a heavy dew that would have soaked him had he been dossing rough. But instead he had enjoyed a fine, dry, restful sleep.

Moving off a ways from the grumbling Flossy, and casting about with a practiced eye, Pertinax managed to spot some untended prairie chicken nests amidst the grassy swales. He robbed them of an egg apiece without compunction (the population of the birds was robust), and soon a fragrant omelet, seasoned with herbs from home, sizzled over a small propane burner. (Pertinax obtained the flammable gas from his universal proseity device, just as he supplied many of his needs.)

After enjoying his meal, Pertinax dispatched a pigeon upward to obtain from the tropospheric mind his positional reading, derived from various inputs such as constellational and magnetic. The coordinates, cloud-blazoned temporarily on the sky in digits meters long, informed Pertinax that Flossy had

carried him nearly one hundred and fifty kilometers during their previous half-day of travel. At this rate, he'd join up with Sylvanus on the morrow, and with the others a day later. Then the five stewards would reach "Chicago" around noon of the fourth day.

Past that point, all certainty vanished. How the Overclockers would react to the arrival of the wardens, how the wardens would dissuade the humans from tampering with the planetary mind, what they would do if they met resistance—all this remained obscure.

Remounting Flossy, Pertinax easily put the uncertainty from his mind. Neither he nor his kind were prone to angst. So, once on his way, he reveled instead in the glorious day and the unfolding spectacle of a nature reigning supreme over an untarnished globe.

Herds of bisons thundered past at a safe distance during various intervals along Pertinax's journey. Around noon a nearly interminable flock of passenger pigeons darkened the skies. A colony of prairie dogs stretching across hectares mounted a noisy and stern defense of their town.

That night replicated the simple pleasures of the previous one. Before bedding down, Pertinax enjoyed a fine display of icy micrometeorites flashing into the atmosphere. The Upflowered had arranged a regular replenishment of Earth's water budget via this cosmic source before they left.

Around noon on the second full day of travel, with the landscape subtly changing as they departed one bioregion for another, Pertinax felt a sudden quivering alertness thrill through Flossy. She had plainly pinged the must of Sylvanus's steed (a stallion named Bix) on the wind, and needed no help from her rider to zero in on her fellow Kodiak Kangemu. Minutes later, Pertinax himself espied Sylvanus and his mount, a tiny conjoined dot in the distance.

Before long, the two wardens were afoot and clasping each other warmly, while their hoppers boxed affectionately at each other.

"Pertinax, you're looking glossy as a foal! How I wish I was your age again!"

"Nonsense, Sylvanus, you look splendid yourself. After all, you're far from old. A hundred and twenty-nine last year, wasn't it?"

"Yes, yes, but the weary bones still creak more than they did when I was a young buck like you, a mere sixty-eight. Some days I just want to drop my duties and retire. But I need to groom a successor first. If only you and Chellapilla—"

Pertinax interrupted his elder friend. "Perhaps Chellapilla and I have been selfish. I confess to feeling guilty about this matter from time to time. But the demands on our energies seemed always to preclude parentage. I'll discuss it with her tomorrow. And don't forget, there's always Cimabue and Tanselle."

Sylvanus clapped a hearty paw-hand on Pertinax's shoulder. "They're fine stewards, my boy, but I had always dreamed of your child stepping into my shoes."

Pertinax lowered his eyes. "I'm honored, Sylvanus. Let me speak of this with Chell."

"That's all I ask. Now I suppose we should be on our way again."

It took some sharp admonishments and a few coercive treats to convince Bix and Flossy to abandon their play for the moment and resume travel, but eventually the two wardens again raced northeast, toward their unannounced appointment with the Overclockers.

That night before turning in, Sylvanus suggested some entertainment.

"I have not viewed any historical videos for some time now. Would you care to see one?"

"Certainly. Do you have a suggestion?"

"What about *The Godfather*?"

"*Part One*?"

"Yes."

"An excellent choice. Perhaps it will help to refresh our understanding of Overclocker psychology. I'll send up a pigeon."

The sleepy bird responded sharply to the directorial seed and verbal instructions, then zoomed upward. While the wardens waited for the tropospheric mind to respond, they arranged their packs and saddles in a comfortable couch that allowed them to lay back and observe the nighted skies.

In minutes a small audio cloud had formed low down near them, to provide the soundtrack. Then the high skies lit with colored cold fires.

The new intelligent meteorology allowed for auroral displays at any latitude of the globe, as cosmic rays were channeled by virgula and sublimula, then bent and manipulated to excite atoms and ions. Shaped and permuted on a pixel level by the distributed airborne mind, the auroral canvas possessed the resolution of a twentieth-century drive-in screen, and employed a sophisticated palette.

Clear and bold as life, the antique movie began to unroll across the black empyrean. Snacking on dried salted crickets, the two stewards watched in rapt fascination until the conclusion of the film.

"Most enlightening," said Sylvanus. "We must be alert for such incomprehensible motives as well as deceptions and machinations among the Overclockers."

"Indeed, we would be foolish to anticipate any rationality at all from such a species. Their ancestors' choice to secede from the Upflowering tells us all we need to know about their unchanged mentality."

Mid-afternoon of the next day found Sylvanus and Pertinax hard-pressed to restrain their rambunctious hoppers from charging toward three other approaching Kodiak Kangemu. At the end of the mad gallop, five stewards were clustered in a congregation of hearty back-slapping and embraces, while the frolicking hoppers cavorted nearby.

After the general exchange of greetings and reassurances, Cimabue and Tanselle took Sylvanus one side to consult with him, leaving Pertinax and Chellapilla some privacy.

Chellapilla smiled broadly, revealing a palisade of blunt

healthy brown teeth. Her large hazel eyes sparkled with affection and her leathery nostrils flared wetly. The past year since their last encounter had seen her acquire a deep ragged notch in one ear. Pertinax reached up to touch the healed wound. Chellapilla only laughed, before grabbing his paw-hand and kissing it.

"Are you troubled by that little nick, Perty? Just a brush with a wounded wolverine when I was checking a trap line for specimens last winter. Well worth the information gained."

Pertinax found it hard to reconcile himself to Chellapilla's sangfroid. "I worry about you, Chell. It's a hard life we have sometimes, as isolated guardians of the biosphere. Don't you wish, just once in a while, that we could live together...?"

"Ah, of course I do! But where would that end? Two stewards together would become four, then a village, then a town, then a city of wardens. With our long life spans, we'd soon overpopulate the world with our kind. And then Earth would be right back where it was in the twenty-second century."

"Surely not! Our species would not fall prey to the traps mankind stumbled into before the Upflowering."

Chellapilla smiled. "Oh, no, we'd be clever enough to invent new ones. No, it's best this way. We have our pastoral work to occupy our intelligence, with the tropospheric mind to keep us in daily contact and face to face visits at regular intervals. It's a good system."

"You're right, I suppose. But still, when I see you in the flesh, Chell, I long for you so."

"Then let's make the most of this assignment. We'll have sweet memories to savor when we part."

Pertinax nuzzled Chellapilla's long furred neck, and she shivered and clasped him close. Then he whispered his thoughts regarding Sylvanus's desired retirement and the needful successor child into her ear.

Chellapilla chuckled. "Are you sure you didn't put Sylvanus up to this? You know the one exemption from cohabitation is the period of parenting. This is all a scheme to get me to clean

your hutch and cook your meals on a regular basis for a few years, isn't it?"

"Yes, I admit it. There's never been a universal proseity device made that was as nice to hold as you."

"Well, let me think about it for the rest of this trip, before I go off my pills. It's true that you and I are not getting any younger, and I am inclined toward becoming a mother, especially if our child will help ease Sylvanus's old age. But I want to make sure I'm not overlooking any complications."

"My ever-sensible Chell! I could have dictated your reply without ever leaving my hutch."

Chellapilla snorted. "One of us has to be the sobersided one."

The two lovers rejoined their fellow stewards. Tanselle immediately took Chellapilla one side, in an obvious attempt to pump her friend for any gossip. The feminine whispers and giggles and sidewise glances embarrassed Pertinax, and he made a show of engaging Cimabue in a complex discussion of the latter's researches. But Pertinax could lend only half his mind to Cimabue's talk of fisheries and turtle breeding, ocean currents and coral reefs. The other half was still contemplating his exciting future with Chellapilla.

Eventually Sylvanus roused them from their chatter with a suggestion that they resume their journey. Bix, Flossy, Amber, Peavine and Peppergrass bore their riders north, deeper into the already encroaching forests of the Great Lakes region.

When they established camp that evening in a clearing beneath a broad canopy of lofty treetops, Sylvanus made a point of setting up a little hearth somewhat apart from his younger comrades. Plainly, he did not want to put a damper on any romantic moments among the youngsters.

The five shared supper together however. Sylvanus kept wrinkling his grizzled snout throughout the meal, until finally he declaimed, "There's a storm brewing. The tropospheric mind must be performing some large randomizations or recalibrations. I suspect entire registers will be dumped."

Baseline weather had been tempered by the creation of an

intelligent atmosphere. Climates across the planet were more equitable and homogenous, with fewer extreme instances of violent weather. But occasionally both the moderately large and even the titanic disturbances of yore would recur, as the separate entities that constituted the community of the skies deliberately encouraged random Darwinian forces to cull and mutate their members.

"I packed some tarps and ropes," said Cimabue, "for just such an occasion. If we cut some poles, we can erect a shelter quickly."

Working efficiently, the wardens built, first, a three-walled roofed enclosure for their hardy hoppers, stoutly braced between several trees, its open side to the leeward of the prevailing winds. Then they fashioned a small but sufficient tent for themselves and their packs, heavily staked to the earth. A few blankets strewn about the interior created a comfy nest, illuminated by several cold luminescent sticks. Confined body heat would counter any chill.

Just as they finished, a loud crack of thunder ushered in the storm. Safe and sound in their tent, the wardens listened to the rain hammering the intervening leaves above before filtering down to drip less heavily on their roof.

Sylvanus immediately bade his friends goodnight, then curled up in his robe in one corner, his back to them. Soon his snores—feigned or real—echoed off the sloping walls.

Swiftly disrobed, Cimabue and Tanselle began kissing and petting each other, and Pertinax and Chellapilla soon followed suit. By the time the foursome had begun exchanging cuds, their unashamed mating, fueled by long separation, was stoked to proceed well into the night.

The reintegrational storm blew itself out shortly after midnight, with what results among the mentalities of the air the wardens would discover only over the course of many communications. Perhaps useful new insights into the cosmos and Earth's place therein had been born this night.

In the morning the shepherds broke down their camp,

breakfasted and embarked on the final leg of their journey to "Chicago." Pertinax rode his hopper in high spirits, pacing Chellapilla's Peavine.

Not too long after their midday meal (Tanselle had bulked out their simple repast with some particularly tasty mushrooms she had carried from home), they came within sight of the expansive lake, almost oceanic in its extent, that provided the human settlement with water for both drinking and washing, as well as various dietary staples. Reckoning themselves a few dozen kilometers south of the humans, the five headed north, encountering large peaceful herds of elk and antelopes along the way.

They smelled "Chicago" before they saw it.

"They're not burning petroleum, are they?" asked Cimabue.

"No," said Sylvanus. "They have no access to any of the few remaining played-out deposits of that substance. It's all animal and vegetable oils, with a little coal from near-surface veins."

"It sure does stink," said Tanselle, wrinkling her nose.

"They still refuse our offer of limited universal proseity devices?" Pertinax inquired.

Sylvanus shook his head ruefully. "Indeed. They are stubborn, suspicious and prideful, and disdain the devices of the Upflowered as something near-demonic. They claim that such cornucopia would render their species idle and degenerate, and destroy their character. When the Upflowered stripped them of their twenty-second-century technology, the left-behind humans conceived a hatred of their ascended brethren. Now they are determined to reclimb the same ladder of technological development they once negotiated, but completely on their own."

Cimabue snorted. "It's just as well they don't accept our gifts. The UPD's would allow them to spread their baneful way of life even further than they already have. We can only be grateful their reproductive rates have been redacted downward."

"Come now," said Chellapilla, "surely the humans deserve as much respect and right to self-determination as any other species. Would you cage up all the blue jays in the world simply because they're noisy?"

"You don't have any humans in your bioregion, Chell. See what you think after you've met them."

The pathless land soon featured the start of a crude gravel-bedded road. The terminus the travelers encountered was a dump site. The oil-stained ground, mounded with detritus both organic and manufactured, repelled Pertinax's sensibilities. He wondered how the humans could live with such squalor, even on the fringes of their settlement.

Moving swiftly down the pebbled roadway, the wardens soon heard a clanking, chugging, ratcheting riot of sound from some ways around the next bend of the tree-shaded road. They halted and awaited the arrival of whatever vehicle was producing the clamor.

The vehicle soon rounded the curve of road, revealing itself to be a heterogeneous assemblage of wood and metal. The main portion of the carrier was a large wooden buckboard with two rows of seats forward of a flatbed. In the rear, a large boiler formed of odd-shaped scavenged metal plates threatened to burst its seams with every puff of smoke. Transmission of power to the wheels was accomplished by whirling leather belts running from boiler to wood-spoked iron-rimmed wheels.

Four men sat on the rig, two abreast. Dressed in homespun and leathers, they sported big holstered side arms. The guns were formed of ceramic barrels and chambers, and carved grips. Small gasketed pump handles protruded from the rear of each gun. Pertinax knew the weapons operated on compressed air and fired only non-explosive projectiles. Still, sometimes the darts could be poison-tipped. A rack of rifles of similar construction lay within easy reach. The driver, busy with his tiller-style steering mechanism and several levers, was plainly a simple laborer. The other three occupants seemed dignitaries of some sort. Or so at least Pertinax deduced, judging from various colorful ribbons pinned to their chests and sashes draped over their shoulders.

Surprised by the solid rank of mounted wardens, looming high over the car like a living wall across the dump road, the

Overclockers reacted with varying degrees of confusion. But soon the driver managed to bring his steam cart to a halt, and the three officials had regained a measure of diplomatic aplomb. The passenger in the front seat climbed down, and approached Pertinax and friends. Leery of the stranger, the Kodiak Kangemus unsheathed their long thick claws a few inches. The awesome display brought the man to a halt a few meters away. He spoke, looking up and shielding his eyes against the sun.

"Hail, wardens! My name is Brost, and these comrades of mine are Kemp and Sitgrave, my assistants. As the Mayor of Chicago, I welcome you to our fair city."

Pertinax studied Brost from above, seeing a poorly shaven, sallow baseline *Homo sapiens* with a shifty air about his hunched shoulders. Some kind of harsh perfume failed to mask completely a fug of fear and anxiety crossing the distance between Brost and Pertinax's sharp nostrils.

Sylvanus, as eldest, spoke for the wardens. "We accept your welcome, Mayor Brost. But I must warn you that we are not here for any simple cordial visit. We have good reason to believe that certain factions among your people are planning to tamper with the tropospheric mind. We have come to investigate, and to remove any such threats we may discern."

The Mayor smiled uneasily, while his companions fought not to exchange nervous sidelong glances among themselves.

"Tamper with those lofty, serene intelligences, who concern themselves not at all with our poor little lives? What reason could we have for such a heinous assault? No, the charge is ridiculous, even insulting. I can categorically refute it here and now. Your mission has been for naught. You might as well save yourself any further wearisome journeying by camping here for the night before heading home. We will bring you all sorts of fine provisions—"

"That cannot be. We must make our own investigations. Will you allow us access to your village?"

Mayor Brost huddled with his assistants, then faced the wardens again. "As I said, the *city* of Chicago welcomes you,

and its doors are open."

Pertinax repressed a grin at the Mayor's emphasis on "city," but he knew the other wardens had caught this token of outraged human dignity as well.

With much back-and-forward-and-back maneuvering, the driver finally succeeded in turning around the steam cart. Matching the gait of their hoppers to the slower passage of the cart, the wardens followed the delegation back to "Chicago."

Beginning with outlying cabins where half-naked children played in the summer dust of their yards along with mongrels and livestock, and continuing all the way to the "city" center, where a few larger buildings hosted such establishments as blacksmiths, saloons, public kitchens and a lone bath house, the small collection of residences and businesses that was "Chicago"—scattered along the lake's margins according to no discernible scheme—gradually assembled itself around the newcomers. Mayor Brost, evidently proud of his domain, pointed out sights of interest as they traversed the "urban" streets, down the middles of which flowed raw sewage in ditches.

"You see how organized our manufactories are," said Brost, indicating some long low windowless sheds flanked by piles of waste byproducts: wood shavings, coal clinkers, metal shavings. "And here's the entrance to our mines." Brost pointed to a shack that sheltered a pit-like opening descending into the earth at a slant.

"Oh," said Cimabue, "you're smelting and refining raw metals these days?"

Mayor Brost exhibited a sour chagrin. "Not yet. There's really no need. We feel it's most in harmony with, uh, our beloved mother earth to recycle the buried remnants of our ancestors' civilization. There's plenty of good metal and plastic down deep where the Upflowered sequestered the rubble they left after their redesign of the globe. Plenty for everyone."

"And what exactly is your population these days, Mayor?" inquired Tanselle.

"Nearly five thousand."

Tanselle shook her head reflectively, as if to say, thought Pertinax, *Would that it were even fewer.*

After some additional civic boosterism the party—considerably enlarged by various gawking hangers-on—arrived at a large, grassy town square, where goats and sheep grazed freely. Ranked across the lawn, tethered securely, were several small lighter-than-air balloons with attached gondolas of moderate size. The shiny lacquered patchwork fabric of the balloons lent them a circus air belied by the solemn unease which the Mayor and his cohorts eyed the balloons.

Immediately, Pertinax's ears pricked forward at this unexpected sight and the humans' nervous regard for the objects. "What are these for?" he asked.

Mayor Brost replied almost too swiftly. "Oh, these little toys have half a dozen uses. We send up lightweight volunteers to spy out nearby bison herds so that our hunting parties will save some time and trouble. We make surveys from the air for our road-building. And of course, the children enjoy a ride now and then. The balloons won't carry much more weight than a child."

"I'd like to examine them."

"Certainly."

Pertinax clambered down off Flossy. Standing among the humans, the top of his head just cleared their belt buckles. He was soon joined by his fellow wardens, who moved through the crowd like a band of determined furry dwarves.

The balloons featured no burners to inflate their straining shapes. Pertinax inquired as to their source of gas.

Highlighting the mechanisms, Mayor Brost recited proudly. "Each balloon hosts a colony of methanogenic bacteria and a food supply. Increasing the flow of nutrients makes more gas. Closing the petcocks shuts them down."

Pertinax stepped back warily from his close-up inspection of the balloons. "They're highly explosive then."

"I suppose. But we maintain adequate safety measures around them."

The wardens regrouped off to one side and consulted quietly

among themselves.

"Any explosion of this magnitude in the tropospheric mind would do no more damage than a conventional rain squall," said Cimabue.

"Agreed," said Chellapilla. "But what if the explosion was meant to disperse some kind of contaminant carried as cargo?"

"Such as?" asked Tanselle.

"No suitably dangerous substance occurs to me at the moment," Sylvanus said, stroking his chin whiskers.

"Nonetheless," cautioned Pertinax, "I have a feeling that here lies the danger facing the tropospheric mind. Let us continue our investigations for the missing part of the puzzle."

Pertinax returned to address the Mayor. "Our mounts need to forage, while we continue our inspection of your town. We propose to leave them here on the green. They will not bother people or livestock, but you should advise your citizens not to molest them. The Kangemu are trained to deal harshly with threats to themselves or their masters."

"There will of course be no such problems," said the Mayor.

Sylvanus advised splitting their forces into two teams for swifter coverage of the human settlement, while he himself, in deference to his age and tiredness, remained behind with their mounts to coordinate the searching. Naturally, Pertinax chose to team up with Chellapilla.

The subsequent hours found Pertinax and his lover roaming unhindered through every part of the human village. Most of the citizens appeared friendly, although some exhibited irritation or a muted hostility at the queries of the wardens. Pertinax and Chellapilla paused only a few minutes to bolt down some cold food around mid-afternoon before continuing their so-far fruitless search.

Eventually they found themselves down by some primitive docks, watching the small fishing fleet of "Chicago" tie up for the evening. The fishermen, shouldering their day's bounty in woven baskets, moved warily past the weary wardens.

"Well, I'm stumped," confessed Pertinax. "If they're hiding

something, they've concealed it well."

Chellapilla said, "Maybe we're going about this wrong. Let's ask what could harm the virgula and sublimula, instead of just expecting to recognize the agent when we see it."

"Well, really only other virgula and sublimula, which of course the humans have no way of fashioning."

"Ah, but what of rogue lobes?"

The natural precipitation cycles brought infinite numbers of virgula and sublimula down from their habitats in the clouds to ground level. When separated from the tropospheric mind in this way, the components of the mind were programmed for apoptosis. But occasionally a colony of virgula and sublimula would fail to self-destruct, instead clumping together into a rogue lobe. Isolated from the parent mind, the lobes frequently went insane before eventually succumbing to environmental stresses. Sometimes, though, a lobe could live a surprisingly long time if it found the right conditions.

"Do you think local factors in the lake here might encourage lobe formations?"

"There's one way to find out," answered Chellapilla.

It took only another half hour of prowling the lakeshore, scrambling over slippery rocks and across pebbled strands, to discover a small lobe.

Thick intelligent slime latticed with various organic elements—pondweeds, zebra mussels, a disintegrating bird carcass—lay draped across a boulder, a mucosal sac with the processing power of a non-autonomous twenty-second-century AI. The slime was liquescently displaying its mad internal thoughts just as a mail cloud did: fractured images of the natural world, blazes of equations, shards of old human culture ante-Upflowering, elaborate mathematical constructions. A steady whisper of jagged sounds, a schizophrenic monologue, accompanied the display.

Pertinax stared horrified. "Uploading this fragment of chaos to the tropospheric mind would engender destabilizing waves of disinformation across the skies. The humans don't even need

to explode their balloons. Simply letting the mind automatically read the slime would be enough."

"We can't allow this to happen."

"Let's hurry back to the others."

"You damned toothy ratdogs aren't going anywhere."

A squad of humans had come stealthily upon Pertinax and Chellapilla while their attentions were engaged by the lobe. With rifles leveled at their heads, the wardens had no recourse but to raise their hands in surrender.

Two men came to bind the wardens. The one dealing with Chellapilla twisted her arms cruelly behind her, causing her to squeal. Maddened by the sound, Pertinax broke free and hurled himself at one of the gun-bearers. But a rifle stock connected with his skull, and he knew only blackness.

When Pertinax awoke, night had fallen. He found himself with limbs bound, lying in a cage improvised from thick branches rammed deep into the soil and lashed together. He struggled to rise, and thus attracted the attentions of his fellow captives.

Similarly bound, Chellapilla squirmed across the grass to her mate. "Oh, Perty, I'm so glad you're awake! We were afraid you had a concussion."

"No, I'm fine. And you?"

"Just sore. Once you were knocked out, they didn't really hurt me further."

Sylvanus's sad voice reached Pertinax as well. "Welcome back, my lad. We're in a fine mess now, and it's all my fault for underestimating the harmful intentions of these savages."

Firelight flared up some meters away, accompanied by the roar of a human crowd. "Where are we?"

"We're on the town green," said Chellapilla. "The humans are celebrating their victory over us. They slaughtered our Kangemu and are roasting them for a feast."

"Barbarians!"

Tanselle spoke. "Cimabue and I are here as well, Pertinax, but he did not escape so easily as you. They clubbed him viciously

when he fought back. Now his breathing is erratic, and he won't respond."

"We have to do something!"

"But what?" inquired Sylvanus.

"The least we can do," said Chellapilla, "is inform the tropospheric mind of our troubles and the threat from rogue lobe infection. Maybe the mind will know what to do."

Pertinax considered this proposal. "That's a sound idea, Chell. But I suspect our pigeons have already served as appetizers." He paused as an idea struck him. "But I know a way to reach the mind. First I need to be free. You three will have to chew my ropes off."

Shielded by darkness, without any guards to note their activities and interfere (how helpless the humans must have deemed them!), his three fellows quickly chewed through Pertinax's bonds with their sturdy teeth and powerful jaws. His first action after massaging his limbs back into a semblance of strength was to take off his robe and stuff it with dirt and grass into a rough recumbent dummy that would satisfy a cursory headcount. Then, employing his own untaxed jaw muscles, he beavered his way out of the cage.

"Be careful, Perty!" whispered Chellapilla, but Pertinax did not pause to reply.

Naked, dashing low across the yard from shadow to shadow, Pertinax reached one of the tethered balloons without being detected. Nearby stood a giant ceramic pot with a poorly fitting lid. Shards of light and sound escaped from the pot, betokening the presence of a malignant rogue lobe within. Plainly, infection of the tropospheric mind was imminent. This realization hastened Pertinax's actions.

First he kicked up the feed on one balloon's colony of methanogens. That vehicle began to tug even more heartily at its tethers. Moving among the other balloons, Pertinax disabled them by snapping their nutrient feed lines. At the very least, this would delay the assault on the mind.

Pertinax leaped onboard the lone functional balloon and

cast off. He rose swiftly to the height of several meters before he was spotted. Shouts filled the night. Something whizzed by Pertinax's head, and he ducked. A barbed projectile from one of the compressed-air guns. Pertinax doubted the weapons possessed enough force to harm him or the balloon at this altitude, but he remained hunkered down for a few more minutes nonetheless.

Would the humans take revenge on their remaining captives? Pertinax couldn't spare the energy for worry. He had a mission to complete.

Within the space of fifteen minutes, Pertinax floated among the lowest clouds, the nearest gauzy interface to the tropospheric mind. Their dampness subtly enwrapped him, until he was soaked and shivering. His head seemed to attract a thicker constellation of fog....

A small auroral screen opened up in the sky not four meters from Pertinax. He could smell the scorched molecules associated with the display.

Don Corleone appeared on the screen: one or more of the resident AIs taking a form deemed familiar from Pertinax's recent past viewing records.

"You have done well to bring us this information, steward. We will now enforce our justice on the humans."

Pertinax's teeth chattered. "Puh-please try to spare my companions."

The representative of the tropospheric mind did not deign to reply, and the screen winked out in a frazzle of sparks.

The nighted sky grew darker, if such was possible. Ominous rumbles sounded from the west. Winds began to rise.

The mind was marshalling a storm. A lightning storm. And Pertinax was riding a bomb.

Pertinax frantically shut off the feeder line to the methanogens. The balloon began to descend, but all too slowly for Pertinax's peace of mind.

The first lightning strike impacted the ground far below, after seeming to sizzle right past Pertinax's nose. He knew the

bolt must have been farther off than that, but anywhere closer than the next bioregion was *too* close.

Now shafts of fire began to rain down at supernatural frequency. Turbulence rocked the gondola. Thunder deafened him. Pertinax's throat felt raw, and he realized he had been shouting for help from the balloon or the mind or anyone else who might be around to hear.

Now the cascade of lighting was nigh incessant, one deadly strike after another on the Overclockers' village. Pertinax knew he could stay no longer with the deadly balloon. But the ground was still some hundred meters away.

Pertinax jumped.

Behind him the balloon exploded.

Pertinax spread out his arms, transforming the big loose flaps of skin anchored from armpits to ankles into wings, wings derived from one of his ancestral strains, the sciuroptera.

After spiraling downward with some control, despite the gusts, Pertinax landed lightly, on an open patch of ground near a wooden sign that announced the "City Limits" of "Chicago."

He had arrived just in time for the twister.

Illuminated intermittently by the slackening lightning, the stygian funnel shape tracked onto land from across the lake and stepped into the human settlement, moving in an intelligent and programmatic fashion among the buildings.

Even at this distance, the wind threatened to pull Pertinax off his feet. He scrambled for a nearby tree and held onto its trunk for dear life.

At last, though, the destruction wrought by the tropospheric mind ended, with the twister evaporating in a coordinated manner from bottom to top.

Pertinax ran back toward the town green.

The many fires caused by the lightning had been effectively doused by the wet cyclone, but still buildings smoldered. Not one stone seemed atop another, nor plank joined to plank. The few Overclocker survivors were too dazed or busy to interfere with Pertinax.

Seared streaks marked the town green, and huge divots had been wrenched up by the twister. Windblown litter made running difficult.

But a circle of lawn around the cage holding the wardens was immaculate, having been excluded from electrical blasts and then cradled in a deliberate eye of the winds.

"Is everyone all right?"

"Perty! You did it! Yes, we're all fine. Even Cimabue is finally coming around."

Within a short time all were freed. Pertinax clutched Chellapilla to him. Sylvanus surveyed the devastation, clucking his tongue ruefully.

"Such a tragedy. Well, I expect that once we relocate the remnant population, we can wean them off our help and back up to some kind of agrarian self-sufficiency in just a few generations."

Pertinax felt now an even greater urgency to engender a heir or two with Chellapilla. The demands on the stewards of this beloved planet required new blood to sustain their mission down the years.

"Chell, have you decided about our child?"

"Absolutely, Perty. I'm ready. I've even thought of a name."

"Oh?"

"Boy or girl, it will have to be Storm!"

WAVES AND
SMART MAGMA

Salt air stung Storm's super-sensitive nose, although he was still several scores of kilometers distant from the coast. The temperate August sunlight, moderated by a myriad, myriad high-orbit pico-satellites, one of the many thoughtful legacies of the Upflowered, descended as a soothing balm on Storm's unclothed pelt. Several churning registers of flocculent clouds, stuffed full of the computational particles known as virgula and sublimula, betokened the watchful custodial omnipresence of the tropospherical mind. Peaceful and congenial was the landscape around him: a vast plain of black-leaved cinnabon trees, bisected by a wide, meandering river, the whole of which had once constituted the human city of Sacramento.

Storm reined to a halt his furred and feathered steed—the Kodiak Kangemu named Bergamot was a burly, scary-looking but utterly obedient bipedal chimera some three meters tall at its muscled shoulders, equipped with a high saddle and panniers—and paused for a moment of reflection.

The world was so big, and rich, and odd! And Storm was all alone in it!

That thought both frightened and elated him.

He felt he hardly knew himself or his goals, what depths or heights he was capable of. Whether he would live his long life totally independent of wardenly strictures, a rebel, or become an obedient part of the guardian corps of the planet. Hence this journey.

A sudden lance of light breaking through a bank of clouds brightened Storm's spirits. Despite the distinct probability that the photons had been deliberately collimated by the tropospheric mind's manipulation of water molecules as a signal to chivvy him onward.

Anything was possible, Storm realized. His destiny rested solely on the strength of his character and mind and muscles, and the luck of the Upflowered. Glory or doom, fame or ignominy, love or enmity.... His fate remained unwritten.

And so far he had not done too badly, giving him confidence for his future.

The young warden had now traveled much further from home than he ever had in his short life. All to barge in upon a perilous restoration and salvage mission whose members had known nothing of Storm's very existence until a short time ago.

A gamble, to be sure, but one he had felt compelled to make. Perhaps his one and only chance for an adventure before settling down.

The death of Storm's parents, the wardens Pertinax and Chellapilla, had left him utterly and instantly adrift. Although by all rights and traditions, Storm should have stepped directly into their role as one of the several wardens of the Great Lakes bioregion, he had balked. The conventional lives his parents had led, in obedience to the customs and innate design of their species did not appeal to Storm's nature—at least not at this moment. Perhaps his unease with his assigned lot in life was due to the unusual conditions of his conception....

Some twenty years ago, five wardens, Storm's parents among them, had undertaken an expedition to the human settlement of "Chicago," one of the few places where those degraded *Homo sap* remnants who had disdained the transcendence of the Upflowering still dwelled. During that dangerous enforcement action, which resulted in the destruction of the human village by the tropospheric mind, Storm had been conceived. Those suspenseful and tumultuous prenatal circumstances seemed to have left him predisposed to a characteristic restless thrill-

seeking.

His conception and birth among the strictly reproductively regulated wardens had been sanctioned so that Storm might grow up to be a replacement for the elderly warden Sylvanus, who, at age one-hundred-and-twenty-eight, had already begun to ponder retirement.

And so Storm was raised in the cozy little prairie home— roofed with pangolin tiles, pots of greedy, squawking parrot tulips on the windowsill—shared by Pertinax and Chellapilla. His first two decades of life had consisted of education and play and exploration in equal measures. His responsibilities had been minimal.

Which explained his absence from the routine surveying expedition where his parents had met their deaths.

A malfunctioning warden-scent broadcaster had failed to protect their encampment from a migratory herd of galloping aurochs, and Storm's parents had perished swiftly at midnight in each other's arms in their tent.

Sylvanus, all gray around his muzzle and ear tufts, his once-sinewy limbs arthritic as he closed in on his second century, condoled with Storm.

"There, there, my poor boy, cry all you want. I know I've drained my eyes already on the trip from home to see you. Your parents were smart and capable and loving wardens, and lived full lives, even if they missed reaching a dotage such as mine. You can be proud of them. They always honored and fulfilled the burdens bestowed on our kind by the Upflowered."

At the mention of the posthumans who had spliced and redacted Storm's species out of a hundred baseline genomes, Storm felt his emotions flip-flopping from sadness to anger.

"Don't mention the Upflowered to me! If not for them, my mother and father would still be alive!"

Sylvanus shook his wise old head. "If not for the Upflowered, none of our kind would exist at all, my son."

"Rubbish! If they wanted to create us, they should have done so without conditions."

"Are you not, then, going to step into my paw prints, so that I might lay down my own charge? You're fully trained now...."

Storm felt a burst of regret that he had to disappoint his beloved old "uncle." But the emotion was not strong enough to countervail his stubborn independence. He laid a paw-hand on Sylvanus's bony shoulder.

"I can't, uncle, I just can't. Not now, anyhow. And in fact, I'm leaving this bioregion entirely. I have to see more of the world, to learn my place in it."

Sylvanus recognized the futility of arguing with the headstrong youth. "So be it. Travel with my blessing, then, and try to return if you can before my passing, for a final farewell. I'll get Cimabue and Tanselle to breed my successor, while I hang in there for a while yet."

And so Storm had set out westward, across the vast continent, braving rain and heat, loneliness and fear, with no goal in mind other than to see what he could see. He and his trusty marsupial avian-ursine mount, Bergamot, foraged off the land, supplementing their herbivore diet with various nutriceuticals conjured up out of Storm's Universal Proseity Device.

Crossing the Rockies, he had encountered the tropospheric mind for the first time since his abdication. He had been deliberately avoiding this massive atmospheric intelligence due to its tendency to impose orders on all wardens. Storm feared chastisement for his rebellion. But traveling this high above sea level, there was no escaping the lower tendrils of the globally distributed artificial intelligence.

A chilly caplet of cloud stuff, rich in virgula/sublimula codec, had formed about his head, polling his thoughts by transcranial induction. Storm squirmed under the painless interrogation, irritated yet helpless to do anything.

A palm-sized high-res wetscreen formed in the air, and on it appeared the current chosen avatar of the tropospheric mind: a kindly sorcerer from some old human epic. (The tropospherical mind contained all the accumulated data of the Earth's digitized culture at the time of the Upflowering, a trove which the

wardens frequently ransacked for their own amusement and edification.)

The sorcerer spoke. "You follow a lonely path, Storm. And a less-than-optimal one, so far as your own development is concerned."

Anticipating harsher rebuke, Storm was taken aback. "Perhaps. But it's my choice."

"Yet you might both extend your own growth and aid me and the world at the same time."

"How is that?"

"By joining a cohort of your fellows now assembling. As you work with them and bind together as a team, you might come to better appreciate your innate talents and how they could best benefit the planet under my direction."

"Your direction! That's always been my quarrel. We're just pawns to you! It was under your direction that my parents died."

Had the sorcerer denied this accusation, Storm would have definitely walked out on the mission. But the sorcerer had the good grace to look apologetic, sad and chagrined, although he did not actually accept responsibility for the deaths.

Mollified, Storm felt he could at least inquire politely about the mission. "What are these other wardens doing?"

"They are building a ship, and will embark from San Francisco Bay for the island of Hawaii, where they will confront my insane sister, Mauna Loa. She has already killed all the resident wardens there, as she seeks to establish her own dominion. No communications or diplomacy I have had with her have changed her plans. You think me a tyrant, but she wants utter control of all life around her."

Storm said, "Maybe she'll listen to reason from us."

"I sincerely doubt it. But you should feel free to try. In any case, I believe the odyssey will offer you the challenges you seek. Even a magnitude more."

Storm's curiosity was greatly piqued. Curse the weather mind! It was impossible to outwit or out-argue something that used a significant portion of the atmosphere as its computational

reservoir. This was precisely why Storm had avoided speaking to the construct.

"If I agree to go on this journey with them, it does not mean I will fall right back into your tidy little schemes for me afterwards."

The sorcerer grinned. "Of course not."

Storm instantly regretted giving his tacit consent. But the lure of the dangerous mission was too strong to resist.

"Allow me," said the tropospheric mind, "to download your optimal route into your UPD."

Utility fog shrouded Storm's panniers, pumping information into his proseity unit as he gee'd up and rode on.

* * * * * * *

Now, so close to his West Coast destination, Storm felt compelled to surrender his nostalgic ruminations for action. He kicked Bergamot into motion, and the biped surged in its odd loping fashion across the fruited plains that had once been covered by human urban blight.

As he passed beneath the cinnabon trees, Storm snatched a few dozen sweet sticky rolls from the branches overhead, filling a pannier with the welcome treats. He tossed several, one at a time, into the air ahead of him, where Bergamot snapped them up greedily with lightning reflexes. Gorging himself, eventually sated, Storm licked his paw-hands and muzzle clean.

Following the directions in his UPD, paralleling the Sacramento River for most of the journey, past the influx of its many tributaries, through its delta, Storm came in good time to the shores of San Pablo Bay. He continued west and south along that body of water, eventually reaching his ordained rendezvous point: the northern terminus of the roadless Golden Gate Bridge, anomalous in the manicured wilderness.

One of the select human artifacts preserved after the Upflowering for its utility and beauty, the span glistened with the essentially dumb self-repair virgula and sublimula that had

maintained it against decay for centuries.

Storm admired the sight for a short time, then homed in on the scent of his fellow wardens. Following a steep path, he reached a broad stony beach. There he found ten wardens finishing the construction of their ship, and ten Kodiak Kangemus picking idly at drifts of seaweed and bivalves.

Six of the wardens worked around a composite UPD device. Their individual reconfigurable units had been slaved together in order to produce larger-than-normal output pieces. Three wardens fed biomass into the conjoined hopper, while three others handled the output, ferrying it to the workers on the ship. Those other four wardens, consulting printed plans, snapped the superwood pieces into place on the nearly completed vessel.

At first no one noticed Storm. But then he was spotted by a female, noteworthy for her unique piebald coloration.

"Ho! It's the supercargo!"

Storm bristled at the slight, but said nothing. He dropped down off Bergamot, shooing the beast towards its companions.

The ten wardens hastened to group themselves around Storm, in a not-unfriendly manner.

"You're Storm," said the pretty pinto female. Her voice was sweet and chirpy, her demeanor mischievous. "I'm Jizogirl. The weather mind told us you'd be here today. Just in time, too! Let me introduce everyone."

During the hellos, Storm uneasily sized up his new companions—all of whom were at least a few years older than he, and in some instances decades.

Pankey, Arp, Rotifero, Wrinkles and Bunter were males. Tallest of the ten, Pankey's bold mien bespoke a natural leadership. Arp managed to look bored and inquisitive simultaneously. Elegant Rotifero paid little attention to Storm, instead preferring to present his best profile to the ladies. Wrinkles plainly derived his name from his exaggerated patagium: the folds of flesh beneath a warden's arms that allowed brief aerial gliding. Bunter, plump as a pumpkin, was sniffing suspiciously in the direction of Storm's panniers.

Beyond the charming Jizogirl: Catmaul exhibited an athlete's lithe strength; Faizai echoed Rotifero's sexual preening; Shamrock was plainly itching to get back to work, as if looking to impress Pankey and secure the number-two slot; and Gumball shyly pondered her own paw-feet rather than make eye-contact with Storm.

"Pleased to meet you all," said Storm. "I'm anxious to learn more about our mission. I hope I'll be an asset."

Pankey spoke. "You are rather the hundredth-and-one leg on a centipede, you know. We had a complete roster without you butting in."

"Pankey! For shame!" Jizogirl made up for her earlier quip about "supercargo" in Storm's eyes with this remonstrance, and he chose to appear unaffected by Pankey's gibe.

"I know I can be of some use. Just tell me what to do."

"Well, we want to sail at dawn, and we still have several hours of work to accomplish before dark. So if you could possibly pitch in—"

"Of course. Just point me toward a task."

"Why don't you collect biomass for now? It's the simplest chore."

Storm bit his tongue against a defense of his own abilities, and merely said, "Sure. Should I slave my UPD to the others?"

Pankey frowned. "I hadn't thought of that. Of course."

Storm did so. Then, removing a sharp, strong nanocellu-lose machete from his panniers (and also some cinnabons for everyone, much welcomed), he headed toward a stand of spartina. Soon, with energetic effort, he had accumulated a surplus of the tall grass, and so was able to take a break. He strolled onboard the ship to learn more about it. He saw that the super-wood components were being grafted into place with various epoxies from the UPD.

Rotifero spied Storm and gestured grandly, eager to abandon his own work and act as tour guide. "The *Slippery Squid*! A sharp ship, isn't she? We should make it to the Sandwich Islands in just five days."

"So fast?"

Rotifero motioned for Storm to look over the side at the ship's unique construction. "The humans called this model the hydroptére. Multi-hulled, very fast. But here's the real secret."

Rotifero walked to the fore of the ship and kicked at a bundle of neatly sorted fabric and lines. "She's a kiteship. Once we get this scoop aloft, the weather mind provides an unceasing wind. We should average fifty knots. Old Tropo even keeps us on the proper heading. No navigation necessary. Which is fine by me, as I don't know a sextant from an astrolabe."

Storm nodded sagely, although the instruments named were unfamiliar to him. "And what do we do when we arrive in Hawaii?"

"Ah, I'd best let Pankey explain all that tonight. He's our leader, you know, and he rather resents anyone stepping on his lines. Say, what do you think of Fazai? Aren't her ears the perkiest and hairiest you've ever seen? You know what they say: 'Ears with tufts, can't get enough!'"

Storm felt hot blood flash beneath his furry face. Wardens lived solitary lives, each responsible for vast bioregions, meeting only infrequently. At such times, mating was lustily indulged in, with gene-regulated, reversible contraceptive locks firmly in place. In his two decades of family-centric life, Storm had not yet managed to meet a free female and mate. In fact, the unprecedented presence of so many of his kind in such proximity rather unnerved him.

"I—I wouldn't know."

Rotifero jabbed an elbow into Storm's ribs. "I realize the ten of us're paired up evenly already, but don't worry. One of the does will probably take pity on you. If any of them have a spare minute!"

Storm's embarrassment flicked to hurt pride in an instant. "Thanks, I'm sure. But I'm used to Great Lakes does. They're much nicer in every way."

Pankey put a stop to any further amatory talk with a shouted, "Hey, you two, back to work!"

Storm spent the rest of the afternoon chopping and hauling spartina, and trying not to think of Faizai's ears.

Twilight brought successful completion of all their tasks. Sailing at dawn was assured, Pankey confirmed. A driftwood fire was kindled, tasty food was fabbed from spartina fed into the now separated UPD's (the same method by which the voyagers would sustain themselves at sea; the proseity units could desalinate seawater as well), and everyone settled down around the flames on UPD-fabbed cushions laid over mattresses of dried seaweed. Conversation was casual, and Storm mainly listened. He soon deduced that the ten wardens all hailed from up and down the Pacific Coast, and knew each other to varying degrees.

When all had finished eating, Pankey stood, and the others, including Storm, snapped to attention.

"I will endeavor to bring our newest member up to speed," said the tall warden, grooming his muzzle somewhat self-consciously. "But this is a good time for anyone else to ask questions as well, if you're unsure of anything.

"We ten—excuse me, we eleven—have been constituted an ERT—an Emergency Response Team—by the tropospheric mind—Old Tropo, if he'll permit the familiarity—and given the assignment of straightening out the mess in Hawaii. All the wardens in that chain of islands have perished, assassinated by Mauna Loa, sister to Tropo, who wishes to enslave all the mobile entities of that biosphere.

"We are all familiar, I believe, with the phenomenon of 'rogue lobes,' isolated colonies of virgula and sublimula which descend to the ground as star jelly. Usually, their lifetimes are extremely short and erratic, given their separation from the main currents of the weather mind. But in the case of Mauna Loa, we have an intelligent and self-sustaining organism, unfortunately quite deranged and exhibiting no signs of possessing any ethical constraints.

"As near as Tropo can determine, a rogue lobe hybridized with two types of extremophile microbe: an endolithic species

and a hyperthermophilic species. The result is smart magma, centered in the active Mauna Loa volcano, with vast subterranean extensions throughout Hawaii's volcanic system and beyond. Mauna Loa's active tubes stretch far out to sea, in fact, and she appears to be trying to extend them to reach other land masses in the Pacific Ring of Fire, to colonize them as well. Meanwhile, aboveground, the magma's agents are local animal species controlled by transcranial inductive caps that consist of a kernel of smart magma insulated by a shell of inert, heat-absorptive material. It is these animal agents which slew our fellows."

Wrinkles stuck up a paw-hand, flaring his broad patagium, and asked a question that had been on Storm's mind.

"How did Mauna Loa ever capture animal agents in the first place?"

"Good question," Pankey said. "Tropo has reconstructed the evolution of the non-fatal cold magma caps along these lines. Mauna Loa would throw out lariats of moderately hot smart magma—its necessarily high temperature downgraded by a radioactive component that served to keep the cooler substance plastic—at any animal that passed near an active flow. In ninety-nine point nine percent of such attacks, the victim would die. But once a single victim, however damaged, survived with a magma patch on its epidermis, Mauna Loa had an agent. And once it recruited an agent with manipulative abilities—such as one of the many extant island simians—it had the ability to place the refined cold magma caps on a great numbers of recruits."

"So we can expect some hassle from these agents," said Jizogirl. Storm risked a glance toward her, admiring her understated bravado, and trying in the firelight to assess once again the degree of tuftedness of her ears.

"Yes. They will run interference to stop us from killing Mauna Loa."

This new talk of killing troubled Storm a bit. "Isn't there any way we might convince Mauna Loa to modify her bad behavior, to fall in line with Tropo's leadership?"

Pankey emitted a derisive blurt. "Reason with a killer volcano! Good luck! I'd like to see you try!"

"Just watch me then!"

Pankey turned disdainfully away from Storm and directed his speech to the rest. "The saner members of the ERT will be employing logic bombs against Mauna Loa. The plan for the bomb has been uploaded to everyone's UPD—yes, Storm, yours as well. This goes a long way toward insuring that at least one of us should reach the volcano and be able to drop the bomb in. The bomb's antisense instructions will replicate and propagate rapidly through the silicaceous medium, and shut down the magma mind."

"Do we have to deliver the bomb right to Mauna Loa herself?"

"No. We can attack Kilauea instead. It's a much smaller, lower, accessible target, and closer to the coast than Mauna Loa herself."

"Why can't we just dump the bomb into the first trickle of lava we see?"

Pankey began to manifest some irritation with Storm's persistent questions, even though he had invited them. "Because Mauna Loa has the ability to pinch off any small tendril of its body, and isolate the antisense wave. But Kilauea is too big and interconnected for that tactic to succeed."

Pankey paused, glaring a bit at Storm as if daring him to pose more stumpers. But Storm was satisfied that he had a grasp of their task. Pankey resumed a greater gravitas before next he spoke.

"And so we should all recognize, I believe, our true position. We stand now on the verge of a dangerous voyage, at the end of which we will face enemies who wish to stop us from crushing a brutal killer and tyrant. May Old Tropo guide our paws."

Concluding the lecture, this solemn invocation engendered a long and ponderous silence amongst the wardens, as they considered their chances for success, and the high stakes at play. Storm still debated internally whether Mauna Loa was really the unreasoning menace portrayed, or whether she could not be

cajoled and reasoned with.

But their grim and thoughtful mood was ultimately leavened by a loud comment from Rotifero.

"Well, if I'm heading to my death, I intend to get in all the mating I can over the next five days! And I advise all my boon comrades to do the same!"

No sooner had this carnal activity been urged than the wardens began pairing off. Storm was disheartened to see Jizogirl beat out Shamrock in a bid for Pankey's attentions. Disgruntled but accepting, Shamrock settled for Arp instead, while Wrinkles and shy Gumball, Bunter and agile Catmaul hooked up.

Surprisingly, while most of the warden couples were already down on their mats, swiftly lost in petting and other foreplay, Rotifero and Faizai had not yet begun. Instead, the two, arms about each others middles, approached Storm.

"Would you care to make it a threesome, Storm? I realize you hardly know us, and it's not much done. But under the circumstances, I thought...."

Storm hungrily drank in Faizai's allure, guttering flames glinting hotly in her liquid eyes. He gulped once, twice, then managed to speak.

"*Urk*— That is, not tonight, thank you. I'm very tired from my travels."

"Maybe some other time," Faizai slurred lusciously.

Storm made no reply, but instead dragged his mat away to lie with the Kodiak Kangemus, their musk and somnolent growls failing to fully mask the squeals and scents from his copulating comrades.

But at last he fell into a light, uneasy sleep.

* * * * * * *

"On three! One, two—three!"

The combined muscle power of all six males succeeded in tossing the bundle of the precisely packed kite a full five meters into the air, as the *Slippery Squid* floated just offshore. The

kite began to unfurl. A perfectly timed wind sent by the tropo-spheric mind caught the MEMS fabric, belling it out to its full extent and lofting it higher, higher— The six tough composite lines fastened to the prow of the *Squid* tautened. The ship began to cut the pristine waters of San Francisco Bay, heading out to open sea.

A collective shout of triumph went up. The wardens hugged and slapped one another on the back. Jizogirl waved to the Kodiak Kangemus on the shore where they milled, reluctant to loose sight of their departing masters. Eventually, they would acknowledge the separation and find their way home.

"Goodbye, Slasher! See you soon!"

Arp said dourly, "You hope."

"Hey now, no defeatist talk," Pankey admonished.

Shamrock came up to the leader and said, "Shouldn't we erect the canopy now? Pretty soon it'll get hot, and we'll appre-ciate the shelter."

"Good idea. Wrinkles, Bunter, Catmaul, Faizai—get to it!"

Poles and a gaily striped awning soon shielded a large portion of the blonde superwood deck from the skies, and a few of the wardens took advantage of the shade to relax. Bunter was drawing a snack from his UPD. No one had gotten much sleep last night. But Storm stayed where he could see and admire the kite, a burnt-orange scoop decorated with the image of a sword-wielding paw and arm.

Jizogirl came up beside Storm. He nervously tightened his grip on the rail, then forced himself to relax. He looked straight at her, and admired the way the wind ruffled her patchwork fur.

"Do you like the picture on our kite, Storm? I designed it myself. No one else cared, but I thought we should have an emblem. I derived it from an old human saga. Lots of daring swordplay! So unlike our humdrum daily routines. The sweep of the action appealed to me. The humans were mad, of course, but so vibrant! I watched the show over and over. Once I played the video on a cloudscreen big as the horizon! Old Tropo indulged me, I guess. Shameful waste of computational power, but who

cares! It was magnificent!"

Storm asked thoughtfully, "Are you okay with this mission? To kill a sentient being, even one accidentally born and malfunctioning?"

Jizogirl grew sober. "You didn't see the footage of the Hawaiian wardens being slaughtered, Storm. Horrible, just horrible. I don't think we have any choice...."

Jizogirl's sincere repugnance and sorrow was a strong argument in favor of the assassination of Mauna Loa, but Storm still felt a shard of uncertainty. He wished he could somehow speak to the rogue magma mind first.

Her natural sprightliness reasserting itself, Jizogirl resumed her light chatter. Grateful that the doe seemed content to conduct a monologue, Storm just smiled and nodded at appropriate places. He found her anecdotes charming. She moved from talk of her viewing habits into a detailed autobiography. She was thirty-two years old. Her assigned marches centered around old human Vancouver. Her father had died when a rotten Sequoia limb had fallen and crushed him, but her mother was still alive....

By the time the *Squid* was out of sight of land, Storm felt he knew Jizogirl as well as he knew old Sylvanus. But Sylvanus had never caused Storm's stomach to flutter, or his heart to thump so loudly.

In return for her story, Storm told his own—haltingly at first, then with a swelling confidence and excitement. Jizogirl listened appreciatively, her ears (distinctly less tufted than Faizai's) making continual microadjustments of attitude to filter out the *thwack* of waves, cries of gulls and cryptovolans, playful loud chatter of their fellow wardens. His story finally caught up with realtime, and Storm stopped, faintly chagrined. He had never talked about himself—about anything!—for such a stretch before. What would she think of such boasting?

Jizogirl smiled broadly, revealing big white shovel-like teeth. "Why, I never could have made such a leap out of my rut when I was your age, Storm! You're so brave and daring. Imagine,

traveling across half the continent on your own!'"

Storm felt his head seemingly inflate, his vision fragment into sparkles. But Jizogirl's next words deflated his elation.

"If I had a little brother, I'd want him to be just like you!"

"Hey, Jizogirl, come look at this funny fish!" The voice belonged to Pankey, but a crumpled Storm could not even feel any twinge of jealousy when Jizogirl begged off and trotted over to see the latest specimen the wardens had caught for their continual cataloguing purposes. He remained at the rail, trying to estimate how long he could stay afloat alone, were he to jump, and why he would bother to prolong his miserable life.

That first day a-sea passed swiftly and easily. With no real duties (a rare condition for any warden), under the benevolent aegis of the weather mind, knowing their heading was correct and no doldrums or foul storms would ever bedevil them, the Emergency Response Team merely romped and rested, joked and petted, carefree as kits. All except Storm, who nursed his romantic disappointment alone.

As twilight swooped in from the east, the sea around the *Squid* came alive with luminescent dinoflagellates, pulsing with electric blue radiance. Storm watched the display for a while before an idea struck him.

The hasty construction of their ship had precluded any infrastructure, such as lights. Storm would provide some.

From his UPD he produced a dozen hollow, transparent spheres of biopolymer, each with a screw-on cap. He made a length of netting. Then he dipped each uncapped netted globe into the plankton flock, filling it to the brim. By the time he had dunked them all, darkness had thickened. But Storm's bioluminescent globes made spectral yet somehow comforting blue hollows in the night.

All his comrades thronged around Storm and his creations. "Brilliant!" "Just what we need!" "Let's get them hung up!"

More netting secured the globes beneath the canopy, and an exotic yet homey ambiance resulted. Arp got busy with his own UPD and produced the parts of a ukulele, which he quickly

snapped together. He strummed a sprightly tune, and Catmaul commenced a sensuous dance, to much clapping and hooting. Bunter concocted some kind of cocktail, which added considerably to the levity.

Storm watched with a blooming jubilation that received its greatest boost in the next moment. From the shadows, Jizogirl appeared to deliver unto Storm a quick hug and a kiss, before rejoining Pankey.

* * * * * * *

The second day of their voyage, the wardens were less sanguine. Hangovers reigned, and the prospect of entertaining themselves for another day seemed less like fun than a duty. Also, the further they drew from home, the larger loomed the grim struggle that awaited them.

Storm affected the most optimism and panache. His triumph last night—the invention of the light globes, the kiss—continued to sustain him. Standing at the bow, he tried to urge the *Slippery Squid* forward faster. He felt the urgent need to meet his destiny, to prove himself, to discover whether the action he had always imagined he craved truly suited him.

Studying the kite that pulled them onward, Storm had a sudden inspiration.

Pankey was scrolling through the headache-tablet templates on his UPD when Storm interrupted him.

"How are we going to fight?"

Pankey looked at Storm as if the youngster had spoken in an extinct human tongue. "Fight? You mean the animal agents Mauna Loa will throw at us? We can't possibly fight them. I counted on stealth. A midnight landing—"

"And if the enemy doesn't cooperate with your plans?"

Pankey waved Storm off. "I've considered everything. Go away now."

Storm retrieved his own UPD and called up the plans for his machete. He tinkered with them, then hit PRINT.

The scimitar-like sword necessarily emerged from the spatially restricted output port in three pre-epoxied pieces that locked inextricably together. The nanocellulose composite was stronger than steel and carried an exceedingly sharp edge.

Out on the open deck, Storm began energetically to practice thrusts, feints and parries alone. Soon he had attracted an audience. He added enthusiastic grunts and shouts to his routine.

Rotifero said, "I actually believe that such vigorous exercise might very well drive these demons out of one's head. Do you have another one of those weapons, Storm?"

Without stopping, Storm said, through huffs and puffs, "Just...hit...'print'...on...my...UPD...."

Soon all eleven wardens, even a grudging Pankey, were sparring vigorously. "Beware my unstoppable blade!" "Take that, foul fruit bat!" "I'll run you through!"

That night was spent mostly attending to various minor cuts and bruises.

Sword practice continued the next day, somewhat less faddishly, until just before noon came a cry of "Land ho!" from Catmaul.

Storm saw a small, heavily treed island at some distance off the port. "Is that Hawaii already?"

Pankey cupped the back of his own neck with one paw and massaged, as if to evoke insight. "Impossible...."

Bunter said, "Look how lush the vegetation is! We might find a species of nice fruit not templated in our UPD's, if we land."

The normally reticent Gumball now laughed and said, "I don't think we want to land on *that* 'island.'"

"Why?" said Pankey.

"I'm surprised none of you have heard of the Terrapin Islands before. Down in Baja, we see them pass by all the time. Just watch."

As the *Squid* came abreast of the island at some remove, a patch of the ocean between island and ship began to bulge, water pouring off a rising humped form several times bigger

than the *Squid*.

The gimlet-eyed scaled head of the gargantuan *Chelonioidea* regarded the vessel with cool reptilian disinterest. Sea grass draped from its jaws. Opening wide its horny mouth, working its tongue, the terrapin inhaled the masses of vegetation like a noodle.

Storm was secretly pleased to find his own nerves holding steady at the sight of the monster. The others reacted variously. Faizai shrieked, Arp clucked his tongue, Bunter gulped. Shamrock urged impossibly, "Get some more speed on here!" Gumball laughed.

"They're harmless! Don't worry!"

True to Gumball's reassurance, the *Squid* slipped past the mammoth grazing landscaped sea turtle without interference, and soon Terrapin Island lay below the horizon.

"And some claim the Upflowered had no sense of humor," Rotifero observed.

That night, long after his companions had passed satedly into deep sleep, Storm could be found awake at the rail, contemplating their luminescent wake.

He liked these people, bucks and does equally. Even Pankey's stern bossiness was fueled by pure and admirable motives. He enjoyed working with them, feeling part of a team. But did that mean he was ready completely to step into Old Tropo's harness? And what of their vengeful mission? Justified, or reprehensible?

The slick shadowy head of some marine creature broke the water then, and Storm jumped back. A dolphin! But capping its skull was a crust of magma! Here was one of Mauna Loa's captives.

The dolphin's precisely modulated squeaks were completely intelligible. "Stop! Don't run away! I just want to talk!"

"Mauna Loa...?"

"Yes. I know who you are, and why you're coming. But you need not fear me. I only want to own a few islands, where I can practice my art. I want to mold life, just as the Upflowered did. Introduce novelty to the world. My tools are crude, though.

Radiation mainly. You could help me gain access to better ones. Join me! Frustrate this mission! Turn it aside somehow."

"I—I don't know. I can't betray my friends. I have to think."

"Take your time then. I won't interfere. I'm harmless, really."

And with that promise, the dolphin was gone, leaving Storm to a troubled sleep.

Days four and five inched by tediously, as the wardens found all attractions equally stale, the monotony of the marine landscape infusing them with a sense of eternal stasis. Unspoken thoughts of the challenge awaiting them weighed them down. Storm tried to conceive of ways to convince his friends of the wrongness of their assault, but failed to come up with any dominant argument.

After their evening meal of the fifth day, Pankey gathered them together and said, "We should sight our destination some time tomorrow. It occurs to me that we should arm ourselves in advance with our logic bombs. Everyone make three apiece, and some sort of bandolier that can also hold your UPD."

Having complied, the wardens tested the fit of their bandoliers that cradled, across their furry muscled chests, the biopolymer eggs stuffed with antisense silicrobes, deadly only to the smart magma mind of Mauna Loa. Storm thought the UPD strapped to his back was a bulky and awkward feature, but refrained from questioning Pankey's orders.

Pankey went around testing and tightening buckles before registering approval.

"Fine. Well done. Now, as to our chosen delivery method. We'll halt offshore by day and study our terrain maps one final time. We'll land under cover of darkness and split up, heading to Kilauea on pawfoot by a variety of routes. At any major vent near the summit caldera, feel free to bomb the living shit out of this volcano bitch!"

Pankey's curse-filled martial bravado rang false and antithetical to Storm, and he noted that the rough talk failed to inspire any signs of gung-ho enthusiasm in the rest.

Storm asked, "Can we expect any support from the weather

mind? Maybe some storm coverage to shock the defenders?"

"I considered asking for that. But any bad weather will impede us just as much as it hurts Mauna Loa's slaves. No, stealth is our best bet."

"What about our swords?"

"Listen, Storm, all that swordplay onboard was good exercise and fun. It took our mind off our problems. But if you need to use those toothpicks on land, it'll be too late for you already. You'd best leave your sword behind. It's just extra weight that'll slow you down."

"I'm taking mine."

Pankey shrugged. "Junior knows best."

Storm noticed that Jizogirl appeared about to second Storm's objection to venturing forth unarmed. But then the doe relented, and said nothing.

Storm slept only fitfully, so angry was he at Pankey's rude dismissal of him. So when dawn was barely a rumor, Storm was already up, alone of the wardens, and defecating over the edge of the vessel.

Looking sleepily into the dark foaming waters that had swallowed his scat, Storm hoped for a return of the dolphin diplomat, for more talk that might help him decide whose side he was really on.

But instead he saw a sleek gray hand and arm emerge to grip a ridge halfway up the hull.

He convulsively tumbled off his lavatory perch to the deck, then scrambled to his feet. A pair of hands now gripped the railing, then another pair, and another—

These were no innocent emissaries. Mauna Loa's promise not to interfere had been a lie. She had just been stalling, till she could outfit these attackers. Suddenly, Storm felt immense guilt at having kept the earlier visit a secret. The wardens could have been prepared for invasion by this route—

"Foes! Foes! Help! Attack!"

A wet torpedo face that seemed all teeth materialized between the first pair of hands. Gills flapped shut, and nostrils

flared opened.

Storm dove for his sword. The other wardens were stirring confusedly. Storm kicked them, slapped them with the flat of his blade.

"Swords! Swords! Get your swords!"

Turning back toward the rail, Storm faced the intruders fully.

The handsharks fused anthropoid and squaline designs into a bipedal monster all gray rugose hide and muscles. Neckless, their shark countenances thrust forward aggressively. Each wore the pebbled slave cap of the magma mind, clamped tight. A fishy carrion reek sublimed off them.

Involuntarily bellowing his anger and fear, Storm rushed forward, sword at the ready.

He got a deep resonant lick in on the ribs of a handshark at the same time he was batted powerfully across the chest. He went down and skidded on his butt across the wet deck. Leaping back to his feet, he confronted another monster—the same one?— and slashed out, blade landing with a squelch across its eyes.

Screams, battle-cries, the thunk of blade into flesh. Storm could get no sense of the whole battle's tide, but only flail about in his little sphere of chaos.

Somehow he slaughtered without being slaughtered himself, until the battle was over.

Weeping, wiping blood from his face, his sword dripping gore, Storm reunited with his comrades.

Those who still lived.

That headless corpse was Bunter. The one with torn throat was Gumball. Half of Arp's torso was gone in a single bite. Faizai lay in several pieces. They never found Shamrock; perhaps a dying handshark had dragged her overboard.

Almost half their team dead, before they even sighted their goal.

There could be no question now of where Storm must place his allegiance. All his doubt and conflicts had evaporated with the lives of his friends. Guilt plagued him as well. He knew the only way to make up for such a transgression was to carry forth

the assault on Mauna Loa with all his wit and bravery. Although beyond the assassination attempt, his future still floated mistily.

Only three handshark corpses littered the deck. Just one more attacker, and all the wardens would probably this moment be dead.

Storm pulled a bloody, sobbing Jizogirl to him, clutched her tightly. He tried to imagine why he had ever sought adventure, and how he could instantly transport himself and Jizogirl and the others safely home. But hard as he pondered, throughout the sad task of creating winding sheets from the UPD, bundling up the bodies of their friends, and consigning them to the sea with a few appeals to the Upflowered, Storm could find no easy solutions.

* * * * * * *

Throughout the battle, and afterwards, their big-bellied kite had continued to pull the *Squid* onward, impelled by the insistent weather mind. The tropospheric intelligence seemed intent on throwing its agents against its rival without delay.

And so by the time the surviving wardens had dumped the handshark corpses overboard, washed their clotted fur, disinfected their wounds and applied antibiotics and synthskin bandages, cleansed their swords, and sluiced the offal from the deck with seawater, the jade-green island of Hawaii had come dominantly into view, swelling in size minute by minute as their craft surged on.

Storm confronted Pankey. "You're not still thinking of hanging offshore till midnight, are you? Mauna Loa obviously knows we're here. We can't face another assault from more sharks."

Pankey appeared unsure and confused. "That plan can still work. We'll just need to put in to shore further away from Kilauea. Let's get the coastal maps...."

Storm's anger and anxiety boiled over. "Bugger that! The longer we have to travel overland, the more vulnerable we are!"

His expression ineffably sad, Faizai-bereft Rotifero said calmly, "I agree with our young comrade, Pankey. We need a different plan."

"All right, all right! But what!"

Jizogirl said, "Let's get in a little closer to shore anyhow. Maybe something we see will give us an idea."

Pankey said, "That makes sense."

Catmaul asked, "How will we get the weather mind to stop blowing us along?"

Normally, communication with the atmospheric entity was accomplished with programmed messenger birds that could fly high enough to have their brain states interpreted on the wing. But the wardens, overconfident about the parameters of their mission, had set out without any such intermediaries.

Pankey's voice conveyed less than total confidence. "Old Tropo is watching us. Surely he'll bring us to a halt safely."

Larger and larger Hawaii bulked. Details along the gentle sloping shore became more and more resolvable.

"Is that some kind of wall?"

"I—I'm not sure..."

As predicted and hoped, when the *Squid* had reached a point several hundred meters offshore, it came to a gradual stop. The weather mind had pinned the kite in a barometrically dead cell between wind tweezers that kept the parasail stationary but aloft.

With their extremely sharp eyes, the wardens stared landward, unbelieving.

Ranked along the beach was a living picket of animal slaves of the volcano queen.

The main mass of the defense consisted of anole lizards. But not kawaii baseline creatures to be held with amusement in a paw. No, these anoles, unfamiliar to the mainlanders, were evidently Upflowered creations, large as elephants. And atop each anole sat a simian carrying a crudely sharpened treebranch spear. Interspersed among the legs of the anoles were a host of lesser but still formidable toothed and clawed beasts. Blotches of

stony gray atop the anoles were certainly slave caps, no doubt to be found on their companions as well. The huge gaudy dewlaps of the lizards flared and shrunk, flared and shrunk ominously, a prelude to attack.

"This—this is not good," murmured Wrinkles.

Pankey said, "We'll sail south or north, evade them—"

Storm grew indignant. He wanted to reach out and shake some sense into Pankey. "Are you joking? Those monsters can easily pace us on land, while we sail a greater distance than they need gallop."

Jizogirl interrupted the argument. "It's academic, my bucks! Look!"

The anoles and their riders were wading into the surf, making straight for the *Squid.*

"This—this is even worse," Wrinkles added—rather superfluously, thought Storm, in an uncanny interval of stunned calmness.

Catmaul began yanking on one of the half-dozen kite tethers. "We have to get away! Now! Why doesn't Tropo help us!"

Rotifero gently pulled the doe away from the cables. "Old Tropo is a stern taskmaster. He brought us here to do a job, and do it we must."

Storm looked up in vain at the unmoving kite.

The kite!

"I have a plan! But we need to ditch our UPD's first. They're too heavy for what I have in mind."

Suiting actions to words, Storm doffed his harness, detached the proseity device, then redonned the bandolier with just logic bombs attached.

"Stash your swords in your harnesses, and follow me!"

Not waiting to see if they obeyed, Storm leaped onto the kite cables and began to climb. He felt a rightness and force to his actions, as he threw himself into battle without thought for his own safety, only that of his comrades, and the success of their necessary mission. Here, then, was the defining moment he had sought, ever since he left home.

The angle of the cables permitted a fairly easy ascent. Soon, Storm belly-flopped onto the wind-stuffed mattress of the kite. Seconds later, his five comrades joined him, with plenty of room to spare.

Below, the swimming anoles had closed half the distance to the ship.

"We have to do this just perfectly. We sever the four inner cables completely, and the two outer ones partially. Pankey and I will do the outer ones. Get busy!"

The composite substance of the cables was only a few Mohs softer than the sword blades, making for an arduous slog. But with much effort, Wrinkles, Jizogirl, Rotifero and Catmaul got the four inner cables completely separated—they fell grace-fully, with an ultimate *splash*!—causing the parafoil configura-tion to deform non-aerodynamically, attached to the ship now only by a few threads at either end.

Storm spared a look down. The anoles were too big to clamber aboard the ship. But the simians weren't. And the apes were approaching the remaining two tethers linking kite and ship.

"Now!

Storm and Pankey sawed frantically and awkwardly in synchrony from their recumbent positions—

Twin loud *pops* from the high-tensioned threads, and the kite was free. Instant winds sent by an alert weather mind grabbed it and pushed it toward land.

Storm allowed himself the tiniest moment of relief and triumph and relaxation. Then he sized up what awaited them.

The terrain below showed rampant greenery of cloud forest far off to every side. But the Kilauea caldera itself loomed off-center in a barren zone of old and new lava flows: the Kau Desert. Twenty-four kilometers away, the mother volcano Mauna Loa reared almost four times higher.

"Can we ride this all the way?" shouted Pankey.

"I hope so!" Storm replied. "Maybe we can bomb one of the magma rifts from up here!"

But his optimism soon received a dual assault.

Several slave-capped gulls stalked their kite, relaying visual feeds to the magma mind. As the kite moved deeper inland, it met attacks.

From an artificially built-up stone nozzle, under concentrated pressure, a laser-like jet of magma shot up high as the kite, narrowly missing the wardens, but spattering them with painful droplets on its broken descent. The kite fabric received numerous smelly burn holes. At the same time a fumarole unleashed billowing clouds of opaque choking sulfurous gases, which the kite sailed blindly through, at last emerging into clear air.

Gasping for breath, wiping his reddened eyes, Storm finally found his voice again.

"We're a big easy target! We have to split up!"

Wrinkles got to his hands and knees. "Me first! I'm the best glider!"

Without any farewells, Wrinkles launched off the unsteady platform. He spread his unusually generous patagium and made graceful curves through the sky.

Jizogirl cried, "Go, Wrinkles, go!"

A lance of red-hot lava shot up from an innocuous spot, and incinerated Wrinkles's entire left side. With a wailing cry he plummeted to impact.

Storm felt gut-punched. "We all need to leap at once! Now! Find a rift and bomb it!"

The remaining five wardens flung themselves free of the kite.

Focused on his gliding, Storm could not keep track of the rest of the Fellowship. Heaven-seeking spears of hot rock burst into existence randomly, a gauntlet of fiery death. Deadly vog—the volcanic fog—stole his sight and breath. He lost track of his altitude, his goal. He thought he heard cries and screams—

Out of the vog he emerged, to see the tortured ground much too close, an eye-searing, writhing active rift bisecting the terrain. He braced for a landing.

His right paw-foot caught in a crevice, and he heard bones snap. The pain was almost secondary to his despair.

Working to free his paw-foot, he heard two thumps behind him.

Pankey and Jizogirl had landed, their fur smoldering, eyes cloudy and tearful.

Jizogirl came to help free Storm's paw-foot.

"Rotifero, Catmaul—?"

Jizogirl just shook her head.

Meanwhile, Pankey had detached a logic bomb from his bandolier, and now darted in toward the living rift. Its incredible heat stopped him some distance away. He made to throw the bomb.

Overhead, the spy gulls circled low. One screeched just as Pankey threw.

A whip of lava caught the bomb in mid-air, incinerating it but prophylactically detaching from the parent flow, frustrating the spread of the released antisense agents backward along its interrupted length.

Pankey rushed back to his comrades. "It's no use. The bombs have to be delivered by hand. It's up to me!"

Jizogirl said, "And me!"

"No! Only if I fail. You and Storm— Just stay with him!"

Before either Storm or Jizogirl could protest. Pankey had taken off at a run.

Storm's nose could smell the scorched flesh of Pankey's paw-feet as the warden dodged one whip after another.

"Remember me—!" the leader of the team called, as he hurled himself and his remaining logic bombs into the rift.

The propagation of the antisense mind-killer agents was incredibly rapid, fueled by the high energies of the system. A deep subterranean rumble betokened the titanic struggle of intelligence against nescience. In a final spasm, the earth convulsed titanically, rippling like a shaken sheet in all directions, tossing Jizogirl down beside Storm, then bouncing them both.

The quake lasted for what seemed minutes, before dying away. Even when the shaking at ground zero had stopped, rumbles and tremors continued to radiate outward into the

surrounding ocean, as the antisense assault propagated. Storm could picture undersea lava tubes collapsing, tectonic plates shifting far out to sea—

Jizogirl got shakily to her paw-feet, and helped Storm stand on his one good leg.

"Is Mauna Loa dead?" she asked.

"I think so...."

Big menacing shapes moved in the vog around them.

"What now?" she asked hopelessly.

Out of the vog, several anoles and their riders emerged. But they no longer exhibited any direction or purpose or malice. One ape clawed at his slave cap and succeeded in ridding himself of it.

Jizogirl suddenly stiffened. "Oh, no! I just thought—We need to get inland, quickly! Up on the lizard!"

The tractable anole allowed Storm to climb onboard, with an assist from Jizogirl. His broken bones throbbed. She got up behind him, grabbed him around the waist.

"How do we make this buggered thing go?"

Storm pulled his sword out and jabbed it into the anole's shoulder. The lizard shot off, heading more or less into the interior.

"Can you tell me why this ride is necessary?"

"Tsunami! You prairie dwellers are so dumb!"

"But how?"

"The self-destruct information waves from the antisense bomb propagated faster than the physical collapse itself. When the instructions hit the furthest distal reaches of Mauna Loa out to sea, they rebounded back and met the oncoming physical collapse in mid-ocean. Result: tsunami!"

Up and up the anole skittered, leaving the Kau Desert behind and climbing the slopes of Mauna Loa. It stopped at last, exhausted, and no amount of jabbing could make it resume its flight.

Storm and Jizogirl dismounted and turned back toward the sea, the doe supporting the buck.

With the sea's recession, the raw steaming seabed lay exposed for several hundred meters out from shore. They saw the *Squid* sitting lopsided on the muck.

Then the crest of the giant wave materialized on the horizon, all spume and glory and destructive power.

"Are we far enough inland, high enough up?"

"Maybe. Maybe not."

The tsunami sounded like a billion lions roaring all at once.

Storm turned his face to Jizogirl's and said, "That kiss you gave me the other night— It was very nice. Can I have another?"

Jizogirl smiled and said, "If it's not our last, then count on lots more."

FARMEARTH

I couldn't wait until I turned thirteen, so I could play FarmEarth. I kept pestering all three of my parents every day to let me download the FarmEarth app into my memtax. What a little makulit I must have been! I see it now, from the grownup vantage of sixteen, and after all the trouble I eventually caused. Every minute with whines like "What difference does six months make?" And "But didn't I get high marks in all my omics classes?" And what I thought was the irrefutable clincher, "But Benno got to play when he was only eleven!"

"Look now, please, Crispian," my egg-Mom Darla would calmly answer, "six months makes a big difference when you're just twelve-point-five. That's four percent of your life up to this date. You can mature a lot in six months."

Darla worked as an osteo-engineer, hyper-tweaking fab files for living prosthetics, as if you couldn't tell.

"But Crispian," my mito-Mom Kianna would imperturbably answer, "you also came close to failing integral social plectics, and you know that's nearly as important for playing FarmEarth as your omics."

Kianna worked as a hostess for the local NASDAQ Casino. She had hustled more drinks than the next two hostesses combined, and been number one in tips for the past three years.

"But Crispian," my lone dad Marcelo Tanjuatco would irrefutably reply (I had taken "Tanjuatco," his last name, as mine, which is why I mention it here), "Benno has a different mito-Mom than you. And you know how special and respected Zoysia

is, and how long and hard even she had to petition to get Benno early acceptance."

Dad didn't work, at least not for anyone but the polybond. He stayed home, cooking meals, optimizing the house dynamics, and of course playing FarmEarth, just like every other person over thirteen who wasn't a maximal grebnard.

The way Dad—and everyone else—pronounced Zoysia's name—all smug, reverential and dreamy—just denatured my proteome, and I had to protest.

"But Benno and I still share your genes and Darla's! That's ninety percent right there! Zoysia's only ten percent."

"And you share ninety-five percent of your genes with any random chimp," said Darla. "And they can't play FarmEarth either. At least not maybe until that new generation of kymes come online."

I knew when I was beaten, so I mumbled and grumbled and retreated to the room I shared with Benno.

Of course, at an hour before suppertime he just had to be there, and playing FarmEarth.

My big brother Benno was a default-amp kid. His resting brain state had been permanently overclocked in the womb, so even when he wasn't consciously "thinking" he was processing information faster than you or me. And when he really focused on something, you could smell the neurons burning.

But no good fairy ever gave a gift without a catch. Benno's outward affect was, well, "interiorized." He always seemed to be listening to some silent voice, even when he was having a conversation with someone. And I'm not talking about the way all of us sometimes pay more attention to our auricular implants and the scenes displayed on our memtax than we do to the person facing us.

Needless to say, puffy-faced Benno didn't have much of social life, even at age sixteen. Not that he seemed to care.

Lying on his back on the lower bunk of our sleeping pod, Benno stared at some unknown landscape in his memtax, working his haptic finger bling faster than the Mandarin's

grandson trying to take down Tony Stark's clone in *Iron Man 10.*

I tried to tap into his FarmEarth feed with my own memtax, even though I knew the dataflow was encrypted. But all that happened was that I got bounced to Benno's public CitizenSpace.

I sat down on the edge of the mattress beside him, and poked him in the ribs. He didn't even flinch.

"Hey, B-man, whatcha doing?"

Benno's voice was a monotone even when he was excited about something, and dealing with his noodgy little brother was low on his list of thrills.

"I'm grooming the desert-treeline ecotone in Mali. Now go away."

"Wow! That is so stellar! Are you planting new trees?"

"No, I'm upgrading rhizome production on the existing ones."

"What kind of effectuators are you using?"

"ST5000 Micromites. Now. Go. Away!"

I shoved Benno hard. "Jerk! Why don't you ever share with me! I just wanna play too!"

I jumped up and stalked off before he could retaliate, but he didn't even bother to respond.

So there you have typical day in the latter half of my thirteenth year. Desperate pleas on my part to graduate to adulthood, followed by admonitions from my parents to be patient, then by jealousy and inattention from my big brother.

As you can well imagine, the six similar months till I turned thirteen passed by like a Plutonian year (just checked via memtax: 248 Earth years). But finally—finally!—I turned thirteen and got my very own log-on to FarmEarth.

And that's when the real frustration started!

* * * * * * *

Kicking a living hackysack is a lot more fun in meatspace than it is via memtax. You can feel muscles other than those in

your fingers getting a workout. Your bare toes dig into the grass. You smell sweat and soil. You get sprayed with salt water on a hot day. You get to congratulatorily hug warm girls afterwards if any are in the circle with you. So even though all the kids gripe about having to leave their houses every day for two whole shared hours of meatspace schooling at the nearest Greenpatch, I guess that, underneath all our complaints, we really like being face to face with our peers once in a while.

That fateful day when we first decided to hack FarmEarth, there were six of us kicking around the sack. Me, Mallory, Cheo, Vernice, Anuta, and Williedell—my best friends.

The sack was an old one, and didn't have much life left in it. A splice of ctenophore, siphonophore, and a few other marine creatures, including bladder kelp, the soft warty green globe could barely jet enough salt water to change its mid-air course erratically as intended. Kicking it got too predictable pretty fast.

Sensing what we were all feeling and acting first, Cheo, tall and quick, grabbed the sack on one of its feeble arcs and tossed it like a basketball into the nearby aquarium—splash!—where it sank listlessly to the bottom of the tank. Poor old sponge.

"Two points!" said Vernice. Vernice loved basketball more than anything, and was convinced she was going to play for the Havana Ocelotes some day. She hugged Cheo, and that triggered a round of mutual embraces. I squeezed Anuta's slim brown body—she wore just short-shorts and a belly shirt—a little extra, trying to convey some of the special feelings I had for her, but I couldn't tell if any of my emotions got communicated. Girls are hard to figure sometime.

Williedell ambled slow and easy in his usual way over to the solar-butane fridge and snagged six Cokes. We dropped to the grass under the shade of the big tulip-banyan at the edge of the Greenpatch and sucked down the cold soda greedily. Life was good.

And then our FarmEarth teacher had to show up.

Now, I know you're saying, "Huh? I thought Crispian Tanjuatco was that guy who could hardly wait to turn thirteen

so he could play FarmEarth. Isn't that parity?"

Well, that was how I felt before I actually got FarmEarth beginner privileges, and came up against all the rules and restrictions and duties that went with our lowly ranking. True to form, the adults had managed to suck all the excitement and fun and thrills out of what should have been sweet as plano-forming—at least at the entry level for thirteen-year-olds, who were always getting the dirty end of the control rod.

"Hi, kids! Who's ready to shoulder-surf some pseudomonads?"

The minutely flexing, faintly flickering OLED circuitry of my memtax, powered off my bioelectricity, painted my retinas with the grinning translucent face of Purvis Mumphrey. Past his ghostlike augie-real appearance, I could still see all my friends and their reactions.

Round as a moon pie, framed by wispy blonde hair, Mumphrey's face revealed, we all agreed, a deep sadness beneath his bayou bonhomie. His sadness related, in fact, to the assignment before us.

Everyone groaned, and that made our teacher look even sadder.

"Aw, Mr. Mumphrey, do we hafta?" "We're too tired now from our game." "Can't we do it later?"

"Students, please. How will you ever get good enough at FarmEarth to move up to master level, unless you practice now?"

Master level. That was the lure, the tease, the hook, the far-off pinnacle of freedom and responsibility that we all aspired to. Being in charge of a big mammal, or a whole forest, say. Who wouldn't want that? Acting to help Gaia in her crippled condition, to make up for the shitty way our species had treated the planet, stewarding important things actually large enough to see.

But for now, six months into our novice status, all we had in front of us was riding herd on a zillion hungry bacteria. That was all the adults trusted us to handle. The prospect was about

as exciting as watching your navel lint accumulate.

At this moment, Mr. Mumphrey looked about ready to cry. This assignment meant a lot to him.

Our teacher had been born in Louisiana, prior to the Deepwater Horizon blowout. He had been just our age, son of a shrimper, when that drilling rig went down and the big spew filled the Gulf with oil for too many months. Now, twenty years later, we were still cleaning up that mess.

So rather than see our teacher break down and weep, which would have been yotta-yucky, we groaned some more just to show we weren't utterly buying his sales pitch, got into comfortable positions around the shade tree (I wished I could have put my head into Anuta's lap, but I didn't dare), and booted up our FarmEarth apps.

Mr. Mumphrey had access to our feeds, so he could monitor what we did. That just added an extra layer of insult to the way we were treated like babies.

Instantly, we were out of augie overlays and into full virt.

I was point-of-view embedded deep in the dark waters of the Gulf, in the middle of a swarm of oil-eating bacteria, thanks to the audiovideo feed from a host of macro-effectuators that hovered on their impellors, awaiting our orders. The cloud of otherwise invisible bugs around us glowed with fabricated luminescence. Fish swam into and out of the radiance, which was supplemented by spotlights onboard the effectuators.

Many of the fish showed yotta-yucky birth defects.

The scene in my memtax also displayed a bunch of useful supplementary data: our GPS location, thumbnails of other people running FarmEarth in our neighborhood, a window showing a view of the surface above our location, weather reports—common stuff like that. If I wanted to, I could bring up the individual unique ID numbers on the fish, and even for each single bacteria.

I got a hold of the effectuator assigned to me, feeling its controls through my haptic finger bling, and made it swerve at the machine being run by Anuta.

"Hey, Crispy Critter, watch it!" she said with that sexy Bollywood accent of hers.

Mumphs was not pleased. "Mr. Tanjuatco, you will please concentrate on the task at hand. Now, students, last week's Hurricane Norbert churned up a swath of relatively shallow sediment north of our present site, revealing a lode of undigested hydrocarbons. It's up to us to clean them up. Let's drive these hungry bugs to the site."

Williedell and Cheo and I made cowboy whoops, while the girls just clucked their tongues and got busy. Pretty soon, using water jets and shaped sonics aboard the effectuators, we had created a big invisible water bubble full of bugs that we could move at will. We headed north, over anemones and octopi, coral and brittle stars. Things looked pretty good, I had to say, considering all the crap the Gulf had been through. That's what made FarmEarth so rewarding and addictive, seeing how you could improve on these old tragedies.

But herding bugs underwater was hardly high-profile or awesome, no matter how real the resulting upgrades were. It was basically like spinning the composter at your home: a useful duty that stunk.

We soon got the bugs to the site and mooshed them into the tarry glop where they could start remediating.

"Nom, nom, nom," said Mallory. Mallory had the best sense of humor for a girl I had ever seen.

"Nom, nom, nom," I answered back. Then all six of us were nom-nom-noming away, while Mumphs pretended not to find it funny.

But even that joke wore out after a while, and our task of keeping the bugs centered on their meal, rotating fresh stock in to replace sated ones, got so boring I was practically falling asleep.

Eventually, Mumphs said, "Okay, we have a quorum of replacement Farmers lined up, so you can all log out."

I came out of FarmEarth a little disoriented, like people always do, especially when you've been stewarding in a really

unusual environment. I didn't know how my brother Benno kept any sense of reality after he spent so much time in so many exotic FarmEarth settings. The familiar Greenpatch itself looked odd to me, like my friends should have been fishes or something, instead of people. I could tell the others were feeling the same way, and so we broke up for the day with some quiet goodbyes.

By the time I got home, to find my fave supper of goat empanadas and cassava-leaf stew laid on by Dad, with both Moms able to be there too, I had already forgotten how bored and disappointed playing FarmEarth had left me.

But apparently, Cheo had not.

* * * * * * *

The vertical play surface at Gecko Guy's Climbzone was made out of MEMs, just like a pair of memtax. To the naked eye, the climbing surface looked like a gray plastic wall studded with permanent handholds and footholds, little grippable irregular nubbins. But the composition of near-nanoscopic addressable scales meant that the wall was instantly and infinitely configurable.

Which is why, halfway up the six-meter climb, I suddenly felt the hold under my right hand, which was supporting all my weight, evaporate, sending me scrabbling wildly for another.

But every square centimeter within my reach was flat.

The floor, even though padded, was a long way off, and of course I had no safety line.

So even though I was reluctant to grebnard out, I activated the artificial setae in my gloves and booties, and slammed them against the wall.

One glove and one bootie stuck, slowing me enough to position my second hand and foot. I clung flat to the wall, catching my breath, then began to scuttle like a crab to the nearest projecting holds, the setae making ripping sounds as they pulled away each time.

A few meters to my left, Williedell laughed and called out, "Ha-ha, Crispy had to go gecko!"

"Yeah, like you never did three times last week! Race you to the top!"

Starting to scramble upward as fast as I could, I risked a glance at Anuta to see if she were laughing at my lameness. But she wasn't even looking my way, just hanging in place and gossiping with Mallory and Vernice.

Sometimes I think girls have no real sense of competition.

But then I remember how much attention they pay to their stupid clothes.

Williedell and I reached the top of the wall at roughly the same time, and gave each other a fist bump.

Down on the floor, Cheo hailed us. "Hey, Crispian, almost got you that time, didn't I!"

Cheo's parents owned the Climbzone, and so the five of us got to play for free in the slowest hours—like now, eight AM on a Sunday. Cheo had to work a few hours on the weekends— mainly just handing out gloves and booties and instructing newbies—so he couldn't climb with us. Of course, he had access via his memtax to the wall controls, and had disappeared my handhold on purpose.

I yelled back, "Next time we're eating underwater goo, you're getting a face full!"

For some reason, my silly remark made Cheo look sober and thoughtful. "Hey, guys, c'mon down! I want to talk about something with you."

The girls must have been paying some attention to our antics, because they responded to Cheo's request and began lowering themselves to the floor. Pretty soon, all five of us were gathered around Cheo.

There were no other paying customers at the moment.

"Let me just close up the place for a few minutes."

Cheo locked the entrance doors and posted a public augie sign saying BACK IN FIFTEEN MINUTES. Then we all went and sat at the snack bar. As always, Williedell made sure we

were all supplied with drinks. We joked that he was going to grow up to be flight attendant on a Amazonian aerostat—but we didn't make the joke too often, since he flared up sensitive about always instinctively acting the host. (I think he got those hospitality habits because he was the oldest in his semi-dysfunctional family and always taking care of his sibs.)

Cheo looked us up and down and then said, "Who's happy with our sludge-eating FarmEarth assignments? Anyone?"

"Nope." "Not me." "I swear I can taste oil and sardines after every run."

That last from Mallory.

"And you know we've got at least another six months of this kind of drudgery until we ramp up maybe half a level, right?"

Groans all around.

"Well, what would you say if I could get us playing at a higher level right away? Maybe even at master status!"

Vernice said, "Oh, sure, and how're you gonna do that? I could see if Crispy here maybe said he had a way to bribe his Aunt Zoysia. She's got real *enchufe*."

"Yeah, well, I know someone with real *enchufe* too. My brother."

Everyone fell silent. Then Anuta said quietly, "But Cheo, your brother is in prison."

As far as we all knew, this was true. Cheo's big brother Adán had got five years for subverting FarmEarth. He had misused effectuators to cultivate a few hectares of *chiba* in the middle of the Pantanal reserve. The charges against him, however, had nothing to do with the actual dope, because of course *chiba* was legal as chewing gum. But he had misappropriated public resources, avoided excise taxes on his crop, and indirectly caused the death of a colony of protected capybaras by diverting the effectuators that might have been used to save them from some bushmeat poachers. Net punishment: five years hospitality from the *federales*.

Cheo looked a bit ashamed at his brother's misdeeds. "He's not in prison anymore. He got out a year early. He racked up

some good time for helping administer FarmEarth among the jail population. You think we got shitty assignments! How would you like to steward *gigundo* manure lagoons! Anyhow, he's a free man now, and he's looking for some help with a certain project. In return, the people he takes on get master status. It may not be strictly aboveboard, but it's really just a kind of shortcut to where we're heading already."

I instantly had my doubts about Adán and his schemes. If only I had listened to my gut, we could have avoided a lot of grief. But I asked, "What is this mysterious project?"

"In jail, Adán hooked up with *Los Braceros Últimos*. You know about them, right?"

"No. What's their story?"

"They think FarmEarth is being run too conservatively. The planet is still at the tipping point. We need to do bigger things faster. No more tip-toeing around with little fixes. No more being over-cautious. Get everybody working on making Gaia completely self-sustaining again. And the *Braceros* want to free up humanity from being Earth's thermostat and immune system and liver."

"Yeah!" said Williedell, pumping his fist in the air. Mallory and Vernice were nodding their heads in agreement. Anuta looked with calm concern to me, as if to see what I thought.

Four to two.

I didn't want to drag everyone else down. And I *was* pretty sick of the boring, trivial assignments we were limited to in FarmEarth. All I could suddenly picture was all the fun that Benno had every day. My own brother! Ninety percent my own brother anyhow. I felt a wave of jealousy and greed that swept away any doubts. The feelings made me bold enough to take Anuta's hand and say, "Count us in too!"

And after that, it was way too late to back out.

* * * * * * *

We met Adán in the flesh just once. The seven of us four-

squared a rendezvous at the NASDAQ Casino where my Mom Kianna worked. The venue was cheap and handy. Because we weren't adults, we couldn't go out onto the gaming floor, where the Bundled Mortgages Craps Table and Junk Bond Roulette Wheels and all the other games of investa-chance were. But the exclusion was good, because that was where Mom hustled drinks, so we wouldn't bump into her.

But the Casino also featured an all-ages café with live music, and I said, "We shouldn't try to sneak around with this scheme. That'll just attract suspicion. We've hung out at the Casino before, so no one will think twice to see us there."

Everyone instantly agreed, and I felt a glow of pride.

So one Friday night, while we listened to some neo-Baithak Gana by Limekiller and the Manatees (the woman playing dholak was yotta-sexy) and sipped delicious melano-rambutan smoothies, we got the lowdown from Cheo's brother.

Adán resembled Cheo in a brotherly way, except with more muscles, a scraggly mustache, and a bad fashion sense that encouraged a sparkly vest of unicorn hair over a bare chest painted with an e-ink display screen showing cycling porn snippets. Grebnard! Did he imagine this place was some kind of Craigslist meat market?

The porn scenes on Adán's chest—soundless, thank god—were very distracting, and I felt embarrassed for the girls—although they really didn't seem too hassled. Now, in hindsight, I figure maybe Adán was trying to unfocus our thinking on purpose.

Luckily the café was fairly dark, and the e-ink display wasn't backlit, so most of the scenes were just squirming blobs that I could ignore while Adán talked.

After he sized us up with some casual chat, he said, "You kids are getting in on the ground floor of something truly great. In the future, you'll be remembered as the greatest generation, the people who had the foresight to take bold moves to bring the planet back from the brink. All this tentative shit FarmEarth authorizes now, half-measures and fallback options and minor

tweaks, is gonna take forever to put Gaia back on her feet. But *Los Braceros Últimos* is all about kickass rejuvenation treatment, big results fast!"

"What exactly would we have to do?" Anuta asked.

"Just steward some effectuators where and how we tell you. Nothing more than you're doing now at school. You won't necessarily get to know the ultimate goal of your work right from the start—we have to keep some things secret—but when it's over, I can guarantee you'll be mega-stoked."

We all snickered at Adán's archaic slang.

"And what do we get in return?" I said.

Adán practically leered. "FarmEarth Master status, under untraceable proxies, to use however you want—in your spare time."

Williedell said, "I don't know. We'll have to keep up our regular FarmEarth assignments, plus yours.... When will we ever *have* any spare time?"

Adán shrugged. "Not my problem. If you really want Master status, you'll give up something else and manage to carve out some time. If not—well, I've got plenty of other potential stewards lined up. I'm only doing this as a favor to my little bro' after all...."

"No, no, we want to sign up!" "Yeah, I'm in!" "Me too!"

Adán smiled. "All right. In the next day or two, you'll find a FarmEarth key in your CitizenSpace. When you use it, you'll get instructions on your assignment. Good luck. I gotta go now."

After Adán left, we all looked at each other a little sheepishly, wondering what we had gotten ourselves into. But then Mallory raised her glass and said, "To the Secret Masters of FarmEarth!"

We clinked rims, sipped, and imagined what we could do with our new powers.

* * * * * * *

The mystery project the six of us were given was called

"Angry Sister," and it proved to be just as boring as our regular FarmEarth tasks.

Three years later, I think this qualifies as some kind of yotta-ironic joke. But none of us found it too funny at the time.

We were tasked with running rugged subterranean effectuators—John Deere Molebots—somewhere in the world, carving out a largish tubular tunnel from Point A to Point B. We didn't know where we were, because the GPS feed from the molebots had been deactivated. We guided our cutting route instead by triangulation via encrypted signals from some surface radio beacons and reference to an engineering schematic. The molebots were small and slow: the six of us barely managed to chew up two cubic meters of stone in a three-hour shift. A lot of time was spent ferrying the detritus back to the surface and disposing of it in the nearby anonymous ocean.

The mental strain of stewarding the machines grew very tiresome.

"Why can't these stupid machines run themselves?" Vernice complained over our secure communications channel. "Isn't that why weak AI was invented?"

Cheo answered, "You know that AI is forbidden in FarmEarth. Don't you remember the lesson Mumphs gave us about Detroit?"

"Oh, right."

A flock of macro-effectuators had been set loose demolishing smart-tagged derelict buildings in that city. But then Detroit's Highwaymen motorcycle outlaws, having a grudge against the mayor, had cracked the tags and affixed them to Manoogian Mansion, the official mayoral residence.

Once the pajama-clad mayor and his half-naked shrieking family were removed from their perch on a teetering fragment of Manoogian Mansion roof, it took only twenty-four hours for both houses of Congress to forbid use of AI in FarmEarth.

"Besides," Mallory chimed in, "with nine billion people on the planet, human intelligence is the cheapest commodity."

"And," said Anuta, "having people steward the effectuators

encourages responsible behavior, social bonding, repentance and contrition for mankind's sins."

Williedell made a rude noise at this bit of righteous FarmEarth catechism, and I felt compelled to stand up for Anuta by banging my drill bit into Williedell's machine.

Vernice said, "All right, all right, I give up! We're stuck here, so let's just do it. And you two, quit your pissing contest!"

The six of us went back to moodily chewing up strata.

After a month of this, our little set had begun to unravel a tad. Each day, when our secret shift of moonlighting was over, none of us wanted to hang together. We were all sick of each other, and just wanted to get away to play with our Master status.

And that supreme privilege did indeed almost make up for all the boredom and tedium of the scut work.

Maybe you've played FarmEarth as a Master yourself. (But I bet you didn't have to worry, like us six fakes did, about giving yourself away to the real Masters with some misplaced comment. The paranoia was mild but constant.) If so, you know what I'm talking about.

You've guided a flock of aerostatic effectuators through gaudy polar stratospheric clouds, sequestering CFCs.

You've guarded nesting mama Kemp's Ridley turtles from feral dogs.

You've quarried the Great Pacific Garbage Patch for materials that artists riding ships have turned on the spot into found sculptures that sell for *muy plata.*

You've draped skyscrapers with vertical farms.

You've channeled freshets into the nearly dead Aral Sea, and restocked those reborn waters.

You've midwifed at the birth of a hundred species of animals: tranked mamas in the wild whose embryos were mispositioned for easy birth, and would have otherwise died.

That last item reminds me of something kinda embarrassing.

Playing FarmEarth with big mammals can be tricky, as I found out one day. They're too much like humans.

I was out in Winnemucca, Nevada, among a herd of wild

horses. The FarmEarth assignment I had picked off a duty roster was to provide the herd with its annual Encephalomyelitis vaccinations. That always happened in the spring, and now it was time.

My effectuator was a little rolligon that barreled across the prairie disguised as tumbleweed. When I got near a horse, I would spring up with my onboard folded legs, grab its mane, give the injection, then drop off quickly.

But after a while, I got bored a little, and so I hung on to this one horse to enjoy the ride. The stallion got real freaky, dashing this way and that, but then it settled down a bit, still galloping. I was having some real thrills.

And that was when my ride encountered a mare.

I hadn't realized that spring was breeding time for the mustangs.

Before I could disengage amidst the excitement and confusion, the stallion was sporting a boner the size of Rhode Island, and was covering the mare.

I noticed now that the mare wore a vaccinating effectuator too.

The haptic feedback, even though it didn't go direct to my crotch, was still having its effect on my own dick. It felt weird and creepy—but too good to give up.

Before I could quite climax in my pants, the titanic horsey sex was over, and the male and female broke apart.

Very cautiously, I pinged the other FarmEarth player. They could always refuse to respond.

Anuta answered.

Back home in my bedroom, my face burned a thousand degrees hot. I was sure hers was burning too. We couldn't even say a word to each other. In another minute, she had broken the communications link.

When we next met in the flesh, we didn't refer to the incident in so many words. But we felt compelled to get away from the others and make out a little.

After a while, by mutual consent, we just sort of dribbled to

a stop, without having done much more than snog and grope.

"I guess," said Anuta, "that unless we mean to go all the way, we won't get to where we were the other day."

"Yeah, I suppose. And even then…."

She nodded her head in silent agreement. Regular people sex was going to have to be pretty special to live up to the equine sex we had vicariously experienced in FarmEarth.

I felt at that moment that maybe FarmEarth Master privileges were kept away from us kids for a reason.

And a few weeks later, when everything came crashing down, I was certain of it.

* * * * * * *

My Moms and Dad were all out of the house that fateful late afternoon. I was lying in bed at home, bored and chewing up subsoils with my pals and their effectuators, eking out a conduit which we had been told, by Adán, represented the last few yards of tunnel, in accordance with our schematics, when I felt a poke in my ribs. I disengaged from FarmEarth, coming out of augie space, and saw my dull-faced brother Benno hovering over me.

"Crispian," he said, "do you know where you are?"

"Yeah, sure, I'm eating up hydrocarbons in the Gulf. Nom, nom, nom, good little Crispy Critter."

"Your statement exists in non-compliance with reality."

"Oh, just go away, Benno, and leave me alone."

I dived back into augie space, eager to get this boring "Angry Sister" assignment over with. We were all hoping that the next task Adán gave us would be more glamorous and exciting. We all wanted to feel that we were big, bold cyber-cowboys of the planet, riding Gaia's range, on the lookout for eco-rustlers, repairing broken fences. But of course, even without star-quality assignments, we still had the illicit Master privileges to amuse—and scare—us.

"Hey," said Mallory when I returned to our subterranean workspace, "where'd you go?"

"Yeah," chimed in Vernice, "no slacking off!"

"Oh, it was just my stupid grebnard brother. He wanted to harass me about something."

Cheo said, "That's Benno, right? Isn't his mom Zoysia van Vollenhoven? I heard he's hot stuff in FarmEarth. Inherited all his Mom's chops, plus more. Maybe he had something useful to tell you."

"I doubt it. He's probably just jealous of me now."

Anuta sounded worried. "You don't think he knows anything about what we're doing?"

"No way. I just mean that he sees me playing FarmEarth eagerly all the time now, so he must have some idea I'm enjoying myself, and that pisses him off. He's always been jealous of me."

At that moment, I felt a hand clamp onto my ankle in meatspace, and I was dragged out of bed with a *thump*! I vacated my John Deere and confronted Benno from my humiliating position on the floor.

"What exactly is the matter with you, Ben? Do you have a short-circuit in your strap-on brain?"

Benno's normally impassive face showed as much emotion as it ever did, like say at Christmas, when he got some grebnard present he had always wanted. The massive agitation amounted to some squinted eyes and trembling lower lip.

"If you do not want to admit your ignorance, Crispian, I will simply tell you where you are. You are at these coordinates: sixty-three degrees, thirty-eight minutes north, and nineteen degrees, three minutes west."

I didn't bother using my memtax to look up that latitude and longitude, because I didn't want to give Benno's accusations any weight. So I just sarcastically asked, "And where exactly is that?"

"You and your crew of naïve miscreants are almost directly underneath the Katla volcano in Iceland. How far down you are, I have not yet ascertained. But I would imagine that you are quite close to the magma reservoirs, and in imminent danger of tapping them with your tunnel. Other criminal crews spaced all

around the volcano are in similar positions. May I remind you that whenever Katla has gone off in the past—the last time was in 1918—it discharged as much toxic substances per second as the combined fluid discharges of the Amazon, Mississippi, Nile, and Yangtze rivers."

Holy shit! Could he be right? My voice quivered a little, even though I tried to control it. "And why would we be in such a place?"

"Because *Los Braceros Últimos* plan to unleash the Pinatubo Option."

Now I started to *really* get scared.

Every school kid from first grade on knew about the Pinatubo Option, named after a famous volcanic incident of the last century. It was a geoengineering scheme of the highest magnitude, intended to flood the atmosphere with ash and other aerosols so as to cut global temperatures by a considerable fraction. Consensus wisdom had always figured it was too risky and uncontrollable a proposition.

"I cannot let you and your friends proceed with this. You must tell them to halt immediately."

For a minute, I had almost felt myself on Benno's side. But when he gave me that order in his know-it-all way, I instantly rebelled. All the years of growing up together, with him always the favored one, stuck in my throat.

"Like hell! We're just doing what's good for the planet in the fastest way possible. *Los Braceros* must have studied everything better than you. You're just a kid like me!"

Benno looked at me calmly with his stoney face. "I am a Master Class Steward, and you are not."

"Well, Mr. Master Class Steward, try and stop me!"

I started to climb to my feet when Benno tackled me and knocked me back down!

We began to wrestle. I expected to pin Benno in a couple of seconds. But that wasn't how things went.

I had always believed my brother was a total lardass from all his FarmEarth physical inactivity. How the heck was I supposed

to know that he spent two hours every weekend in some kind of martial arts training? Was I in charge of his frigging schedule? We didn't even share the same mito-Mom!

I found myself snaffled up in about half a minute, with Benno clamping both my wrists together behind my back with just one big strong hand.

And then, with the other hand, he rawly popped out my memtax, being none too gentle.

I felt blinded! Awake, yet separated from augie space for more than the short interval it takes to swap in fresh memtax, I couldn't access the world's knowledge, talk to my friends, or even recall what I had had for breakfast that morning.

Next Benno stripped me of my haptic bling. Then he said, "You wait right here."

He left, locking the bedroom door behind him.

I sat on the bed, feeling empty and broken. I couldn't even tell you now how much time passed.

The door opened and in walked Benno, followed by his mito-Mom, Zoysia van Vollenhoven.

Aunt Zoysia always inspired instant guilt in me. Not because of anything she said or did, or any overbearing, sneering attitude, but only because of the way she looked.

Aunt Zoysia was the sexiest female I knew—and not in any kind of bulimic high-fashion designer-label manner either, like those thoroughbreds the Brazilians engineer for the runways of the world. I always thought that if Gaia could have chosen to incarnate herself, she would have looked just like Aunt Zoysia, all overflowing breasts and hips and wild mane of hair, lush wide mouth, proud nose and piercing eyes. She practically radiated exuberant joy and heartiness and sensuality. In her presence, I always got an incipient stiffy, and since she was family—even though she and I shared no genes—the stiffy was always instantly accompanied by guilt.

But this was the one time I didn't react in the usual manner, I felt so miserable.

Aunt Zoysia came over and sat on the mattress beside me and

hugged me. Even those intimate circumstances did not stir up any horniness.

"Crispian, dear, Benno has described to me the trouble you've gotten into. It's all right, I completely understand. You just wanted to play with the big boys. But now, I think you'll admit, things have gone too far, and must be brought to a screeching halt. Benno?"

"Yes, mother?"

"Please find a fresh pair of memtax for your brother. We will slave Crispian's to ours, and bring him along for the shutdown of *Los Braceros Últimos*. It will be highly instructional."

Benno went out and came back with new memtax in their organic blister pack. I wetted them and inserted them, and put on my restored haptic bling. I booted up all my apps, but still found myself a volitionless spectator to the shared augie space feed from Zoysia and Benno.

"All right, son, let's take these sneaky bastards down."

"Ready when you are, Mom."

You know, I thought I was pretty slick with my Master Class privileges, could handle effectuators and the flora and fauna of various biomes pretty deftly. But riding Zoysia's feed, I realized I knew squat.

The first thing she and Benno did was to go into God Mode, with Noclip Option, Maphack, Duping and Smurfing thrown in. That much I could follow—barely.

But after that, I was just along for the dizzying ride.

Zoysia and Benno took down *Los Braceros Últimos* like a military sonic cannon disabling a pack of kittens. Racing around the globe in augie space, they undercut all the many plans of the Pinatubo-heads, disabling rogue effectuators and even using legal machines in off-label ways, such as to immobilize people in meatspace. I think the wildest maneuver though was when they stampeded a herd of springboks through the remote Windhoek encampment where some of the conspirators were operating from. The eco-agitators never knew what hit them.

The whole roundup lasted barely an hour. I found myself back in my familiar and yet somehow strange-seeming bedroom, actually short of breath and sweaty. Zoysia and brother Benno were unruffled.

"Now, Crispian," said my Aunt sweetly, no sign of the moderate outlaw blood she had spilled evident on her perfect teeth or nails, "I hope you've learned that privileges only come to those who have earned them, and know how to use them."

"Yes'm."

"Perhaps if you hung out a little more with your brother, and consented to allow him to mentor you...."

I turned to glare at Benno, but his homely, unaggressive expression defused my usual impatience and dislike. Plus, I was frankly a little frightened of him now.

"Yes'm."

"Very well. I think then, in a few years, given the rare initiative and skills you've shown—even though you chose to follow an illegal path with them—you should be quite ready to join us in ensuring that people do not abuse FarmEarth."

And of course, as I've often said to Anuta, wise and sexy Aunt Zoysia predicted everything just right.

Which is why I have to say goodbye now.

Something somewhere on FarmEarth is *wrong*!

ESCAPE FROM
NEW AUSTIN

The song was a few years older than Amy Gertslin, but it still spoke to her and her plight.

"Redneck Woman," by Gretchen Wilson.

Amy sang along to the tune pumping through the wireless earbuds of her fifth-generation iPod, the model that held 50,000 songs in a unit the size of a Triscuit cracker, which Amy wore on a necklace of living synthetic seaweed.

"'Cause I'm a redneck woman, and I ain't no high-class broad. I'm just a product of my raisin', and I say 'hey y'all' and 'yee haw'!"

Amy's skinny fifteen-year-old arms and legs flailed about as she emulated the playing of various air-instruments. She indulged in high kicks and thunderous stomps, weird line-dancing shuffles and slides. Plainly, she had a lot of pent-up energy to release.

The door to Amy's bedroom opened just as she was bellowing out the line about knowing all the words to every Tanya Tucker song. In the doorway stood her father, Batch Gertslin.

Batch was short for Batchelder: a maternal family name used as a given name in this instance. The Gertslins descended in part from the famed Boston Batchelders, bioindustry pioneers. A branch of the family, verifying the legendary strength of the Boston-to-Austin cultural axis, had relocated to the former capital of Texas a couple of generations ago. So although Amy and the rest of her family were Texas natives, they also boasted

a rich Agnostica pedigree.

Only fitting, since Austin was nowadays an integral if non-contiguous part of Agnostica, an azure island in the crimson sea of Faithland.

Batch Gertslin possessed a somewhat moony face, shadowed by a messy thatch of black hair and generally expressive of an amiable curiosity and frisky intellect. But now he was definitely irked.

"Amy! You're bringing the ceiling in my office down!"

Batch Gertslin was a freelance ringtone, screen-wallpaper, emoticon and dingbat designer, and worked from home.

Amy pretended not to hear. "What?!"

"Turn that music off!"

Batch's face was shading into purple—a nice bi-national mix of red and blue, actually—and so Amy dropped her pretense of non-comprehension. A flick of her tongue against her Bluetooth dental implant controller deactivated the iPod. Her earbuds resumed their default task of ambient sound enhancement and noise filtering.

Batch's face regained a measure of composure and normal coloration. "Thank you. Listen, Amy. Your mother and I don't ask very much of you. You're almost an adult, we realize, and deserving of being treated as such. For the most part. But this senseless caterwauling has got to stop. It's most annoying."

Amy felt her own face coloring now, heating up with anger. "'Senseless caterwauling!' You're talking about some of the greatest music ever made! The music I love!"

Batch advanced into the room, holding out his hands in a paternally placating gesture. "I know you don't like any of the music your mother and I enjoy, Amy. That's only natural between generations. After all, you weren't raised on classic acts such as Eminem and Linkin Park and Ol' Dirty Bastard the way your mother and I were. Those old-school performers and their modern heirs are just not for you."

"Damn straight! You know I hate all that emo-crunk-harsh-metal shit! Classic country-western is my zome!"

"Fine, fine. But why do you have to favor the, ah, more downmarket acts in that genre? Couldn't you at least try some of those other artists I've suggested. Lyle Lovett, k. d. lang, Alison Krauss—"

"Oh, *Dad*! You're making my neurons go all apoptosis! Those wimps, those feebs, those posers, those *zygotes*! Charlie Daniels would eat them all for breakfast and still be hungry enough to swallow Shania Twain whole."

Batch assumed a dreamy look. "Shania Twain. What a hottie. Now there was a singer...."

"Ugh! Dad, I promise not to rattle the plaster anymore. Just leave me alone now. Unless you had something else to say—"

"I do. Your mother wants you downstairs now to help with dinner."

"Why can't Hilary do it?"

"Your little brother is busy studying for his Virus Construction finals. And besides, he helped last night."

"Arrrrgh! Okay, I'm coming!"

Batch left, and Amy waited the maximum amount of time before she knew she would receive a second notice to show up in the kitchen. Only then did she grudgingly tromp downstairs.

Phillipa Gertslin stood by the methane-fueled gas range, stirring a pot of free-range-turkey chili. Phillipa's parents had been —still were—a famous team of young-adult writers, whose current series—involving a budding teenaged paleontologist trapped by accident of birth into an intolerant Faithland community—was a best-seller all across Agnostica. They had named their daughter in honor of Philip Pullman and his quintessential Agnostica fictions.

This evening Phillipa wore loose white cotton trousers and a plain black short-sleeved cotton top. For the nth time, Amy sized up her mother's slim figure, wondering if her mother's decidedly non-voluptuous shape was to be her lot too. Why couldn't Philippa Gertslin have had an endowment of Dolly Parton magnitude to pass on to her daughter, or at least one of Shelby Lynne proportions? Oh, well, Amy would just have to go

in for an outpatient boob job when she came into her majority next year.

"Mom, you look like some kind of robot *sushi* chef! Don't you ever feel like glamming it up a little?"

Phillipa regarded Amy's own embroidered red synthetic shirt, rhinestone-studded denim pants, and hand-stitched cowboy boots with a barely concealed distaste.

"You know I don't believe in regional fashions, dear, however ironically worn. Clothes are critical signifiers. I don't want my outfits proclaiming some false allegiance to Faithland, of all places."

Phillipa Gertslin taught popular culture at Howard Zinn University—what used to be known as UT Austin, before the Agnostica-Faithland split. Her last published book had been titled *The Hermeneutics of Hypocrisy* and concerned itself with the frequent preacher sex scandals that continued to plague Faithland at regular intervals without, inexplicably, managing to undermine in any way the basic beliefs of the heartland.

"Now, please," Phillipa continued, "if you could just set the table without offering any more fashion critiques...? I've got to nuke these duck tortillas."

Grumbling, Amy took down a stack of four clunky, hand-fired plates from the cupboard. Each plate weighed as much as brick.

"Why can't we get a set of those faunchy e-paper plates? The ones that let you eyeball content while you eat?"

"Paper? I'd rather eat off the backs of exploited migrant laborers. Who knows what horrid toxins might leach out of that e-paper? It's only been around for a couple of years. I know the government says it's safe, but I hope you realize just how far you can trust our elected officials—even our Agnostica politicians need to be kept on a short rein"

Amy set the weighty plates down on the table with enough force to have shattered a lesser vessel. "And that's another thing. How come you and Dad are always talking trash about our government? Whatever happened to, like, patriotism in this

house? 'Agnostica Number One! My half of the USA right or wrong!'"

Phillipa dumped a bag of blue-corn chips into a handwoven Guatemalan basket and carried it to the table. She looked at her daughter as if Amy had suddenly sprouted bat wings. "Now you're just being ridiculous. You know that no one in Agnostica talks or thinks that way. It's only in Faithland that you'll hear people shouting those mindless chants. Our mode of government is based on rationalism and skepticism. It's only through constant questioning of the empirical that—"

Amy rattled a tray of silverware to cover the sound of her mother's voice. "La, la, la, la! Can't hear the semiotic discourse!"

Phillipa didn't pursue the argument, but just frowned and shook her head, then went back to her meal preparations.

A short time later, the Gertslin family assembled for their evening meal. From his seat across the table from Amy, her brother, Hilary, sneered and said, "Hey, shitkicker, pass the tortillas."

Hilary was a smart, wiry tweener who, unlike the others in his family, boasted a natural skin coloration the shade of a dusky plum. Hilary had been adopted by the Gertslins when he was just months old, an African child orphaned during the post-Mugabe chaos in Zimbabwe. He was as much a product of Agnostica as Batch or Phillipa, even down to his given name. Hilary had been named after the politician Hilary Clinton, who, during the year of little Hilary's birth, 2010, had been elected the first president of Agnostica.

Batch objected now to his son's language. "Hilary, I warned you about using that form of address."

"Aw, Dad, it's a compliment. Isn't that right, Amy? You're proud of being a country girl, aren't you? Barefoot and pregnant all the time? Double-wide trailer living? *Coon*-hunting? Am I right?"

Amy shoved her chair backwards and stood up, stiff as a vibrating board. "That did it! I don't have to sit here and be insulted! None of you understand me at all! This bleeding-heart

family sucks! This tight-ass city sucks! This whole peachy, super-sensitive, liberal *country* sucks!"

Fleeing to hide her tears, Amy ran upstairs to her bedroom.

Several hours of sobbing and listening to Alan Jackson and Lee Ann Womack, a long interval during which no one came to console her, convinced Amy of one thing.

She had to run away to Faithland right now. Defect. She couldn't stand to wait a year till she was legally an adult.

But where would she go in that unknown land?

The answer dawned on her almost immediately.

Nashville. The home and source of the music she loved.

Gretchen Wilson was still alive, Amy knew, though the woman had retired from the music business some years ago. Maybe Amy could track her down in Nashville, become her *protégée*....

Amy began packing. She stuffed a few extra clothes into a backpack, along with her favorite plush toy, an alligator bearing a stitched tourist motto from the Everglades, which she had found discarded in a thrift store and named Mr. Taxes. From the closet she grabbed a black cowboy hat. The hat was still crisp and unworn, since too many local people made fun of Amy when she appeared in public wearing it. But where she was going, it would command respect.

While waiting until the rest of her family had gone to sleep, Amy studied road maps on her pocket ViewMaster. It looked like she could pick up Route 35 North to Oklahoma City, then catch Route 40 West and barrel straight on into Nashville.

That is, if she could get past the border.

Two AM, and everyone in the Gertslin home was asleep save Amy.

Out on the lawn, Amy looked back without regret at the only home she had ever known. Goodbye to its solar cells and rain-collecting system, its weedy lawn planted in a water-conserving mix of native plants, its faded political poster from the recent election: RE-ELECT STERLING FOR MAYOR.

Red River Street was quiet. Amy felt as if the neighborhood

was already a ghostly figment of her past.

A few blocks to the west, she knew she could catch one of the hydrogen-fueled mass-transit buses heading north to the city limits, one step closer to the border; the bus-stop was adjacent to the former State House, in a safe neighborhood.

When Austin joined Agnostica in the 2010 division of the USA, renaming itself New Austin, the Texas state capitol had perforce relocated to Houston. Nowadays, the former home of the governor served as the Waldrop Museum and Cultural Center.

Amy had to wait only a few minutes at the bus shelter. It was a little scary to be out alone this late at night, but luckily no one bothered her. The most frightening person she saw was a man with patches of armadillo skin grafted onto his bare arms, and he seemed more concerned with reading a manga on his ViewMaster than in bothering a skinny teenager.

Finally onboard her bus, Amy tried to imagine how she would get past the Customs and Immigration officials at the limits of New Austin.

When the partitioning of the country was first being adjudicated, New Austin had managed to claim an irregular circle of land some sixty miles in diameter around the urban core. This allowed the city to retain many natural attractions and resources, not the least of which was The Salt Lick BBQ Restaurant in Driftwood. Texas could afford to be magnanimous: the chunk was the only tiny bite that Agnostica had managed to take out of the mammoth, imperturbable Faithland corpus of the state.

Route 35 exited New Austin territory at the small burg named Georgetown. There, Amy would have to undergo scrutiny by two sets of inspectors, those of both Agnostica and Faithland. They would ask to see her ID and inquire about her reasons for leaving one country and entering another, demanding her destination and intentions. First, she'd be busted for being an unescorted minor. Even if she could get around that, she had no definite arrangements in Nashville or en route to offer as legitimate support for her trip.

Well, no point in worrying about that now. With the innate optimism of her years, convinced of the rightness of her quest, Amy assumed some option would present itself when she got to the border.

So she sat back, relaxed, and played some George Jones.

At the outskirts of New Austin proper, Amy had to change to the long-range bus for Georgetown, which she did without trouble. Luckily, she had her life savings—five hundred and ten euros—available via her personal chopcard. Amy wasn't sure what the exchange rate for Agnostica euros versus Faithland dollars was at the moment, but she hoped it was favorable.

She fell asleep for the last twenty miles of the bus ride, her head cradled on Mr. Taxes, awaking only when the driver called out via the onboard PA, "End of the line, folks."

Only half-awake, Amy stumbled out.

The Customs and Immigration plaza was a vast expanse of parking-slot-demarcated pavement hosting many restaurants, motels and duty-free shops, as well as some official government buildings. A hundred yards from where her bus had deposited her, near an Au Bon Pain, a single lane of traffic—fairly light at this hour—crawled toward the lone inspection checkpoint that remained open.

Amy went inside the restaurant, hoping to assemble her thoughts. She ordered a *pain chocolat* and a *café au lait*. Sitting at a table near the door, she nursed her refreshments and tried to come up with a scheme to circumvent the inspectors.

After half an hour of pointless cogitation, nothing had revealed itself to her. So she activated her earbuds and began quietly singing along to a Loretta Lynn tune.

A shadow fell across Amy's field of vision, and she looked up to see a man standing by her table.

The fellow was about six feet four, possessed of an enormous red beard matched in impressiveness only by his beer gut. He wore a one-piece outfit that looked like the inner lining of a taikonaut's suit, with various hookups and jacks.

For a moment, Amy was frightened. But then she noticed

that there were tears in the man's eyes.

The stranger seemed to want to address her, so Amy deactivated her iPod to allow them to talk.

"Honey," said the man, "I ain't thought of that song in nigh on fifteen years, since my Mama died. She loved that song, and used to sing it pert near every day. 'Course, she could actually nurse a tune, not strangle it like you. Nonetheless, it done my heart good to hear you attempt it. Pertickly here, 'midst all these Chardonnay-swillers."

Amy chose to ignore the insult to her singing abilities, as well as the blanket categorization of her fellow New Austinites as foreign- wine imbibers—especially since the latter accusation was true. The man seemed friendly enough, and might know some way of getting her across the border.

"Thanks, mister. I'm purely sorry to hear you lost your mama, even iffen it were a hound dog's age ago."

Amy was surprised to find herself falling into the speech patterns and diction of the stranger, a mode of speech that resembled the vernacular of the songs she loved. She had never allowed herself to indulge in such an affectation before, for fear of ridicule by her peers. But now that she had cut loose from her old life, nothing seemed more natural than to talk this way.

"I appreciate the sentiment, little lady." The man extended his hand. "Bib Bogardus is the name, and I hail from Pine Mountain, Georgia. What's yourn?"

"Amy Gertslin."

"Pleased to meet you, Amy." Bib lowered his bulk precariously into a seat at her table. "Now, just call me a nosy nelly if I'm stepping on any toes with my curiosity, but what brings you out to this place all alone at this hour?"

Amy hesitated a minute, then decided to confide everything to this friendly ear.

Bib listened to her story attentively and without condemnation. When she had finished, he said, "Waal, I can't say I'd be totally happy iffen my own daughter upped and hit the road. She's just about your own age, you know. Name of Jerilee. But

I can unnerstand how a young'un has to find her own destiny. Especially when you're trapped in such a hellhole as New Austin. Why, did you know that you can't even buy a Lone Star beer in this whole territory anymore?"

Emboldened by Bib Bogardus's sympathy, Amy leaned toward him. "Is there any way you could help me scoot past these revenooers, Bib? What do you do anyhow? How come you're here?"

"I drive a big rig, Amy. Carrying a load of tomacco from Mexico to Oklahoma City."

"Why, that's just where I'm going! I figure on hitching a ride from there straight to Nashville. I'm gonna try to get into the music biz."

Bib scrached his beard ruminatively. "Hmmm, best you concentrate on being a producer or songwriter, with them pipes. But hail, who'm I to say what you can do, once you put your mind to it. They got plenty of tricks to sweeten up anyone's voice these days. Just look at thet there little Simpson gal. If it weren't for her mother, Ashlee, pushing her, she'd probably be serving grits at a Waffle House. Or whatever similar place they got in Agnostica. Caviar at the French Embassy, I guess."

"So you'll help me?"

Bib got to his feet. "I sure will. C'mon with me, darling."

Amy, holding her pack by the straps, followed Bib outside to Bib's rig, an enormous, streamlined, diesel-powered tractor-trailer combo bearing the proud name *Dixie Belle* on its prow in cherry-red letters. Amy was awed.

"Does this actually run on *fossil fuels*?"

"You bet, honeychile. I know that's an illegal substance in Agnostica, but they give us truckers an exemption so long as we're just passing through. You won't catch me driving one of those water-farting hydrogen creepers, no sir! Take me twice as long just to break even on my routes."

Bib opened the passenger-side door and removed a crinkly silver suit identical to the one he wore.

"Here, darling, slip into this."

"Do I have to get naked?"

Bib laughed. "Well, you would if you were planning to drive 24/7 like yours truly. Then you'd want to be hooked into the *Dixie Belle's* waste-recycling system, epidermal scrubber, nutrient feeds and booster drips. But since we're only gonna use this suit to fool the *federales*, it just needs access to one of your veins. So roll up your right sleeve."

Amy did as requested, then snugged into the suit, which seamed invisibly at the rear and automatically shrunk to fit her. Then she and Bib got into the tractor cab.

"Wow! This looks like the inside of the *Long March* Mars ship!"

"Waal, we ain't going quite so far as Mars, but I do believe in comfort and technology. Jack yerself in at that port there—"

Once Amy's suit was plugged into the dash, she felt a deft pinprick on her arm. She worried for an instant that Bib was going to drug her and deliver her to the harem of some Yemeni prince. But when nothing happened to her as the big man started the mighty yet purring engine of the truck, she relaxed.

"Just let me do the talking at Customs, 'kay?"

"Sure."

The *Dixie Belle* ambled throatily up to the crossing.

On the New Austin side, the border was protected by a variety of biological barricades, many of them with Batchelder Bioengineering pedigrees: hedges of thorny plants, troops of fire ants, pods of mini-shoggoths. On the Georgetown, Faithland, side, the barriers were strictly inanimate: robot lenses and gun muzzles, monomolecular wire, gluball anti-personnel mines. This natural-artificial interface was as clear a political state-ment of the differences between Agnostica and Faithland as any tract.

Two New Austin inspectors came up to the stopped truck. The first, a short, stocky Latina, led a redacted dog, a Rhodesian Ridgeback with a hypertrophied snout. This mutant canine proceeded to sniff all around the tractor and trailer, while the women inspected the intelligent seals placed on the trailer at its

point of origin. The second inspector, an African-Agnostican with a jaunty goatee, came around to Bib's door.

"Blood sample, please."

"Sure thing, officer." Bib extended his hand and pressed his thumb into the sampling pad on the inspector's ViewMaster. Then the guardian of the gates came around to Amy's side, and she did the same, stifling her reluctance to reveal her identity.

Surely the game was up now...?

In a few seconds, both inspectors seemed satisfied.

"You and your daughter go safe now, Mr. Bogardus."

"Will do, *compadre!*"

Once through the New Austin arch, the *Dixie Belle* sailed beyond the corresponding Georgetown gate and its comparable procedures just as easily.

Once they were a few miles down Route 35, Amy finally felt it was safe to speak.

"'Daughter?' How did you—?"

Bib patted the dashboard affectionately. "The ol' *Dixie Belle* has a handful of useful genomic codes on file. She just injected you with a batch of silicrobes that had a tropism for the cells of your thumb. Once they got there, they started scavagening up all your original blood cells and making replacement blood with different DNA in it. For a second or two, your thumb belonged to somebody else. Then they put everything right again and croaked. Otherwise, you woulda had one helluva immune reaction."

Now that Bib had explained things to her, Amy could sense a faint soreness in her thumb. "Oh. So I can't pull that trick again?"

"Nuh-huh. Not unless you're hooked up to the *Dixie Belle*. 'Fraid you're on your own otherwise."

"Well, I guess I'll just have to hope I don't have any more run-ins with the *federales* on my way to Nashville."

"Not too likely. Faithland's perty quiet these days on the homeland security front, ever since President O'Reilly unleashed that sweet little global virus."

Amy remembered learning about this Faithland anti-terrorist measure in school. Forgetting to employ her new accent and diction, she said, "You mean the Glowworm Patch? The one that spreads by touch and retroengineers into humans a luciferase gene that's activated by certain high-order brain chemistry patterns?"

"That's the one, honeychile. Mighty hard to commit terrorism when thinking about it make you glow bright blue in public."

Amy gave vent to a huge yawn at this point.

Bib regarded Amy tenderly. He paid no attention to the road, since the *Dixie Belle* was on cyber-control. "Maybe you should get some sleep now, honeychile."

"You wouldn't mind...?"

"No, I'll just punch up some Government Mule in my earbuds and do my road-warrior thing."

"'Kay. Thanks...."

Before she knew it, Amy was asleep.

When she awoke, daylight reigned outside, and they were approaching a major metropolitan area.

"Is that—?"

"Oklahoma City? Sure enough. Here's where you and me gotta part ways, I fear. I'm gonna drop you off at the Grayhound terminal. I figger you prolly got enough cash for a ticket to Nashville. Or do you need some bits on your chop?"

"No, no, I'm all set, Bib. Thank you so much for all you've done. You been—you been sweeter to me than mama's ice tea."

"Waal, Amy, you done reminded me of my own little princess, so warn't no way in God's creation I could let you be disappointed. You take care now, y'hear, on the rest of your trip. Faithland's a mighty safe place for the most part, but there's always folks out there looking to score."

Stripped of the truck's passenger suit, wearing her backpack, Amy stood on the sidewalk outside the bus terminal, waving goodbye to the *Dixie Belle*.

So much for all the horrible things the Agnosticans liked to say about the Faithlanders. Amy felt confirmed in her decision

to leave the elite enclave into which she had been born.

She looked around now at the streets of the first Faithland city she had ever visited, expecting to see immense differences from home. Truth to tell, however, many of the same franchises occupied various storefronts, although a few names were new to her. She wondered if JENNA'S PEIGNOIRS was equivalent to VICTORIA'S SECRET.

It would've been nice to explore a little, but Nashville beckoned.

The ticket to Nashville took almost fifty of Amy's euros, which she exchanged for forty dollars at an ATM in the terminal. She even had a few dollars left over for breakfast at the terminal cafe.

A few hours later, Amy was on her bus, heading east. She had taken what appeared to be the seat with possibly the most congenial companion: an Asian woman not much older than Amy herself. Although conventionally pretty, the woman had chosen to downplay her looks with a lack of makeup, severe hairstyle and drab clothing.

After a dozen miles of mutual silence, the woman turned to Amy and introduced herself in a perky manner.

"Hi, there, my name's Cindy Lou Hu."

The woman's English was excellent, but accented. After Amy volunteered her own name, she asked, "Are you from, like, another country?"

"Yes, of course. Shanghai, China. I'm here to visit Brother Ray's Gospel Mission in Nashville."

"Huh?"

Cindy Lou explained that her family had been evangelical Christians for two generations, ever since adopting the creed from American missionaries. Now she was returning to the source of her faith for instruction in spreading the gospel even further.

"Faith is one of your country's last, best exports. No one sells religion abroad like Faithland. Brother Ray and his peers are everywhere around the world. They might assign me to Latin

America or Africa or Mongolia even. It all depends. Wherever I can do the most good bringing the word of Jesus to unbelievers. Are you a believer, Amy?"

Amy began to squirm. This kind of conversation was never encountered in Agnostica. "Uh, well, I guess I'm kind of a, um, secular humanist."

Cindy Lou's smile did not waver, but definitely acquired a steely gleam. "Oh, you must read some of these tracts I happen to have with me. Right now. And then we'll talk about them. We've got *tons* of time."

Fifteen hours later, as the bus pulled into Nashville, Amy's brain felt as if it had been extracted, pureed and reinserted into her skull. She was convinced that the friendly "dialogue" on Jesus and all matters Biblical that Cindy Lou had subjected her to was a form of torture banned by the Geneva Convention.

Still, Amy had not crumbled. She managed to refuse Cindy Lou's repeated importunings to stay at Brother Ray's mission. And engaging in a mass baptism was definitely ruled out. So as the two women parted around midnight outside the Nashville terminal, Amy was finally left extensively on her own, for the first time since she had escaped from New Austin.

The first thing she did was find cheap lodgings with her ViewMaster. In the Ikea capsule hotel on Commerce, not far from the Cumberland River, Amy gratefully rested her head on her thin pillow the size of a handkerchief—a Snööli, according to its label—knowing that she was only a short distance away from all the famous musical sites she had come so far to see.

And perhaps close in time as well to a career in music.

The next morning Amy was up early, eager to see all the attractions that Nashville had to offer. Surely by nightfall she would have connected through some magical serendipity with the forces that would transform her life and allow her musical talent to blossom.

The first place she intended to visit after breakfast was Music Row, the district where all the famous recording studios thrived. Here had so many of her favorite songs been digitized. The side-

walks practically gleamed golden with glory in Amy's mind.

But when Amy arrived at Music Row, she quickly found the district to be a hollow recreation of what she had envisioned, a series of museums and shops without any professional musicians around at all. Only fatuous tour guides and sullen giftshop cashiers afforded any connection to the fabulous heritage of Nashville.

A few simple inquiries soon revealed that Music Row had been obsoleted about ten years ago, by the ultimate perfection of home-recording software and the changed nature of music distribution. Music Row was now distributed unevenly across all of Faithland, in a thousand garages and bedrooms, of tract houses and mansions alike.

Saddened but still hopeful after touring the simulated remnants of the district, Amy decided to treat herself to some barbecue. She found a place called Hog Heaven on 27th Street and walked the long blocks there. But the meal disagreed with her. Tennessee barbecue, it turned out, wasn't anything like New Austin's. Weird sauces, weird coleslaw, weird beans, weird cornbread.

But even this disappointing repast failed to dim Amy's excitement at the thought of what awaited her tonight. The Grand Ole Opry was performing in the historic Ryman auditorium, and she had snagged a cheap ticket with her ViewMaster.

Amy spent the remainder of the afternoon strolling around the clean and pretty city. She listened to the locals talk, working on her own accent. Despite a few letdowns, Amy felt sure she would still settle here. There must be a club scene through which she could meet like-minded fans and aspiring artists.

A brief nap back in her hotel room refreshed her for the Opry.

At the theater, Amy debated buying some snacks to serve in lieu of supper. But her money was rapidly dwindling, and she held out despite the grumblings of her stomach.

Inside, Amy settled into her seat, full of anticipation. Even the snickers of some nearby girls her own age—who apparently had nothing better to do than make fun of Amy's outfit—failed

to quash her fervor.

But with the very first act, her faith evaporated, and she knew she was in for heartache.

None of these performers were familiar to her. Favoring the old-time classic singers, Amy had not kept up with the latest voices and faces. Still, she could have become emotionally invested in their songs if they hadn't been all tarted up with synthetic sounds and pop arrangements. Where was the soul and heart of a Willie Nelson or Hank Williams III? Nowhere, it was obvious by intermission.

Amy didn't even stay for the rest of the show, but instead trudged downheartedly back to her hotel, where she deluged Mr. Taxes with a monsoon of tears.

In the morning, Amy realized she had one last place to go that would reaffirm her connection with this city, would justify her arduous trip here, would inspire her future course.

The Country Music Hall of Fame.

With a lighter step, Amy hurried down to the corner of Demonbreun and 5th, arriving just as the museum opened.

She went immediately to the Gretchen Wilson exhibit.

Gretchen, Amy knew, had retired five years ago, after a long and fruitful career. But perhaps the exhibit would contain updated information about her current whereabouts (surely Gretchen still called Nashville home). Or perhaps—hope sprang eternal—there would be notice of a comeback tour.

At the Gretchen Wilson display, Amy synced her ViewMaster with the kiosk there and brought up onto her screen all the information the Country Music Hall of Fame had to offer on her heroine. The digital guide's voice came through her earbuds.

"Since retiring from the road, Gretchen Wilson has invested much of her wealth in Batchelder Bioengineering and now resides in New Austin where she can more closely monitor her business affairs...."

Amy found herself out on the sidewalk without any memory of having exited the museum. For a long time she just stood rooted to the spot as foot traffic surged around her. Then she

turned toward her hotel to reclaim her pack and check out.

As she walked, she punched up some Johnny Cash.

"Lead me gently home, father, lead me gently home…."

FEMAVILLE 29

La Palma is a tiny mote in the Canary Islands, a mote that had certainly never intruded into my awareness before one fateful day. On La Palma, five hundred billion tons of rock in the form of an unstable coastal plateau awaited a nudge, which they received when the Cumbre Vieja volcano erupted. Into the sea a good portion of the plateau plunged, a frightful hammer of the gods.

The peeling off of the face of the island was a smaller magnitude event than had been feared; but it was a larger magnitude event than anyone was prepared for.

The resulting tsunami raced across the Atlantic.

My city had gotten just twelve hours warning. The surreal chaos of the partial evacuation was like living through the most vivid nightmare or disaster film imaginable. Still, the efforts of the authorities and volunteers and good Samaritans ensured that hundreds of thousands of people escaped with their lives.

Leaving other hundreds of thousands to face the wave.

Their only recourse was to find the tallest, strongest buildings and huddle.

I was on the seventh floor of an insurance company when the wave arrived. Posters in the reception area informed me that I was in good hands. I had a view of the harbor, half a mile away.

The tsunami looked like a liquid mountain mounted on a rocket sled.

When the wave hit, the building shuddered and bellowed like a steer in an abattoir euthanized with a nail-gun. Every window

popped out of its frame, and spray lashed even my level.

But the real fight for survival had not yet begun.

The next several days were a sleepless blur of crawling from the wreckage and helping others do likewise.

But not everyone was on the same side. Looters arose like some old biological paradigm of spontaneous generation from the muck.

Their presence demanded mine on the front lines.

I was a cop.

I had arrested several bad guys without any need for excessive force. But then came a shootout at a jewelry store where the display cases were incongruously draped with drying kelp. I ended up taking the perps down okay. But the firefight left my weary brain and trembling gut hypersensitive to any threat.

Some indeterminate time afterwards—marked by a succession of candy-bar meals, digging under the floodlights powered by chuffing generators, and endless slogging through slimed streets—I was working my way through the upper floors of an apartment complex, looking for survivors. I shut off my flashlight when I saw a glow around a corner. Someone stepped between me and the light source, casting the shadow of a man with a gun. I yelled, "Police! Drop it!", then crouched and dashed toward the gunman. The figure stepped forward, still holding the weapon, and I fired.

The boy was twelve, his weapon a water pistol.

His mother trailed him by a few feet—not far enough to escape getting splattered with her son's blood.

Later I learned neither of them spoke a word of English.

One minute I was cradling the boy, and the next I was lying on a cot in a field hospital. Three days had gotten lost somewhere. Three days in which the whole world had learned of my mistake.

They let me get up the next day, ostensibly healthy and sane enough, even though my pistol hand, my left, still exhibited a bad tremor. I tried to report to the police command, but found

that I had earned a temporary medical discharge. Any legal fallout from my actions awaited an end to the crisis.

I tried being a civilian volunteer for another day or two amidst the ruins, but my heart wasn't in it. So I took the offer of evacuation to Femaville 29.

*　*　*　*　*　*　*

The first week after the disaster actually manifested aspects of an odd, enforced vacation. Or rather, the atmosphere often felt more like an open-ended New Year's Eve, the portal to some as-yet undefined millennium where all our good resolutions would come to pass. Once we victims emerged from the shock of losing everything we owned, including our shared identity as citizens of a large East Coast city, my fellow refugees and I began to exhibit a near-manic optimism in the face of the massive slate-cleaning.

The uplift was not to last. But while it prevailed, it was as if some secret imperative in the depths of our souls—a wish to be unburdened of all our draggy pasts—had been fulfilled by cosmic fiat, without our having to lift a finger.

We had been given a chance to start all over, remake our lives afresh, and we were, for the most part, eager to grasp the offered personal remodeling.

Everyone in the swiftly erected encampment of a thousand men, women and children was healthy. The truly injured had all been airlifted to hospitals around the state and nation. Families had been reunited, even down to pets. The tents we were inhabiting were spacious, weather-tight and wired for electricity and entertainment. Meals were plentiful, albeit uninspired, served promptly in three shifts, thrice daily, in a large communal pavilion.

True, the lavatories and showers were also communal, and the lack of privacy grated a bit right from the start. Trudging through the chilly dark in the middle of the night to take a leak held limited appeal, even when you pretended you were camping.

And winter, with its more challenging conditions, loomed only a few months away. Moreover, enforced idleness chafed those of us who were used to steady work. Lack of proper schooling for the scores of kids in the camp worried many parents.

But taken all in all, the atmosphere at the camp—christened with no more imaginative bureaucratic name than Femaville Number 29—was suffused with potential that first week.

My own interview with the FEMA intake authorities in the first days of the relocation was typical.

The late September sunlight warmed the interview tent so much that the canvas sides had been rolled up to admit fresh air scented with faint, not unpleasant maritime odors of decay. Even though Femaville 29 was located far inland—or what used to be far inland before the tsunami—the wrack left behind by the disaster lay not many miles away.

For a moment, I pictured exotic fish swimming through the streets and subways of my old city, weaving their paths among cars, couches and corpses. The imagery unsettled me, and I tried to focus on the more hopeful present.

The long tent hosted ranks of paired folding chairs, each chair facing its mate. The FEMA workers, armed with laptop computers, occupied one seat of each pair, while an interviewee sat in the other. The subdued mass interrogation and the clicking of keys raised a surprisingly dense net of sound that overlaid the noises from outside the tent: children roistering, adults gossiping, birds chattering. Outside the tent, multiple lines of refugees stretched away, awaiting their turns.

The official seated across from me was a pretty young African-American woman whose name-badge proclaimed her HANNAH LAWES. Unfortunately, she reminded me of my ex-wife, Calley, hard in the same places Calley was hard. I tried to suppress an immediate dislike of her. As soon as I sat down, Hannah Lawes expressed rote sympathy for my plight, a commiseration worn featureless by its hundredth repetition. Then she got down to business.

"Name?"

"Parrish Hedges."

"Any relatives in the disaster zone?"

"No, ma'am."

"What was your job back in the city?"

I felt my face heat up. But I had no choice, except to answer truthfully.

"I was a police officer, ma'am."

That answer gave Hannah Lawes pause. Finally, she asked in an accusatory fashion, "Shouldn't you still be on duty then? Helping with security in the ruins?"

My left hand started to quiver a bit, but I suppressed it so that I didn't think she noticed.

"Medical exemption, ma'am."

Hannah Lawes frowned slightly and said, "I hope you don't mind if I take a moment to confirm that, Mr. Hedges."

Her slim, manicured fingers danced over her keyboard, dragging my data down the airwaves. I studied the plywood floor of the tent while she read my file.

When I looked up, her face had gone disdainful.

"This explains much, Mr. Hedges."

"Can we move on, please?"

As if I ever could.

Hannah Lawes resumed her programmed spiel. "All right, let's talk about your options now...."

For the next few minutes, she outlined the various programs and handouts and incentives that the government and private charities and NGO's had lined up for the victims of the disaster. Somehow, none of the choices really matched my dreams and expectations engendered by the all-consuming catastrophe. All of them involved relocating to some other part of the country, leaving behind the shattered chaos of the East Coast. And that was something I just wasn't ready for yet, inevitable as such a move was.

And besides, choosing any one particular path would have meant foregoing all the others. Leaving this indeterminate interzone of infinite possibility would lock me into a new life

that might be better than my old one, but would still be fixed, crystallized, frozen into place.

"Do I have to decide right now?"

"No, no, of course not."

I stood up to go, and Hannah Lawes added, "But you realize, naturally, that this camp was never intended as a long-term residence. It's only transitional, and will be closed down at some point not too far in the future."

"Yeah, sure," I said. "We're all just passing through. I get it."

I left then and made way for the next person waiting in line.

* * * * * * *

The tents of Femaville 29 were arranged along five main dirt avenues, each as wide as a city boulevard. Expressing the same ingenuity that had dubbed our whole encampment, the avenues were labeled A, B, C, D and E. Every three tents, a numbered cross-street occurred. The tents of one avenue backed up against the tents of the adjacent avenue, so that a cross-block was two tents wide. The land where Femaville 29 was pitched was flat and treeless and covered in newly mowed weeds and grasses. Beyond the borders of our village stretched a mix of forest, scrubby fields and swamp, eventually giving way to rolling hills. The nearest real town was about ten miles away, and there was no regular transportation there other than by foot.

As I walked up Avenue D toward my tent (D-30), I encountered dozens of my fellow refugees who were finished with the intake process. Only two days had passed since the majority of us had been ferried here in commandeered school buses. People—the adults, anyhow—were still busy exchanging their stories—thrilling, horrific or mundane—about how they had escaped the tsunami or dealt with the aftermath.

I didn't have any interest in repeating my tale, so I didn't join in any such conversations.

As for the children, they seemed mostly to have flexibly put behind them all the trauma they must have witnessed. Reveling

in their present freedom from boring routine, they raced up and down the avenues in squealing packs.

Already, the seasonally withered grass of the avenues was becoming dusty ruts. Just days old, this temporary village, I could feel, was already beginning to lose its freshness and ambiance of novelty.

Under the unseasonably warm sun, I began to sweat. A cold beer would have tasted good right now. But the rules of Femaville 29 prohibited alcohol.

I reached my tent and went inside.

My randomly assigned roommate lay on his bunk. Given how the disaster had shattered and stirred the neighborhoods of the city, it was amazing that I actually knew the fellow from before. I had encountered no one else yet in the camp who was familiar to me. And out of all my old friends and acquaintances and co-workers, Ethan Duplessix would have been my last choice to be reunited with.

Ethan was a fat, bristled slob with a long criminal record of petty theft, fraud and advanced mopery. His personal grooming habits were so atrocious that he had emerged from the disaster more or less in the same condition he entered it, unlike the rest of the survivors who had gone from well-groomed to uncommonly bedraggled and smelly.

Ethan and I had crossed paths often, and I had locked him up more times than I could count. (When the tsunami struck, he had been amazingly free of outstanding charges.) But the new circumstances of our lives, including Ethan's knowledge of how I had "retired" from the force, placed us now on a different footing.

"Hey, Hedges, how'd it go? They got you a new job yet? Maybe security guard at a kindergarten!"

I didn't bother replying, but just flopped down on my bunk. Ethan chuckled meanly at his own paltry wit for a while, but when I didn't respond, he eventually fell silent, his attentions taken up by a tattered copy of *Maxim*.

I closed my eyes and drowsed for a while, until I got hungry.

Then I got up and went to the refectory.

That day they were serving hamburgers and fries for the third day in a row. Mickey Dee's seemed to have gotten a lock on the contract to supply the camp. I took mine to an empty table. Head bowed, halfway through my meal, I sensed someone standing beside me.

The woman's curly black hair descended to her shoulders in a tumbled mass. Her face resembled a cameo in its alabaster fineness.

"Mind if I sit here?" she said.

"Sure. I mean, go for it."

The simple but primordial movements of her legs swinging over the bench seat and her ass settling down awakened emotions in me that had been absent since Calley's abrupt leave-taking.

"Nia Horsley. Used to live over on Garden Parkway."

"Nice district."

Nia snorted, a surprisingly enjoyable sound. "Yeah, once."

"I never got over there much. Worked in East Grove. Had an apartment on Oakeshott."

"And what would the name on your doorbell have been?"

"Oh, sorry. Parrish Hedges."

"Pleased to meet you, Parrish."

We shook hands. Hers was small but strong, enshelled in mine like a pearl.

For the next two hours, through two more shifts of diners coming and going, we talked, exchanging condensed life stories, right up to the day of disaster and down to our arrival at Femaville 29. Maybe the accounts were edited for maximum appeal, but I intuitively felt she and I were being honest nonetheless. When the refectory workers finally shooed us out in order to clean up for supper, I felt as if I had known Nia for two weeks, two months, two years—

She must have felt the same. As we strolled away down Avenue B, she held my hand.

"I don't have a roomie in my tent."

"Oh?"

"It's just me and my daughter. Luck of the draw, I guess."

"I like kids. Never had any, but I like 'em."

"Her name's Izzy. Short for Isabel. You'll get to meet her. But maybe not just yet."

"How come?"

"She's made a lot of new friends. They stay out all day, playing on the edge of the camp. Some kind of weird new game they invented."

"We could go check up on her, and I could say hello."

Nia squeezed my hand. "Maybe not right this minute."

* * * * * * *

I got to meet Izzy the day after Nia and I slept together. I suppose I could've hung around till Izzy came home for supper, but the intimacy with Nia, after such a desert of personal isolation, left me feeling a little disoriented and pressured. So I made a polite excuse for my departure, which Nia accepted with good grace, and arranged to meet mother and daughter for breakfast.

Izzy bounced into the refectory ahead of her mother. She was seven or eight, long-limbed and fair-haired in contrast to her mother's compact, raven-haired paleness, but sharing Nia's high-cheeked bone structure. I conjectured backward to a gangly blond father.

The little girl zeroed in on me somehow out of the whole busy dining hall, racing up to where I sat, only to slam on the brakes with alarming precipitousness.

"You're Mr. Hedges!" she informed me and the world.

"Yes, I am. And you're Izzy."

I was ready to shake her hand in a formal adult manner. But then she exclaimed, "You made my Mom all smiley!" and launched herself into my awkward embrace.

Before I could really respond, she was gone, heading for the self-service cereal line.

I looked at Nia, who was grinning.

"And this," I asked, "is her baseline?"

"Precisely. When she's really excited—"

"I'll wear one of those padded suits we used for training the K-9 squad."

Nia's expression altered to one of seriousness and sympathy, and I instantly knew what was coming. I cringed inside, if not where it showed. She sat down next to me and put a hand on my arm.

"Parrish, I admit I did a little Googling on you after we split yesterday, over at the online tent. I know about why you aren't a cop anymore. And I just want to say that—"

Before she could finish, Izzy materialized out of nowhere, bearing a tray holding two bowls of Technicolor puffs swimming in chocolate milk, and slipped herself between us slick as a greased eel.

"They're almost out of food! You better hurry!" With a plastic knife, Izzy began slicing a peeled banana into chunks thick as Oreos that plopped with alarming splashes into her bowls.

I stood up gratefully. "I'll get us something, Nia. Eggs and bacon and toast okay?"

She gave me a look which said that she could wait to talk. "Sure."

During breakfast, Nia and I mostly listened to Izzy's chatter.

"—and then Vonique's all like, 'But the way I remember it is the towers were next to the harbor, not near the zoo.' And Eddie goes, 'Na-huh, they were right where the park started.' And they couldn't agree and they were gonna start a fight, until I figured out that they were talking about two different places! Vonique meant the Goblin Towers, and Eddie meant the Towers of Bone! So I straightened them out, and now the map of Djamala is like almost half done!"

"That's wonderful, honey."

"It's a real skill, being a peacemaker like that."

Izzy cocked her head and regarded me quizzically. "But that's just what I've always been forever."

In the next instant she was up and kissing her mother, then out the hall and raising puffs of dust as she ran toward where I

could see other kids seemingly waiting for her.

Nia and I spent the morning wandering around the camp, talking about anything and everything—except my ancient, recent disgrace. We watched a pickup soccer game for an hour or so, the players expending the bottled energy that would have gone to work and home before the disaster, then ended up back at her tent around three.

Today was as warm as yesterday, and we raised a pretty good sweat. Nia dropped off to sleep right after, but I couldn't.

Eleven days after the flood, and it was all I could dream about.

* * * * * * *

Ethan was really starting to get on my nerves. He had seen me hanging out with Nia and Izzy, and used the new knowledge to taunt me.

"What's up with you and the little girl, Hedges? Thinking of keeping your hand in with some target practice?"

I stood quivering over his bunk before I even realized I had moved. My fists were bunched at my hips, ready to strike. But both Ethan and I knew I wouldn't.

The penalty for fighting at any of the Femavilles was instant expulsion, and an end to government charity. I couldn't risk losing Nia now that I had found her. Even if we managed to stay in touch while apart, who was to say that the fluid milieu of the post-disaster environment would not conspire to supplant our relationship with another.

So I stalked out and went to see Hannah Lawes.

One complex of tents hosted the bureaucrats. Lawes sat at a folding table with her omnipresent laptop. Hooked to a printer, the machine was churning out travel vouchers branded with official glyphs of authenticity.

"Mr. Hedges. What can I do for you? Have you decided to take up one of the host offerings? There's a farming community in Nebraska—"

I shook my head in the negative. Trying to imagine myself relocated to the prairies was so disorienting that I almost forgot why I had come here.

Hannah Lawes seemed disappointed by my refusal of her proposal, but realistic about the odds that I would've accepted. "I can't say I'm surprised. Not many people are leaping at what I can offer. I've only gotten three takers so far. And I can't figure out why. They're all generous, sensible berths."

"Yeah, sure. That's the problem."

"What do you mean?"

"No one wants 'sensible' after what they've been through. We all want to be reborn as phoenixes—not dray horses. That's all that would justify our sufferings."

Hannah Lawes said nothing for a moment, and only the minor whine of the printer filigreed the bubble of silence around us. When she spoke, her voice was utterly neutral.

"You could die here before you achieve that dream, Mr. Hedges. Now, how can I help you, if not with a permanent relocation?"

"If I arrange different living quarters with the consent of everyone involved, is there any regulation stopping me from switching tents?"

"No, not at all."

"Good. I'll be back."

I tracked down Nia and found her using a piece of exercise equipment donated by a local gym. She hopped off and hugged me.

"Have to do something about my weight. I'm not used to all this lolling around."

Nia had been a waitress back in the city, physically active eight or more hours daily. My own routines, at least since Calley left me, had involved more couch-potato time than mountain climbing, and the sloth of camp life sat easier on me.

We hugged, her body sweaty in my arms, and I explained my problem.

"I realize we haven't known each other very long, Nia, but

do you think—"

"I'd like it if you moved in with Izzy and me, Parrish. One thing the tsunami taught us—life's too short to dither. And I'd feel safer."

"No one's been bothering you, have they?"

"No, but there's just too many weird noises out here in the country. Every time a branch creaks, I think someone's climbing my steps."

I hugged her again, harder, in wordless thanks.

We both went back to Lawes and arranged the new tent assignments.

When I went to collect my few possessions, Ethan sneered at me.

"Knew you'd run, Hedges. Without your badge, you're nothing."

As I left, I wondered what I had been even with my badge.

* * * * * * *

Living with Nia and Izzy, I naturally became more involved in the young girl's activities.

And that's when I learned about Djamala.

By the end of the second week in Femaville 29, the atmosphere had begun to sour. The false exuberance engendered by sheer survival amidst so much death—and the accompanying sense of newly opened horizons—had dissipated. In place of these emotions came anomie, irritability, anger, despair, and a host of other negative feelings. The immutable, unchanging confines of the unfenced camp assumed the proportions of a stalag. The food, objectively unchanged in quality or quantity, met with disgust, simply because we had no control over its creation. The shared privies assumed a stink no amount of bleach could dispel.

Mere conversation and gossip had paled, replaced with disproportionate arguments over inconsequentials. Sports gave way to various games of chance, played with the odd pair of

dice or deck of cards, with bets denominated in sex or clothing or desserts.

One or two serious fights resulted in the promised expulsions, and, chastened but surly, combatants restrained themselves to shoving matches and catcalls.

A few refugees, eager for stimulation and a sense of normality, made the long trek into town—and found themselves returned courtesy of local police cars.

The bureaucrats managing the camp—Hannah Lawes and her peers—were not immune to the shifting psychic tenor of Femaville 29. From models of optimism and can-do effectiveness, the officials began to slide into terse minimalist responses.

"I don't know what more we can do," Hannah Lawes told me. "If our best efforts to reintegrate everyone as functioning and productive members of society are not appreciated, then—"

She left the consequences unstated, merely shaking her head ruefully at our ingratitude and sloth.

The one exception to this general malaise were the children.

Out of a thousand people in Femaville 29, approximately two hundred were children younger than twelve. Although sometimes their numbers seemed larger, as they raced through the camp's streets and avenues in boisterous packs. Seemingly unaffected by the unease and dissatisfaction exhibited by their guardians and parents, the kids continued to enjoy their pastoral interlude. School, curfews, piano lessons—all shed in a return to a prelapsarian existence as hunter-gatherers of the twenty-first century.

When they weren't involved in traditional games, they massed on the outskirts of the camp for an utterly novel undertaking.

There, I discovered, they were building a new city to replace the one they had lost.

Or, perhaps, simply mapping one that already existed.

And Izzy Horsley, I soon learned (with actually very little surprise), was one of the prime movers of this jovial, juvenile enterprise.

With no tools other than their feet and hands, the children had cleared a space almost as big as a football field of all vegetation, leaving behind a dusty canvas on which to construct their representation of an imaginary city.

Three weeks into its construction, the map-cum-model had assumed impressive dimensions, despite the rudimentary nature of its materials.

I came for the first time to the site one afternoon when I grew tired of continuously keeping Nia company in the exercise tent. Her own angst about ensuring the best future for herself and loved ones had manifested as an obsession with "keeping fit" that I couldn't force myself to share. With my mind drifting, a sudden curiosity about where Izzy was spending so much of her time stole over me, and I ambled over to investigate.

Past the ultimate tents, I came upon what could have been a construction site reimagined for the underage cast of *Sesame Street*.

The youngest children were busy assembling stockpiles of stones and twigs and leaves. The stones were quarried from the immediate vicinity, emerging still wet with loam, while sticks and leaves came from a nearby copse in long disorderly caravans.

Older children were engaged in two different kinds of tasks. One chore involved using long pointed sticks to gouge lines in the dirt: lines that plainly marked streets, natural features and the outlines of buildings. The second set of workers was elaborating these outlines with the organic materials from the stockpiles. The map was mostly flat, but occasionally a structure, teepee or cairn, rose up a few inches.

The last, smallest subset of workers were the architects: the designers, engineers, imagineers of the city. They stood off to one side, consulting, arguing, issuing orders, and sometimes venturing right into the map to correct the placement of lines or ornamentation.

Izzy was one of these elite.

Deep in discussion with a corn-rowed black girl and a pudgy

white boy wearing smudged glasses, Izzy failed to note my approach, and so I was able to overhear their talk. Izzy was holding forth at the moment.

"—Sprankle Hall covers two whole blocks, not just one! C'mon, you gotta remember that! Remember when we went there for a concert, and after we wanted to go around back to the door where the musicians were coming out, and how long it took us to get there?"

The black girl frowned, then said, "Yeah, right, we had to walk like forever. But if Sprankle Hall goes from Cleverly Street all the way to Khush Lane, then how does Pinemarten Avenue run without a break?"

The fat boy spoke with assurance. "It's the Redondo Tunnel. Goes under Sprankle Hall."

Izzy and the black girl grinned broadly. "Of course! I remember when that was built!"

I must have made some noise then, for the children finally noticed me. Izzy rushed over and gave me a quick embrace.

"Hey, Parrish! What're you doing here?"

"I came to see what was keeping you guys so busy. What's going on here?"

Izzy's voice expressed no adult embarrassment, doubt, irony or blasé dismissal of a temporary time-killing project. "We're building a city! Djamala! It's someplace wonderful!"

The black girl nodded solemnly. I recalled the name Vonique from Izzy's earlier conversation, and the name seemed suddenly inextricably linked to this child.

"Well," said Vonique, "it *will* be wonderful, once we finish it. But right now it's still a *mess*."

"This city—Djamala? How did it come to be? Who invented it?"

"Nobody *invented* it!" Izzy exclaimed. "It's always been there. We just couldn't remember it until the wave."

The boy—Eddie?—said, "That's right, sir. The tsunami made it rise up."

"Rise up? Out of the waters, like Atlantis? A new continent?"

Eddie pushed his glasses further up his nose. "Not out of the ocean. Out of our minds."

My expression must have betrayed disbelief. Izzy grabbed one of my hands with both of hers. "Parrish, please! This is really important for everyone. You gotta believe in Djamala! Really!"

"Well, I don't know if I *can* believe in it the same way you kids can. But what if I promise just not to *dis*believe yet? Would that be good enough?"

Vonique puffed air past her lips in a semi-contemptuous manner. "Huh! I suppose that's as good as we're gonna get from anyone, until we can show them something they can't ignore."

Izzy gazed up at me with imploring eyes. "Parrish? You're not gonna let us down, are you?"

What could I say? "No, no, of course not. If I can watch and learn, maybe I can start to understand."

Izzy, Vonique, and Eddie had to confer with several other pint-sized architects before they could grant me observer's status, but eventually they did confer that honor on me.

So for the next several days I spent most of my time with the children as they constructed their imaginary metropolis.

At first, I was convinced that the whole process was merely some over-elaborated coping strategy for dealing with the disaster that had upended their young lives.

But at the end of a week, I was not so certain.

So long as I did not get in the way of construction, I was allowed to venture down the outlined HO-scale streets, given a tour of the city's extensive features and history by whatever young engineer was least in demand at the moment. The story of Djamala's ancient founding, its history and contemporary life, struck me as remarkably coherent and consistent at the time, although I did not pay as much attention as I should have to the information. I theorized then that the children were merely re-sorting a thousand borrowed bits and pieces from television, films and video games. Now, I can barely recall a few salient details. The Crypt of the Thousand Martyrs, the Bluepoint

Aerial Tramway, Penton Park, Winkelreed Slough, Mid-winter Festival, the Squid Club— These proper names, delivered in the pure, piping voices of Izzy and her peers, are all that remain to me.

I wished I could get an aerial perspective on the diagram of Djamala. It seemed impossibly refined and balanced to have been plotted out solely from a ground-level perspective. Like the South American drawings at Nazca, its complex lineaments seemed to demand a superior view from some impossible, more-than-mortal vantage point.

After a week spent observing the children—a week during which a light evening rain shower did much damage to Djamala, damage which the children industriously and cheerfully began repairing—a curious visual hallucination overtook me.

Late afternoon sunlight slanted across the map of Djamala as the children began to tidy up in preparation for quitting. Sitting on a borrowed folding chair, I watched their small forms, dusted in gold, move along eccentric paths. My mind commenced to drift amidst wordless regions. The burden of my own body seemed to fall away.

At that moment, the city of Djamala began to assume a ghostly reality, translucent buildings rearing skyward. Ghostly minarets, stadia, pylons—

I jumped up, heart thumping to escape my chest, frightened to my core.

Memory of a rubbish-filled, clammy, partially illuminated hallway, and the shadow of a gunman, pierced me.

My senses had betrayed me fatally once before. How could I ever fully trust them again?

Djamala vanished then, and I was relieved.

* * * * * * *

A herd of government-drafted school buses materialized one Thursday on the outskirts of Femaville 29, on the opposite side of the camp from Djamala, squatting like empty-eyed yellow

elephants, and I knew that the end of the encampment was imminent. But exactly how soon would we be expelled to more permanent quarters not of our choosing? I went to see Hannah Lawes.

I tracked down the social worker in the kitchen of the camp. She was efficiently taking inventory of cases of canned goods.

"Ms. Lawes, can I talk to you?"

A small hard smile quirked one corner of her lips. "Mr. Hedges. Have you had a sudden revelation about your future?"

"Yes, in a way. Those buses—"

"Are not scheduled for immediate use. FEMA believes in proper advance staging of resources."

"But when—"

"Who can say? I assure you that I don't personally make such command decisions. But I will pass along any new directives as soon as I am permitted."

Unsatisfied, I left her tallying creamed corn and green beans.

Everyone in the camp, of course, had seen the buses, and speculation about the fate of Femaville 29 was rampant. Were we to be dispersed to public housing in various host cities? Was the camp to be merged with others into a larger concentration of refugees for economy of scale? Maybe we'd all be put to work restoring our mortally wounded drowned city. Every possibility looked equally likely.

I expected Nia's anxiety to be keyed up by the threat of dissolution of our hard-won small share of stability, this island of improvised family life we had forged. But instead, she surprised me by expressing complete confidence in the future.

"I can't worry about what's coming, Parrish. We're together now, with a roof over our heads, and that's all that counts. Besides, just lately I've gotten a good feeling about the days ahead."

"Based on what?"

Nia shrugged with a smile. "Who knows?"

The children, however, Izzy included, were not quite as sanguine as Nia. The coming of the buses had goaded them to

greater activity. No longer did they divide the day into periods of conventional playtime and construction of their city of dreams. Instead, they labored at the construction full-time.

The ant-like trains of bearers ferried vaster quantities of sticks and leaves, practically denuding the nearby copse. The grubbers-up of pebbles broke their nails uncomplainingly in the soil. The scribers of lines ploughed empty square footage into new districts like the most rapacious of suburban developers. The ornamentation crew thatched and laid mosaics furiously. And the elite squad overseeing all the activity wore themselves out like military strategists overseeing an invasion.

"What do we build today?"

"The docks at Kannuckaden."

"But we haven't even put down the Mocambo River yet!"

"Then do the river first! But we have to fill in the Great Northeastern Range before tomorrow!"

"What about Gopher Gulch?"

"That'll be next."

Befriending some kitchen help secured me access to surplus cartons of pre-packaged treats. I took to bringing the snacks to the hard-working children, and they seemed to appreciate it. Although truthfully, they spared little enough attention to me or any other adult, lost in their make-believe, laboring blank-eyed or with feverish intensity.

The increased activity naturally attracted the notice of the adults. Many heretofore-oblivious parents showed up at last to see what their kids were doing. The consensus was that such behavior, while a little weird, was generally harmless enough, and actually positive, insofar as it kept the children from boredom and any concomitant pestering of parents. After a few days of intermittent parental visits, the site was generally clear of adults once more.

One exception to this rule was Ethan Duplessix.

At first, I believed, he began hanging around Djamala solely because he saw me there. Peeved by how I had escaped his taunts, he looked for some new angle from which to attack me,

relishing the helplessness of his old nemesis.

But as I continued to ignore the slobby criminal slacker, failing to give him any satisfaction, his frustrated focus turned naturally to what the children were actually doing. My lack of standing as any kind of legal guardian to anyone except, at even the widest stretch of the term, Izzy, meant that I could not prevent the children from talking to him.

They answered Ethan's questions respectfully and completely at first, and I could see interest building in his self-serving brain, as he rotated the facts this way and that, seeking some advantage for himself. But then the children grew tired of his gawking and cut him off.

"We have too much work to do. You've got to go now."

"Please, Mr. Duplessix, just leave us alone."

I watched Ethan's expression change from greedy curiosity to anger. He actually threatened the children.

"You damn kids! You need to share! Or else someone'll just take what you've got!"

I was surprised at the fervor of Ethan's interest in Djamala. Maybe something about the dream project had actually touched a decent, imaginative part of his soul. But whatever the case, his threats gave me a valid excuse to hustle him off.

"You can't keep me away, Hedges! I'll be back!"

Izzy stood by my side, watching Ethan's retreat.

"Don't worry about him," I said.

"I'm not worried, Parrish. Djamala can protect itself."

The sleeping arrangements in the tent Nia, Izzy and I shared involved a hanging blanket down the middle of the tent, to give both Izzy and us adults some privacy. Nia and I had pushed two cots together on our side and lashed them together to make a double bed. But even with a folded blanket atop the wooden bar down the middle of the makeshift bed, I woke up several times a night, as I instinctively tried to snuggle Nia and encountered the hard obstacle. Nia, smaller, slept fine on her side of the double cots.

The night after the incident with Ethan, I woke up as usual in

the small hours of the morning. Something urged me to get up. I left the cot and stepped around the hanging barrier to check on Izzy.

Her cot was empty, only blankets holding a ghostly imprint of her small form.

I was just on the point of mounting a general alarm when she slipped back into the tent, clad in pajamas and dew-wet sneakers.

My presence startled her, but she quickly recovered, and smiled guiltlessly.

"Bathroom call?" I whispered.

Izzy never lied. "No. Just checking on Djamala. It's safe now. Today we finished the Iron Grotto. Just in time."

"That's good. Back to sleep now."

Ethan Duplessix had never missed a meal in his life. But the morning after Izzy's nocturnal inspection of Djamala, he was nowhere to be seen at any of the three breakfast shifts. Likewise for lunch. When he failed to show at super, I went to D-30.

Ethan's sparse possessions remained behind, but the man himself was not there. I reported his absence to Hannah Lawes.

"Please don't concern yourself unnecessarily, Mr. Hedges. I'm sure Mr. Duplessix will turn up soon. He probably spent the night in intimate circumstances with someone."

"Ethan? I didn't realize the camp boasted any female trolls."

"Now, now, Mr. Hedges, that's most ungenerous of you."

Ethan did not surface the next day, or the day after that, and was eventually marked a runaway.

The third week of October brought the dreaded announcement. Lulled by the gentle autumnal weather, the unvarying routines of the camp, and by the lack of any foreshadowings, the citizens of Femaville 29 were completely unprepared for the impact.

A general order to assemble outside by the buses greeted every diner at breakfast. Shortly before noon, a thousand refugees, clad in their donated coats and sweaters and jackets, shuffled their feet on the field that doubled as parking lot, breath

pluming in the October chill. The ranks of buses remained as before, save for one unwelcome difference.

The motors of the buses were all idling, drivers behind their steering wheels.

The bureaucrats had assembled on a small raised platform. I saw Hannah Lawes in the front, holding a loud-hailer. Her booming voice assailed us.

"It's time now for your relocation. You've had a fair and lawful amount of time to choose your destination, but have failed to take advantage of this opportunity. Now your government has done so for you. Please board the buses in an orderly fashion. Your possessions will follow later."

"Where are we going?" someone called out.

Imperious, Hannah Lawes answered, "You'll find out when you arrive."

Indignation and confusion bloomed in the crowd. A contradictory babble began to mount heavenward. Hannah Lawes said nothing more immediately. I assumed she was waiting for the chaotic reaction to burn itself out, leaving the refugees sheepishly ready to obey.

But she hadn't countered on the children intervening.

A massed juvenile shriek brought silence in its wake. There was nothing wrong with the children gathered on the edges of the crowd, as evidenced by their nervous smiles. But their tactic had certainly succeeded in drawing everyone's attention.

Izzy was up front of her peers, and she shouted now, her young voice proud and confident.

"Follow us! We've made a new home for everyone!"

The children turned as one and began trotting away toward Djamala.

For a frozen moment, none of the adults made a move. Then, a man and woman—Vonique's parents—set out after the children.

Their departure catalyzed a mad general desperate rush, toward a great impossible unknown that could only be better than the certainty offered by FEMA.

Nia had been standing by my side, but she was swept away. I caught a last glimpse of her smiling, shining face as she looked back for a moment over her shoulder. Then the crowd carried her off.

I found myself hesitating. How could I face the inevitable crushing disappointment of the children, myself, and everyone else when their desperate hopes were met by a metropolis of sticks and stones and pebbles? Being there when it happened, seeing all the hurt, crestfallen faces at the instant they were forced to acknowledge defeat, would be sheer torture. Why not just wait here for their predestined return, when we could pretend the mass insanity had never happened, mount the buses and roll off, chastised and broken, to whatever average future was being offered to us?

Hannah Lawes had sidled up to me, loud-hailer held by her side.

"I'm glad to see at least one sensible person here, Mr. Hedges. Congratulations for being a realist."

Her words, her barely concealed glee and schadenfreude, instantly flipped a switch inside me from off to on, and I sped after my fellow refugees.

Halfway through the encampment, I glanced up to see Djamala looming ahead.

The splendors I had seen in ghostly fashion weeks ago were now magnified and recomplicated across acres of space. A city woven of childish imagination stretched impossibly to the horizon and beyond, its towers and monuments sparkling in the sun.

I left the last tents behind me in time to see the final stragglers entering the streets of Djamala. I heard water splash from fountains, shoes tapping on shale sidewalks, laughter echoing down wide boulevards.

But at the same time, I could see only a memory of myself in a ruined building, gun in hand, confronting a shadow assassin.

Which was reality?

I faltered to a stop.

Djamala vanished in a blink.

And I fell insensible to the ground.

I awoke in the tent that served as the infirmary for Femaville 29. Hannah Lawes was sitting by my bedside.

"Feeling better, Mr. Hedges? You nearly disrupted the exodus."

"What—what do you mean?"

"Your fellow refugees. They've all been bussed to their next station in life."

I sat up on my cot. "What are you trying to tell me? Didn't you see the city, Djamala? Didn't you see it materialize where the children built it? Didn't you see all the refugees flood in?"

Hannah Lawes's cocoa skin drained of vitality as she sought to master what were evidently strong emotions in conflict.

"What I saw doesn't matter, Mr. Hedges. It's what the government has determined to have happened that matters. And the government has marked all your fellow refugees from Femaville 29 as settled elsewhere in the normal fashion. Case closed. Only you remain behind to be dealt with. Your fate is separate from theirs now. You certainly won't be seeing any of your temporary neighbors again for some time—if ever."

I recalled the spires and lakes, the pavilions and theaters of Djamala. I pictured Ethan Duplessix rattling the bars of the Iron Grotto. I was sure he'd reform, and be set free eventually. I pictured Nia and Izzy, swanning about in festive apartments, happy and safe, with Izzy enjoying the fruits of her labors.

And myself the lame child left behind by the Pied Piper.

"No," I replied, "I don't suppose I will see them again soon."

Hannah Lawes smiled at my acceptance of her dictates, but only for a moment, until I spoke again.

"But then, you can never be sure."

ABOUT THE AUTHOR

PAUL DI FILIPPO's fiction has been appearing in print for over thirty years now. He's aiming to beat Jack Williamson's career record, but is counting on medical science to help. He lives in Providence, Rhode Island, amidst daily reminders of Lovecraft's tenure in that town. His mate of nearly forty years is Deborah Newton, and their companions at the moment are Penny Century, a calico cat, and Brownie, a chocolate-colored cocker spaniel.